All the King's Men

A P Bateman

Copyright © 2024 by Anthony Bateman

All rights reserved.

No part of this book may be reproduced in any form or by any electronic or mechanical means, including information storage and retrieval systems, without written permission from the author, except for the use of brief quotations in a book review.

For Clair, Summer and Lewis

Also by A P Bateman

The Rob Stone Series:

1) The Ares Virus
2) The Town
3) The Island
4) Stone Cold
5) The Cartel

The Alex King Series:

1) The Contract Man
2) Lies and Retribution
3) Shadows of Good Friday
(a series prequel/standalone)
4) The Five
5) Reaper
6) Stormbound
7) Breakout
8) From the Shadows
9) Rogue
10) The Asset
11) Last Man Standing
12) Hunter Killer
13) The Congo Contract
(a series prequel/standalone)

14) Dead Man Walking
15) Sovereign Power
16) Kingmaker
(A series prequel/standalone)
17) Untouchable
18) The Enemy
19) Die Trying
20) All the King's Men
21) The Eagle's Talon

The DI Grant Series

1) Vice
2) Taken

Standalone Novels:

Never Go Back
The Most Dangerous Game

Short Stories:

The Perfect Murder?
Atonement (an Alex King thriller)

Chapter One

There were only a few jobs more stressful than that of air traffic controller, but Peter Wright wouldn't know what any of them were, and he would likely not believe anyone who told him. He wouldn't have cared, either because he enjoyed his work, enjoyed the stress in a pseudo masochistic way, and he liked the hours. Six shifts on, followed by four days off. His days were never longer than ten hours and he would never be required to start a shift until he had taken nine hours off from the previous shift. He enjoyed the night shifts the most because he liked coffee and generally suffered from insomnia and found that lying awake in bed through the night a lonely place since his divorce. At least when he slept through the day it could be on the sofa with the curtains drawn and the low hum of daytime tv in the background. He slept better that way as well. His shift started today at six am and he would be done by four. In late summer that gave him plenty of time to head deep into the Surrey countryside and blow off the cobwebs on his mountain bike, and still chill out in the garden with a beer and his record collection into the evening. Vinyl was back, and he had taken his records out of his parents' attic and was reliving his youth now that Kate had the boys and had moved in with her new partner. He would have preferred not to be a forty-year-old with a receding hairline and stubborn stomach bulge on the dating scene, but needs must when you were on the shelf and he hadn't had the practice that his wife had, because he hadn't been the one to have the affair, but he had lost the kids and family home as a direct result of hers. Dating was not working out for him, perhaps it was the aura of desperation surrounding him, or perhaps his heart wasn't really in it. But the records brought back some nostalgia and nostalgia was a comfortable and unthreatening place to live.

He had seven flights on his monitor, and he was handling landings for the next hour. He liked it when they stacked up and liked it when challenges arose.

"EmiratesEK537, this is Gatwick tower, fly heading zero-nine-zero, you have a clear path for runway two, two thousand metres, altitude four-thousand feet, verify."

"EmiratesEK537, roger that, affirmative, runway two, zero-nine-zero..."

"Peter?"

Peter Wright pulled out the pad of his right headphone and looked at the man to his left. "What is it, Chris?" he asked, somewhat impatiently. He had a line-up of seven aircraft and the wind had been gusting all morning, which meant they could be using runway one at any moment and that would require some planes getting back up to altitude and start holding patterns that would cause delays close to an hour for flights six back in the line and beyond.

"British Airways flight BA0106 from DBX Dubai, no

response to checks from ATC. Lining up on beacon prompts, looks like full auto-land has been initiated."

Wright frowned. "Frequency changes?" he asked before taking a sip of coffee.

"Nothing works."

"Comms failure, maybe?"

"That still doesn't explain the activation of full auto-land."

"No..." he swallowed; his throat instantly dry despite the coffee.

"Have you ever had a case of auto-land?" asked Chris tentatively.

Peter Wright shook his head. He'd been in the game for fourteen years and he'd experienced every scenario from crashes to hijackings, travel rage and mass strike action, and all had affected his working day, but he had never experienced, nor knew of a case of auto-land. "No, I haven't. Okay, let's get the next three down as quickly as we can, send four backwards onto a holding pattern and make way for BA0106 on runway two," he said decisively. Gatwick had two runways and only one could operate at a time because of the wind direction. Airplanes generally took off and landed into the wind for maximum lift, there were a few exceptions, but jet airliners were not one of them. "And let's get airport rescue and firefighting services dispatched."

"External as well?"

Wright watched the dot on his screen, accompanied by its flight number steadily crossing the screen right to left in a text box. The aircraft was on a downward trajectory. It was in full descent. "Let's see what's what when she's on the apron."

"This sort of thing doesn't happen often, boss..."

He nodded. He wasn't sure that it ever had. Partial auto-land had to be programmed by one of the pilots in case one or both were incapacitated. A full system auto-land meant that something bad had happened. Gatwick Airport was about to make the news. "Alright," Wright said. "Call the airport manager and tell them what we've got."

Chapter Two

There were two sentries on the bridge and another on the far riverbank. To his left the weir increased the flow of the water as if it had suddenly reached a conveyer belt, pulling the slow-moving flotsam and jetsam and swirling it into gentle spirals, ever faster until the leaves and twigs and weed and patches of oil seemed caught in a vortex in the middle of the river, before going over the edge of the weir cascading down to the frothy white water some twenty feet below. He could rule out crossing any closer to the weir. To his right, the water still moved slowly and looked deep. The sentry was pacing slowly up and down the bank, his eyes scanning left and right. Fifty paces one way, a slow and steady perusal of the opposite riverbank, before pacing fifty or so steps in the other direction. He neither looked in a sense of high-alert, and nor was he bored and lethargic. He was simply keeping a steady watch and would likely spot movement or hear a splash over the monotonic sound of crashing water further downstream.

Luger cursed the military boots that he wore without laces. He could ditch them now, but he would not get far without them on the other side of the river. The great coat was already soddened from last night's rain, but if he fastened it and tied the cuffs, then he could get some air into it along with the boots and use it to float to the other side. He couldn't hope to swim with the boots dragging him down, and he knew that he would need them if he was going to get away.

The sentries were met by a soldier driving an old Land Rover 110. They held a conflab, then one of the men waved and beckoned the sentry on the riverbank over to them. This was it. There was no better time. Luger removed the soaked great coat and buttoned and zipped it. He slipped the boots inside and bundled the whole thing together as he slipped into the icy water. It was late summer, but the water had come down from the Black Hills and the night's rain had chilled it further. Without making a splash, he pushed off, his legs in frog stroke, his arms cradling the bundle. The gentle current helped, and he soon made it to the reeds and heaved himself out.

"Cadet Luger!" one of the men shouted, but Luger could see that the man was not looking in his direction. "Cadet Luger!"

The other sentry cupped his hands and shouted, "End ex! End ex!"

That was the sentence that should have finally made him relax. Forty-eight hours in the Welsh and Herefordshire countryside trying to escape the soldiers of the Parachute Regiment, straight after the gruelling 'Fan Dance' – the twenty-four-kilometre footrace and navigation challenge over Pen Y Fan, the highest mountain in the Brecon Beacons. He had never known exhaustion like it. But even now, having tagged along with the Special Air Service selection phase for a week, he found himself in fear of being tricked. But even the Paras wouldn't pull such a low trick, would they? He had been briefed that they looked forward to their role on SAS selection. Many of them would try out soon, after all, sixty percent of the SAS ranks were filled with ex-Paras. He had been roughed up by a few, as had the other recruits, and he couldn't help feeling that they would resort to dirty tricks to catch him, but 'end-ex' was sacrosanct. It was as much a de-escalation of tensions as a health and safety point. There had to be trust that the exercise had ended.

"Cadet Luger, end-ex!" the soldier shouted, briefly looking his way. He turned towards the opposite riverbank and shouted again, "End-ex! You have a call from someone called Ramsay!"

Luger smarted. He had so wanted to prove himself, even though he would never complete the course – he was only here for fitness evaluation and experience – but he at least wanted to complete the three phases that he had been put forward in. He staggered out of the reeds and the soldiers waved him over when they caught sight of him.

He was greeted with a blanket and a bacon roll wrapped in tin foil that had long-since cooled. The driver poured him hot tea with milk and sugar from a flask as he dried himself with the towel and bit ravenously into his first food for forty-eight-hours. The sweet tea was sickening, and he never drank it normally, favouring strong, black coffee, but he was so cold that he did not care. The soldiers all regarded him warily. He was not one of them, and for a 'civvy' to be on SAS selection, much speculation had already been made in the mess.

He was driven in silence back to Stirling Lines and given ten minutes to shower and pack his things, then driven across the base to the helicopter landing pads where he was met by a familiar face, but one that filled him with dread.

"Oi, oi!" shouted Flymo.

"What have I done to deserve this?" Luger chided.

Flymo was a Londoner of Afro-Caribbean descent who had flown helicopters in the army air corps and later in 658 Squadron, which flew the SAS and SBS on their missions. He was one of the best pilots a soldier could wish for because he was brave, reckless, and thus far – lucky. His moniker came from the lawnmower brand that hovered on a cushion of air – and nothing or nobody could hover lower than Flymo. After getting mixed up with one of their missions, Flymo later came to work with MI5, and now with Neil Ramsay's secretive department of special operations. There was no name for the department yet, and Ramsay hadn't been looking to find one.

"Got to double time it, too." Flymo led the way to a AgustaWestland 109 in glossy, navy blue. Ramsay had precured many things, and this was undoubtedly his department's most valued asset.

"Great..." Luger replied, but he was not enthused.

It took a little over an hour to make the one-hundred-and forty-eight-mile straight line journey and all was well until Flymo banked hard and flew far too low for the approach, but he rode the nose high, the rear rotors just inches from the ground and the craft pausing like a striking cobra, before lowering and touching down gently on its wheels.

"Bloody hell!" Luger protested, but it fell on deaf ears as Flymo chuckled in delight. He shifted in his seat and stared at him. "What do you do in between flying us about? Do you just fly off someplace quiet and do loop-the-loops all day?" he asked, his tone purely one of sarcasm.

"Hah! If you only knew!" Flymo chuckled. "Anyways, I'll see you later," he said over the intercom, keeping the engines at revs and the rotors spinning. "Don't forget to duck... I don't want to have to wash the rotors again..."

Luger took off the headset and hung it on the grab handle as he got out, carrying his leather travel bag with him. His muscles ached after the past seventy-two hours, and he still felt chilled to the bone. He jogged away from the helicopter to the waiting black Jaguar saloon. Jim Kernow was behind the wheel. A tough Cornishman in his mid-fifties he had retired from the Metropolitan Police and now worked as Ramsay's driver and minder. He nodded a greeting at the young man, but nothing more.

"Jim's seen it, and it's bad," said Ramsay as Luger got into the back seat beside him. Jim caught Luger's eye in the rear-view mirror, and his expression confirmed as much. "The police haven't had access yet," he said. "But we can only hold them off for so long." He passed Luger a device around the size of a smartphone that had a USB jack protruding. Luger noticed that the USB jack could fold and swing between standard and micro-USB. "I want you to get everything off the main computer," he said. "And I want the black box as well."

"Can I take that away?" he asked. "I wouldn't even know where to begin to look for it."

"The Air Accidents Investigation Branch, or AAIB have a representative waiting at the plane. They come under the Department of Transport, and the Prime Minister has given us access to the black box for twenty-four hours, and the AAIB representative will work with us for that time." Luger nodded as they drew near to the 787 Dreamliner. The aircraft was vast and the ring of emergency vehicles surrounding it looked tiny by comparison.

Jim Kernow stopped beside a group of people in high-vis vests and jackets, all holding clipboards. A woman stepped forwards as Jim and Luger opened their doors. "There she is," Ramsay told him. "Lillia Bailey. And don't be pulled in by those looks. She may well look like she should be on the cover of Vogue, but she's one of the county's leading aircraft crash investigators."

Luger nodded. "Well, the aircraft appears to be in one piece, so..."

"Just go onboard, assess the crime scene, and download what you can from the computer. Ms Bailey will show you where this can be done."

Luger nodded. He got out, closed the door, and walked briskly to the woman heading towards him. He had always viewed Ramsay as an asexual person, far more at home with his work and puzzles, although he knew the man to be married with two children. But however he had viewed him, the man knew a good-looking woman when he saw one, because Lillia Bailey was on another level. Flawless. Luger tried his hardest not to stare at her as she greeted him somewhat solemnly.

"Jack Luger," he said.

"Lillia Bailey, senior investigating officer," she replied, offering her hand. Luger reciprocated a little too firmly, and she looked uncomfortable. He cursed inwardly, embarrassed that she might have looked at it as toxic masculinity. Thankfully, she moved on quickly by saying, "You're with MI5, I understand?"

"Yes."

"Can I see some ID?"

"No," he replied. "My department doesn't really go in for that sort of thing."

"Oh," she said, quite taken aback.

"Shall we?" he asked, heading for the aircraft.

She followed and at the base of steps she said, "I haven't seen it, yet."

Luger frowned. "Who has?"

"The ground crew, then the transport police, and then your boss's associate." Lillia paused. "This is unprecedented. The aircraft landed via the full auto-land procedure…"

"That's a hundred percent automated?" he asked. "They can do that?"

"Yes. But it's not something ever initiated unless one of the pilots is incapable of flying. The process being that auto-land will do the bulk of the work with the remaining pilot making tiny corrections on approach. Full auto-land is similar but initiates when contact with the controls has been lost. The tiny corrections can't be made if both pilots are incapacitated, but it's worked in practice, and as far as I can discover, has never been successfully fully automated until now." She paused as they reached the steps. "Anyway, when the aircraft landed and was still uncontactable by radio, ground crew opened her up, called it in and that's when every emergency response vehicle in London turned up…"

Luger frowned, climbing the steps tentatively. It was all incredibly circumspect. Ramsay had given nothing away on the short drive over, and Jim Kernow, although having been Ramsay's eyes in lieu of access, had said nothing.

"And nobody else has been onboard?"

"No. The transport police looked, but then sealed it. It became a matter of national security. As I said, your boss's associate peered inside, came out looking green, then stopped anybody else from going in," she said, then added, "And now *you're* here."

Luger reached the top step, unsure if she had sounded impressed by his arrival, or sarcastic, but he shrugged it off as the smell reached his nostrils. "That's unpleasant," he commented.

"Ground crew reported a hiss of air when they opened the aircraft, the smell unbearable. After they looked inside, they withdrew immediately."

Two cabin crew greeted them. One was on her knees, her head slumped against her chest, the bulkhead propping her up. Beside her a male colleague was lying face down on the floor. Luger took a foul breath to steady himself and made his way to the right.

"This aircraft was configured for two-hundred and eighty-seven seats... all taken, eight cabin crew and the cockpit had three personnel. One being a trainee pilot," Lillia said over his shoulder.

Luger did the mental arithmetic and came up with two-hundred and ninety-eight people onboard. He couldn't see them all from here, but he could see a body in every seat.

"Three-hundred and two souls," she commented flatly.

Luger turned around, puzzled. "I make it two nine eight."

Lillia nodded, her expression grim. "Four babies in lap harnesses..."

"Oh..."

"I must say, I usually have to pick through the wreckage and body parts, so this is... weird to say the least..."

Luger ignored her and made his way down the aisle. The first thing that struck him was the peaceful expressions on the faces of the dead. He hadn't seen many bodies before, but those he had seen had died with their eyes remaining open. He shuddered as he thought about the man who he had recently killed in Russia to avoid being captured by the police and FSB. The man's expression had been one of shock, his eyes wide. Even with the night sky so dark, he had seen enough for the man's expression to be imprinted on his brain. But this was different. Everybody looked as if they were merely asleep.

"The smell is urine and faeces," she commented. "They went peacefully enough to relax and... well, let go..."

Luger was glad of the cabin crew station, and he cut through, stepping over the body of a female cabin crew and headed back down the opposite aisle. It was easier progress because walking back down the aircraft he did not have to see the faces of the dead. "No oxygen masks," he commented. "I thought they go off with decompression?"

"No, well yes, they do. But the aircraft is not showing any signs of decompression, and I can't say without a pathologist's report, but there are no signs of the bodies having frozen and then defrosted. The bodies would be wet."

"Really? Frozen?"

"Absolutely. Unless the altitude could be decreased dramatically at the point of decompression, then it would have been minus forty-five Celsius, and that's four times colder than a domestic freezer."

"But if it wasn't decompression, then it must have been carbon dioxide or carbon monoxide. If the levels were high, then the masks would have deployed..."

"Agreed."

"A problem with the oxygen tanks, then?"

"I can't see how. Prior to this aircraft's design, then pulling down on your oxygen mask manually, or when activated on mass automatically, it removes the firing pin of the generator igniting a mix of sodium chlorate and iron powder and that explosion initiates the oxygen flow." Lillia paused.

"The Boeing seven-eight-seven is different, a decentralised gaseous system, often called a pulse oxygen system, is in place. These systems have a small high pressure gas cylinder to support the number of masks located within the box. All the boxes are separate and supply a direct block of seats. The system is not controlled centrally, and does not require an accumulator bag, simply giving a pulse of air when the user breathes, rather like an aqua lung in scuba diving."

"In English?" he asked, pausing in the aisle to look at her.

Lillia shrugged. "It's not one central oxygen tank started by a small explosion. It's lots of smaller tanks working under a lot of smaller systems. The entire system cannot fail as a whole."

"And yet, it did." Luger turned and headed down the aisle to the cockpit.

He hesitated at the door to the cockpit and Lillia entered a five-digit code, looking at the notes on her clipboard as she did so. The gruesome story was the same in the cockpit. A middle-aged captain in the lefthand seat and a woman of around thirty in the right in the role of first officer. Behind her, on a booster seat, a young man in his early twenties. He would be the trainee pilot that Lillia had mentioned. All three of them appeared to be asleep.

"The auto-land system shut down the engines and locked the brakes when it became stationary."

"Wow, it can do that?"

She shrugged. "Nobody has ever seen it done other than in testing."

"These things can really fly themselves..." he shook his head. "Incredible."

"In theory. But there is no auto-take-off and this is the

first time auto-land has ever been initiated for real. The flight plan has been crazy because of it with flights diverted all over the country, and to France just because auto-taxiing clearly isn't a thing yet, and we now have a seven-eight-seven sat on Gatwick's only serviceable runway." Lillia Bailey paused. "The sooner you're done here, the sooner we can clear the plane and get it towed out of the way. However, protocol dictates that she stays where she is until the AAIB clear her."

"Can you show me the main computer?"

"Of course," she replied, bending down, and removing a carpeted cover within a chrome-edged square in the carpeted floor. A ladder was visible and led down to the nose of the aircraft. She stood aside and Luger slid down the ladder with the skill of an ex-naval officer. Dimly lit by the lights of motherboards, he used the torch app on his phone to get a better look.

Lillia followed him down, one rung at a time. "What are you looking for?" she asked somewhat incredulously.

Luger took out the data catcher. "I need to download all computer activity for the flight."

"I'll get the black box for you."

"I want that as well, but my boss wants to see all data. In particular, the IP identity of the wireless internet and computer actions."

Lillia frowned. "You don't think this is an accident? A malfunction of the system?"

"No."

She shook her head incredulously. "Your boss thinks somebody took control of the computer mid-air and shut off the air?"

"The system recirculates cabin air. If that circulation was switched off, along with carbon dioxide and carbon monoxide sensors, then the oxygen masks wouldn't deploy." He paused. "And if they could be switched off remotely..."

"My god..." she said, horrified at the prospect.

The computer was exactly as Luger had imagined. A series of motherboards with tiny bulbs indicating processing in action. He had worked with similar systems aboard naval vessels, and ashore. He found a USB port and inserted the data catcher. Ramsay's programme would do the rest. "How many commercial aircraft do you reckon are in the air at any one time," he asked ponderously.

Lillia frowned. "There is an average of nine-thousand-eight-hundred planes in the air at any given time. That's around one million, three hundred souls. Crew would take it up to anywhere between another sixty and a hundred thousand souls."

"Interesting..."

"Interesting? More like terrifying."

"And souls? Why not say passengers or people?"

"It's always been souls." She paused. "I suppose it stops crew being disregarded when it's reported that a plane crashed with two-hundred passengers dead. It stops marginalisation."

"Interesting..."

"I'll get the black box," she said tersely. "Your department has been granted twenty-four hours and the sooner the experts can start investigating this tragedy, the better."

Luger ignored the jibe, appreciating that her nose had been put out of joint by MI5. "What will you do when you find out what happened?"

She shrugged. "The AAIB will publish their findings and pass it on to Boeing, British Airways and Gatwick Airport. If there's shown to be someone specifically at fault, then the Crown Prosecution Service will call upon the AAIB as a material witness."

"That's great. But we take *our* findings and hunt down those responsible before they can do this to every plane in the air and kill one and a half million people at once." He paused. "So, I'm sorry if twenty-four hours is an inconvenience, but those *souls* up there aren't going to get any more dead because my department are having a looksee first."

Lillia Bailey looked taken aback, but her expression mellowed, and she shrugged. "I suppose," she said, then added, "Sorry..."

Not a problem, he thought. "You can make it up to me by agreeing to have dinner with me tonight..."

She flushed red, but quickly recovered. "I *have* a boyfriend," she replied sharply.

"Well, he can't come," Luger replied lightly. "Shall we say, eight at The Ivy. I prefer the original on West Street. We can talk more about this, and what needs to be done to prevent it happening again."

"Just dinner," she agreed.

"And drinks, of course."

"And drinks..."

Luger smiled. "It's a date, then."

"Not a date," Lillia said firmly. "Just dinner and drinks, and shop talk about this incident." She paused and said, "Now, I'll retrieve the black box while you finish downloading the data."

Luger nodded, but as she turned away, he smiled knowingly. In his experience women in healthy relationships didn't agree to have dinner with men they had just met. And the only reason that a woman would stipulate 'just dinner' was because they were probably attracted to them, too, but did not want to appear morally loose. As far as Luger was concerned, beyond dinner was a done deal.

He checked the data catcher and the display read that the download was complete. Pocketing it and looking around him for Lillia, he noticed a rubber wall with a zipper door and went for a closer look. Curiosity got the better of him and he unzipped it and stepped through into the service bay where drinks, food lockers and trolleys were stored beside a lift so narrow that it did not seem feasible that a person could fit inside. Beyond this was the luggage bay and he opened a heavy door and stepped inside. The luggage was stored in sections, and he could hear whining ahead of him. After walking halfway down the fuselage, he saw a black labrador in a cage. The dog was curled up, looking forlorn, but very much alive. Luger frowned. The air down here should have been as toxic as in the cabins, but the fact that it had not been corrupted showed that this had been an isolated, targeted piece of programming. Luger checked the cage, then took out his Leatherman and sliced the cable ties securing the door. Tentatively, he reached for the dog and received a lick across the fingers. He opened the cage fully, and noticed the rope lead coiled and tucked into a webbing strap on top of the cage. He fastened the loop around the dog's neck and encouraged him out of the cage. The dog started to wag its tail and followed and as Luger walked him past the food service trolleys, he snatched a couple of individual packets of crackers and opened them while the dog sat attentively, its tail brushing to and fro across the floor. The animal snatched the biscuits and held up a paw for more.

"Silly thing..." he said to it quietly, then opened another packet and tossed it for the dog to catch mid-air.

"What on earth are you doing?" Lillia said from behind. "How the hell did the dog survive?"

Luger looked at the black box in her hand, which contrary to popular belief and all general reasoning, was in fact bright orange. "Well, whatever is recorded on that, we know that shutting off the air was targeted, and not done throughout the entire aircraft. Otherwise, Fido here wouldn't have made it."

"This is crazy," she said heavily. "*How* could someone... *why* would someone do such a thing?"

"Hopefully, that's what we are about to find out."

Chapter Three

"Lillia Bailey said that it's plug and play," Luger said, sipping some of his strong, black coffee.

Ramsay put down the black box and frowned, "How long is that thing going to be here?"

Luger patted the dog on its head and said, "It depends upon whether someone claims him."

"You can't just keep someone's dog," commented Mae, placing Ramsay's tea beside him. "Aw, he is cute, though. What are you calling him?"

"Nothing. He's calling him nothing because it needs to go through quarantine, then get returned to its late owner's next of kin." Ramsay turned the black box on its side. At five kilos it was surprisingly heavy for its dimensions.

"Not a fan, Mr Ramsay?" asked Mae. She was a matronly woman with grey hair tidied back in a tight bun. She served as Ramsay's secretary and personal assistant and had formerly been with GCHQ, and later with MI5 before Ramsay had poached her ahead of a purge at Thames House in favour of new blood. She had an analytical eye for detail and was working on the perfect filing system, despite computerised records. She thought that in the age of cyber-crime a tangible account was both beneficial, if not essential.

"I don't like creatures that poo on the pavement," Ramsay said, not taking his eyes off the screen in front of him now that the black box was connected. For fear of data corruption or viruses, the black box was connected to a tower which had neither Wi-Fi nor mainframe access.

"Will there be anything else, Mr Ramsay?" asked Mae, hovering at the door.

"No, thank you," Ramsay replied, glancing up briefly before returning his attention to the screen.

"Is this what you think is their E.L.E?" asked Luger, slipping a biscuit to the dog.

In the heart of the Scottish Highlands, at a manor house in his department's portfolio of assets, two members of Iron Fist – an axis-of-evil consisting of five countries making up each finger of the fist – a former Russian GRU officer turned mafia boss, and his Chinese counterpart, had been undergoing 'enhanced' questioning. It had been two months since their last significant mission, and it had taken two months for the Chinese agent to start talking. He had spoken of an E.L.E, or Extinction Level Event. That had been just four days ago.

"The maths doesn't add up," Ramsay replied. "If they took down every commercial airliner in this manner – if that is what's happened – then it's a million to a million and a half people. That's a terrible event, but it's only double the worldwide flu deaths each year. It's hardly an E.L.E."

Luger understood Ramsay's comparison, but the man had the ability to say things with little or no emotion.

Personally, if he could help save a million and a half lives, then Luger would consider it a good day at work.

"What about nuclear power stations?" Luger asked. "If airliners can be controlled remotely using their own failsafe systems, then what if they were to be flown into nuclear reactors?"

"It's impossible to destroy a nuclear reactor with a commercial airliner. They have already been tested in that way, up to Boeing seven-four-seven airliners." He paused. "After all, an airliner is merely an aluminium tube. Look how they disintegrated when they hit the Twin Towers." Ramsay looked up at him intently. "It was aviation fuel that brought down the towers. The fires were so fierce that they melted and weakened the steel structure. Once the integrity of the structure was compromised, weight and gravity did the rest. The impacts themselves did very little damage to the buildings, the aftermath of the fires, however, was quite different."

"If they can hack the systems of an airliner, switch off the air recirculation and shut down the fail safes, then what else can they do?" Luger mused, then drank some more of his strong, black coffee.

"I shudder to think..." Ramsay replied somewhat distractedly, then said, "Ah, here we are... Shortly after take-off from Dubai, the air recirculation modular system was closed to half. The alarm was disabled a few minutes later. Oxygen cylinders disabled on the next command. Then, the system was shut down completely as the aircraft reached Egyptian airspace. As it entered Italian airspace, the pilots failed to adjust to a new heading and auto-pilot remained in operation. Again, over Switzerland, then German airspace when adjustments were called for by air traffic control, auto-pilot remained unchanged. The full auto-land system was initiated automatically as the aircraft flew out over the North Sea before heading west on the pre-programmed landing approach." He paused. "After entering Italian airspace there are no further communications either from the cockpit, or between the three pilots. We can, therefore, assume that they were either unconscious or dead by that time."

"What has the prisoner said about this extreme event?" Luger asked. "Can the interrogators steer the prisoner down this road? We know enough about the flight to unnerve him. He may start to spill more if he does not know how much we know."

"It's a fine line," replied Ramsay. "If he discovers that we are way off the mark, then he may well clam up altogether."

"We need to find the IP of whoever entered the instructions into the airplane's computer system."

Ramsay unplugged the black box and pressed the intercom. Mae opened the door and Ramsay said, "Mae, please take this downstairs to Charlotte and see what she can find. It's important that she treats it as a virus threat, so no connection to our mainframe." He paused as she lifted it off his desk, clearly surprised by its weight. "We're looking for a signature, a location... anything that gives us somewhere to start looking."

Mae nodded, but she paused at the door and said, "I know I'm just the admin around here..."

Ramsay looked at her with interest and said, "Not at all, Mae. Do go on..."

"Perhaps the point of it all is that it's not one specific threat, but a test." She paused. "Because if it's possible to kill everybody in the air, and land a plane from behind a laptop, then what else could they do?"

Ramsay stared for a moment at the door as it closed solidly behind his personal assistant. "What else, indeed?" he mused.

Chapter Four

San Jose, California (Silicon Valley)

Like Kim Jong Un, the tyrannical leader of North Korea, Hong Gil-dong had attended the private International School of Berne in Gümligen, Switzerland for five years, after which he spent four years in attendance of the Liebefeld Steinhölzli state school in Köniz, near Bern. The North Korean regime had facilitated this using forged passports purchased by secret agents in Brazil. However, whereas the Korean despot had gone on to attend military academy, Hong Gil-dong had been sent to the Massachusetts Institute of Technology (MIT) on the visa and passport of a South Korean student, who as far as Hong Gil-dong knew, had been snatched and was still rotting in a North Korean prison camp, having been chosen and seized specifically for the task. Over the next fifteen years, Hong Gil-dong had been employed by various tech companies including

Microsoft, Apple and Sony, and became a top programmer and developer of AI concepts. Life had been good in California. He had learned to surf, drove a classic Porsche and a new BMW, and lived in a beach-front condominium. He earned good money, dated women, used high-class escort agencies, but was never allowed to forget why he was there by his masters. The secret agents of the RGB – the Reconnaissance General Bureau would call on him without notice, and they had the nasty habit of making their appearance both ominous and intimidating. He remembered while living at Long Beach, working for a web design start up, being on a date at a new and exciting restaurant in Santa Monica, when he had been approached by two North Korean agents in the restrooms. They had threatened him, their words direct from the Supreme Leader's mouth, and he had been left a quivering wreck. Once back at the table his date had assumed that he had just done several lines of cocaine in the cubicle and took offence. Another time, they had followed him around his local convenience store in San Jose as he filled his shopping basket, then they had simply disappeared. He knew what was expected of him, and he knew what would happen to his family if he did not go through with it. Nine years in English-speaking schools in Switzerland, three years at MIT and fifteen years in the tech industry with the unseen weight and the influence of the RGB behind him, had been a constant reminder of his duty. He remembered taking a job with Microsoft after he had been pipped to the post by another applicant. A weeklong interview where applicants completed tasks, presentations and interviews and were whittled one-by-one until only two remained. The successful applicant had died in a road traffic collision in the early hours apparently drunk at the wheel after celebrating his new job. Hong Gil-dong had got to know the applicant over the week and knew that the man did not drink. He had also seen the RGB men the night before when he had to tell them that he had not been successful in his application. The next day, Hong Gil-dong had been contacted by HR at Microsoft and given his employment contract. Over the years Hong Gil-dong had suspected the RGB of paving or shaping the way for his career. At times he had considered making a break for it. Were his mother and father even alive still? They would be in their late sixties by now and people did not reach a grand old age in a country where food was rationed, and medical care was so poor. Where work was chosen for people and refusal to labour in your given career found them sent to concentration camps. His sisters and brother would be alive, but for how long if he ran? And where would he go? He could ditch the ridiculous fake name, the Korean equivalent of John Doe – and that's exactly how he felt, a dead man - but how would he restart his life, his career? His work history, credit and visas were in a false name. No, he was duty-bound to continue his work, if not for his country, then for his siblings and the memory of a wonderful mother and father, whom he knew not to be dead or alive.

Hong Gil-dong's fingers glided across the keyboard with the rhythm, poise, and dexterity of a concert pianist as he wrote the pathways for the AI programme to generate. It was an easy enough target this time because there was a friendly element interwoven into the firewall. The Chinese-built nuclear power station had been a win for the *Yǒnghéng de Shēngmìng* power company, known as *Eternal Life Energy,* outside of China. A legitimate energy company with such an infrastructure and foresight that it could afford to win most tenders that it bid for because of its unique profit share flexibility. Eternal Life Energy was a nuclear energy company that provided governments and domestic energy companies around the globe with safe nuclear power and made up for its losses in supply and construction by negotiating a profit share of just fifteen percent of gross revenue. The fact that the company had an ongoing vested interest in the uninterrupted supply of electricity and the safe running of the plant and infrastructure filled governments and energy companies with confidence. However, what the directors of Eternal Life Energy did not know was that there was a Chinese equivalent of Hong Gil-dong who had been working with their computer systems for years. That quiet and unassuming man who wrote the firewall programmes and coding for Eternal Life Energy had been a sleeper agent for Iron Fist for years before the intelligence world had even heard of them.

Hong Gil-dong sat back in his chair and rubbed his hands together, working the joints of his fingers, which grew stiff and ached after heavy coding sessions, his digits unable to keep pace with his thoughts and slowing down his mental processing ability. If only there was thought-to-programme capabilities, and he made a mental note to start working on it. It could be done. His AI programming was all but there, but his task load was incredible and there were barely enough hours in the day as he worked on the demands of his handlers - the thugs from the RGB, who he suspected were from the department known as 'Bureau 35' – the special operations and assassination wing of the RGB.

Hong Gil-dong had not so much penetrated the firewalls, as glided straight through them, thanks to the coding written by his unknown Chinese counterpart. He wondered whether the unfortunate man or woman worked for money, patriotism or through fear. A little for the money, a little for patriotism and lot out of fear, he suspected.

All the King's Men

Unlike Hong Gil-dong, who now worked and existed from fear alone.

Chapter Five

London

"Cottage pie?"

"Of course!" Luger grinned.

"Here of all places?"

"They're famous for it!" He paused. "It's their signature dish!"

"I thought this place was meant to be fancy..."

"It's superb," Luger replied. "Not disappointed, are you?"

Lillia looked embarrassed. "No, no, I just..."

"Never had a good cottage pie growing up?" he teased. "Anyway, once I tasted this, I won't order anything else."

"Well, I'm going for the tempura nobashi prawns, followed by the fish pie..."

"Fish pie?" he goaded her. "That's just the seafood equivalent of a cottage pie!"

"I know, I know," she replied cheerfully. "But it sounds far classier with scallops, prawns and bass!"

Lillia looked around the art deco themed restaurant with its elegant naked nymph statuettes and coloured glass panes. The lighting was from dozens of ornate art deco lamps, and on top of the white linen tablecloths the cutlery gleamed, and the glassware sparkled. The waiter arrived and topped up their glasses with champagne. Luger relayed their orders and waited while another waiter placed bread and various butters on the table, giving a brief explanation of the butters.

"I once had bacon butter at a pub in Wiltshire," Luger told her when the waiter had left them.

"Bacon butter! That's weird," Lillia replied.

Luger pulled a face of mock indignancy. "No, it was amazing! Crispy smoked bacon diced finely and mixed into homemade butter." He paused. "Buttered onto warm ciabatta, each mouthful was like a delicious bacon sandwich."

"You love fine food, I see." She paused to take a mouthful of the bread, and spoke somewhat elegantly, considering that her mouth was full. "Oh my god! How can bread taste so good?"

"It's one of the greatest pleasures in food and eating, warm, freshly baked bread and good butter or oil. You don't need anything else." Luger smiled and shrugged humbly. "I'm not really a foodie, per se, I went to boarding school, so the food was bloody awful. Boarding schools are a business at the end of the day. And profitable businesses at that, so the food was bloody minimal as well. You could always tell a boarder from a day pupil, because there was never a fat boarder..." He paused, buttering some of the sour dough bread with seaweed butter, then took a bite. When he finished chewing, he added, "And the Royal Navy was basic canteen fare. There was the occasional officers' functions, but nothing special. Four course hotel function cuisine. Like three-star hotels, at that."

"And a food snob, to boot!" she exclaimed. "No, you're definitely a foodie!"

Luger shrugged. "I enjoy some of the finer things in life," he said, staring into her eyes. "That's why I asked you out to dinner..."

"Flatterer."

Luger shrugged. "If you're with someone and he's not telling you how great you are, or how amazing you look, then you're with the wrong person."

"I *did* say I have a boyfriend..."

"I know, and I feel sorry for him."

"Really...?"

"Yes. He must live in constant fear of someone better coming along," Luger replied, then added, "Like tonight, for instance." Lillia was about to respond when two waiters arrived, each placing their starters in front of them simultaneously. A third topped up their glasses with champagne and refilled their water glasses. Lillia picked ponderously at her prawns, as if choosing which to spear first with her fork. "Okay, I lied," he said. "I don't feel sorry for him at all..."

"You're very *confident*, aren't you?"

"By the sound of it, I think you meant to say arrogant..."

"Perhaps," she grinned.

Luger ate some of his crispy duck and smacked his lips. "That's delicious," he said. "I don't mind sharing."

"I think you just want one of my prawns..."

"If one is going, then I wouldn't say no." She smiled and scooped one onto her fork, making sure that she had some of the wasabi mayonnaise coating it. Luger leaned forward and gratefully accepted it into his mouth. He noticed that she did not mind sharing her fork, which boded well for what he had planned later. "That's delicious," he announced as he chewed. He hadn't been after her food, just the knowledge that she would be willing to share. "Would you like some duck?"

Lillia wrinkled her nose in disgust. "No, it had a face!" She paused, laughing at his reaction to her comment. "I don't eat animals that have faces..."

"That prawn would have taken offence," he chuckled. "Before it was deep fried, that is..."

"You know what I mean," she blushed. "Ducks are cute, that's all. Prawns, lobsters, crabs, and cod fish aren't exactly pretty things."

"I sort of get it," he replied. "Don't put a face to something; don't feel guilty."

"Exactly!"

"Like your boyfriend, for instance," he said. "I can't picture his face and feel nothing at all."

"That's mean of you," she replied, sipping her champagne as she regarded him closely.

But not mean enough for you to leave and rush back to him? he thought, smiling at the notion that she was still here. *Perhaps she just enjoyed the food?*

"Fair enough," he replied. "It *was* just dinner after all." Did he detect disappointment in her eyes? Possibly. He knew the game some women played, but they were not the only players in the game. He had been invited to play, too. Her game was about impressions and virtue, maintaining a persona. She had been hurt before; thrown caution to the wind and given herself too early, too quickly. She had felt worthless afterwards and judged. She did not want to make the same mistake again. Would she sleep with him? Yes.

Undoubtedly. Would she let him know that she was thinking about it? Definitely not. Not yet at least. "So, how did you become a crash investigator? It seems like one of those careers you hear about, but never normally meet someone who actually does it."

"Just like an MI5 agent."

"Officer," he corrected her.

"What's the difference?" she asked incredulously.

"Buggered if I know," he shrugged, then looked at her seriously. "Agents are people often referred to as assets who work unofficially for the Security Service or the Secret Intelligence Service, or MI6 as most people call them."

"Them? You don't work closely?"

"What, those shits across the river? Not if we can help it." He paused. "Anyway, these agents provide information in return for money or patriotism and are run by officers." He shrugged. "I don't do that, but I'm an officer all the same. Anyway, we were talking about you and your unusual career."

She smiled. He was playing her game, finally. Enough about him, let's hear everything about you. "I was a commercial pilot," she told him. "Still am, although I haven't flown commercial in five years. I do, however, fly test flights for new equipment and analyse the data."

"That's incredible," he said, genuinely impressed. "A test pilot. Wow!"

"Would you have thought so if I weren't a woman?" she asked him, studying his reaction.

"Yes," he lied. In truth, he found it altogether more impressive, and knew that he shouldn't have because he was as good as fresh out of the Royal Navy, where women were dominating key roles and there had been more than a few female career trailblazers. Pilots included. But he supposed it was because she was so attractive, that such a specialist career made it genuinely surprising, and he realised that he was falling into the toxic masculinity trap. So, what if she could model for Vogue? Lillia Bailey had intellect as well as beauty, and it appeared that she thought only the former to matter. "Actually, I lied. I was taken in by your looks. A commercial airline pilot is a hugely impressive career, but to be at the top of your game in air crash investigations is the icing on the cake. Being a test pilot is pretty much the candle on top of the icing." He paused. "You *do* know that you could model for the biggest names in the industry, don't you?"

She chuckled. "That's quite patronising, actually..."

"I'm sorry."

"It's okay, I'm used to it." She shrugged and placed her cutlery down on her plate. "Looks are nothing," she said. "If you are unfortunate enough to have a car accident, or get savaged by a dog, then what have you got? If you haven't got brains and drive and personality, then you've lost the only attribute you ever had. Age comes to us all, and nobody looks as good at fifty as they did at twenty. Modelling is a great career for some, but certainly not for me."

"God, I must sound like a dickhead," he said heavily. "Okay, if you agree just to finish this dinner with me, then I promise not to be condescending for the rest of the evening."

"Do you think you can manage that?"

Luger laughed and raised his champagne glass. "I'll toast to giving it a shot!"

Lillia clinked glasses with him and shrugged. "Okay, so enough about my career and looks, what about you?" She leaned forwards and whispered, "Or can't secret agents, or *officers*, talk about that?" She looked up, her doe-like eyes glossy and brown with the purist whites he thought he had ever seen. The waiters knew that they had interrupted at an inopportune moment, so cleared quickly and efficiently, crumbing down with silver hand rollers. When they bustled away, she continued, "Sorry, but I've always wondered how secret the *secret service* really is..."

Luger smiled. He wasn't about to get into the semantics of which service did what, or where they operated from and simply said, "I work for the Security Service. We deal with threats to national security to the United Kingdom and the Commonwealth. It's not glamorous, and the pay is poor," he smiled.

"Hence dinner at The Ivy," she grinned.

He shrugged. "I'm from a wealthy family," he told her with neither pride nor ignominy. "I have money."

"Oh..."

"But that's why I do it because I'm not money orientated. I joined because of a sense of duty and wanting to make a difference. I was in the Royal Navy but left after someone convinced me to work for the Security Service."

"Who convinced you, a woman?"

"Yes."

"Were you close?"

"Yes. She's dead now."

"Oh..."

He shrugged. "What about you?" he asked. "Pilot to crash investigator in what can only be a reasonably short time."

"I gained my pilot's licence after self-funding, and some company sponsorship, then flew commercial airliners, starting with domestic flights from London to Manchester and London and Glasgow, then short haul to the Costa's and then eventually long-haul. I met my fiancé on the job.

He was an airline pilot as well." She paused heavily. "His plane went down over the Indian Ocean. No survivors."

"Crikey, I'm sorry…" Luger said quietly.

She smiled thinly; the memory of his death still raw. "I think it was the process of investigating the crash that kept me going. I wasn't involved, of course, but I awaited the findings and imagined that when the inquest was closed there would be a direct cause attributed and someone would be to blame." She sighed heavily in pause, then said, "They attributed it to pilot error…" Luger reached across the table and touched her hand. She did not move hers, seemingly taking comfort in the gesture. "It was bullshit," she said acidly. "Aviation and aeronautic companies, airlines, and corporate lawyers… the lead investigator was a corrupt bastard and took a bribe. Of course, I can't prove it, but I vowed that I would do my part to see that it never happened again, or at least under my watch."

Luger shook his head. "I can't believe that goes on."

"Nor could I, but Brad was a fantastic pilot, it couldn't have been pilot error. A bad landing, perhaps. But out in the middle of the Indian Ocean? I can't see what he could have done wrong. They said he failed to engage autopilot and made a mistake entering the headings into the navigation system. But that's what co-pilots are for. You don't simply make mistakes like that because it's a two-person process."

Luger thought on this. He was no amateur psychiatrist, but he thought that her career move had more to do with her inability to grieve and accept her loss, than to address the crash investigation sector's failings. He still found it hard to believe a bribe could be made for an investigation to be corrupted. "And the black box?" he asked, realising he had been silent too long.

"Never recovered. These things are bright orange and

have a GPS beacon that emits a signal underwater for close to a week." She paused. "If you can't find the wreckage, you can generally find the black box."

The waiters arrived in a trio with their main courses and vegetables, and once again, topped up their champagne, draining the bottle. Luger asked for another and when they had gone, he said, "So, what about today?"

Lillia put down her knife and fork. "I can't believe we're doing this. Not here, in all this decadence..." She paused. "I mean, that woman over there, she reads the News at Ten sometimes."

"I know. She looks younger on the tv," he chided. "And that man near the bar, he's..."

"Oh my god! It is as well; I loved his latest film!"

"I didn't see it," Luger commented. "But I thought he'd be taller..."

"Ouch!"

Luger laughed. "Anyway, we've got to eat," he said lightly, but realised that it belayed the heaviness he felt when he thought of the bodies of the passengers on the aircraft.

"Your boss has until tomorrow evening before I get the black box back and access to the aircraft's computer. The black box recorder is one thing, but do you think he will find anything significant from the download?"

"Undoubtedly," Luger replied. "He has the best computer whizzes in the business."

"That's a technical term," she chided. "Whizzes?" she laughed.

"Techies, then."

"Not technical yourself?"

"Not really," he lied. In the Royal Navy his specialism had been weapons systems, namely missiles and countering enemy defence strategies against them. That and naval intelligence. But she did not need to know that. "I struggle with my smartphone most of the time," he added lightly.

Lillia looked past him, and he got the distinct impression that someone was behind him. He turned in his seat, his heart racing as recognition dawned on him.

"Hello, Jack..." she said, bending to kiss his cheek. Her perfume reminded him of their time in his bed, just two months ago, but the memory washed over him like a surging shore break. "My, I certainly started something bringing you here, and cottage pie again, to boot!" She smiled at Lillia and said, "Hello sweetie, I'm Harriet..."

"Lillia," she replied stoically.

"Colleague, or a date?" Harriet smiled pleasantly, glancing at Luger. "Oh, please not a date, Jack. You'll break my cold, cold heart..."

Lillia hesitated a moment too long, then said, "Colleague, I guess."

"Oh, wonderful!" Harriet ran a hand across Luger's shoulder and said to him, "My heart at least remains whole for now."

"And still cold," Lillia smiled innocently.

"Oh, sharp as a tack, and such a pretty thing as well," Harriet smirked.

"It's good to see you, too, Harriet," Luger said thinly. "We must talk about my recent trip to Russia sometime."

"Old news, darling," she replied, sounding more like *dahhling*. "All's well that ends well." She bent down and kissed him on the cheek again, and to his annoyance he felt a surge of passion rush through him, his heart hammering against the wall of his chest. "So lovely to see you again, we *must* catch up soon..." She straightened up, her figure every bit as wonderful as Lillia's, with her sequined cocktail dress glistening in the light. "Nice to meet you, Lilly."

"I'm sure," Lillia replied not bothering to correct her. She waited until Harriet returned to her seat opposite a girlfriend who looked equally as glamorous. "An ex?" she asked awkwardly.

"No," Luger replied. "An associate."

"She seems to think it was a lot more than that…"

"Well, it wasn't and it's not."

Lillia sipped a mouthful of champagne and said, "Do excuse me, I have to go to the ladies…" She stepped out from her leather bench seat, clutching her handbag close to her.

Luger stood; the years of public school still ingrained in him. He sat back down as she made her way out through the oak and glass doors and downstairs to the toilets. He sipped some champagne awkwardly, not continuing to eat while she had absented herself. Inside he was seething. Harriet had been instrumental in setting him up on his last operation, the MI6 officer wining, dining, and sleeping with him, all the while knowing that he was the unwitting pawn in a mole hunt to verify a double agent. He had been lucky to make it out of Russia alive. And yet… The sound of her voice – a soft purr – the scent of her, the perfume, her touch… He had been a fool, but he knew he would do it all again for another chance to be with her. He had never known sex like it.

His thoughts were eventually interrupted by the head waiter, who bent discreetly beside him and said, "I am afraid madam has asked me to apologise, and that she has been taken unwell." He paused. "She has settled the bill and said feel free to order dessert. I must add, sir, that she has left a substantial gratuity…"

Luger nodded, embarrassed and feeling vulnerable with

his back to the room. He had been left sitting there – his fellow diners watching and judging – and he knew that the other diners would be assuming that they had argued, or that he was a drunk, a boar, who had seen off his date. He waited for the head waiter to finish his table checks around him, then left quietly without looking at Harriet and all the while, feeling her eyes boring into the back of his skull. Was she smiling? He almost certainly felt so.

Outside, people were exiting the small theatre opposite. He looked both ways down West Street, then saw Lillia climbing into a taxi and he ran after her. She saw him as she slid inside, making the briefest of eye contact, then the taxi pulled away.

"Damn it!" he shouted out loud, watching the taillights until they were swallowed up by the night-time London traffic.

Chapter Six

Notting Hill, London

Satisfied that there were no hidden cameras in the property, Rashid removed his woollen hood and rubbed his face. The flat was small, but exquisitely furnished and no expense had been spared in the décor and soft furnishings. As Rashid studied the furniture, fittings and finish, it was clear to see that Harriet had used an interior designer or had indeed missed her true calling.

"This is what I'd like my place to look like when it's finished," Jo Blyth commented. "Only with cushions from The Range instead of Harrods..." She was new to the team, having only worked on one assignment, but had proved to be both smart and intuitive, and had shown great integrity. She was barely thirty and had served in the Metropolitan Police Service before joining GCHQ and had then been poached by Ramsay for his new department.

"I'll have to come by one evening with a bottle of wine and see it for myself."

"You'd need an invite first."

"Is that likely?"

"Nope." She spread a sheet on the carpet and took off her backpack, resting it in the centre of the sheet. Rashid did the same. "I don't like wine, anyway."

"Beer, then."

"Yuk..."

"What do you drink, then?"

"Bourbon," she replied. "Anyway, you're a Muslim, aren't you? You're not meant to drink."

"So many rules," he quipped. "You sound like my mother..."

Jo did not respond and started to unpack the equipment. She checked her phone, the trace on Harriet's phone showing her location as on West Street. She pulled back the image of the map on the screen, showing Harriet's banker husband still at Canary Wharf, where he often worked late to make calls to New York, Chicago, and Los Angeles. All good, unless they left their phones behind.

Rashid had started on the plug sockets, removing the facias, and replacing them with ones with built-in microphones and pinhole cameras. The electrical connection still worked with appliances, while keeping the surveillance equipment remained constantly powered. He studied the facias, then set about copying some scratches onto one with his penknife, carefully copying the marks on the facia in his hand. Details mattered.

Jo made her way into the main bedroom and looked around carefully. She had voiced her opinion on cameras in the bedroom and bathroom, suggesting audio only, but Ramsay had been unequivocal and said that they would be discreet when viewing, but they were all grown-ups and discretion had no place in intelligence gathering. She entered the bathroom and chose the dome light above and the shaving/electric toothbrush socket on the wall away from the sink. As she left, she checked the bathroom again, making sure that she had not left any footprints on the floor tiles, but the PPE socks over her trainers had avoided that.

"Get something with her DNA on it," Rashid said from behind her. "Something that only she would use. Hairbrush, straighteners, that sort of thing."

"We need her DNA?" she asked, quite surprised at the notion.

Rashid shrugged. "We're only here once so it pays to be thorough."

Jo nodded, taking out her phone. "The husband is on the move." She checked the other marker then said, "And it looks like Harriet is leaving. Speed ten miles per hour so she's in a taxi." She knew this because Harriet's Tesla was in the garage below, along with her husband's Maybach. Her husband was a big name in finance and the couple owned a house in Berkshire, which they had already given the same treatment, including the ability to control the couple's existing CCTV system remotely.

"We're done here," said Rashid. "This'll pay her back for bugging Jack's place."

Luger discovered a listening device in his flat after Harriet had visited, and he had to confess to Ramsay and the team that he had been compromised for a month. By his own admission, he had done nothing to compromise the team, he had received no visitors since she had been in the flat, and few telephone conversations, but the team knew what the two of them had got up to, and the MI6 officer had taken the opportunity to set devices while he had been in the shower.

"I'm not sure what it will achieve," she replied.

"Ramsay's game of chess," said Rashid pointedly. "MI6 played a silly game with us, they also put Jack's life at risk. They then made a scapegoat of the embassy man, Carter. That's an extreme measure to take just to cover their backs, having someone try and run the poor bloke over."

"So, this is what? Tit for tat?" she asked, carefully packing the equipment and tools away and checking around her, making sure that no detail had been overlooked.

"No. It's hedging our bets." Rashid slung the bag over his shoulder and headed for the door, satisfied that they had left nothing incriminating behind them. He reset the alarm, then closed the door quietly and relocked the lock with his set of lockpicks. "MI6 knows that we know what they were up to, and now we have to wait and see who blinks first..."

Chapter Seven

Jack Luger sipped his coffee, studying the document as Ramsay sat with his back to him, watching the Thames. Rashid and Jo sat either side of Luger studying the same document.

"What's a coding fingerprint?" Rashid asked. Both Jo and Luger had tech backgrounds, but his was merely in soldiering. There were times when his skills were called for, and days like these when he felt out of the loop.

"It means that the person who wrote the code accidently left a piece of them within the programme," Ramsay said, wheeling himself around to address them. "Rather like morse code operators who could be identified by what was termed their 'hand'. Just the slight elongating of letters, the rhythm, the pause..." he said thoughtfully. "Coding is the same. However, there is an opening in this programme, a gap in the firewall. Anti-corruption coding will turn away attempts to corrupt the programme, but this particular string of code has an opening. Once through the opening..." He shrugged. "I suppose we could think of it as malware, can corrupt the code and an operator can gain control and rewrite the programme, thus defeating the pre-programmed instructions, or any AI interaction."

"So, whoever shut down the aircraft's air recirculation system and emergency oxygen countermeasures made a mistake?" Rashid asked.

"Yes and no," Ramsay replied. "Yes, an opening is there. But I cannot for the life of me, imagine someone with these coding skills did that by mistake. The team downstairs can't see it as a mistake, either. And they're the best in the business." He paused heavily. "Or so I thought until I saw the coding work of this genius. It both frightens me and intrigues me in equal measures."

"Is it a trap?" Rashid asked.

"I think it's something else," Ramsay mused. "But what? I have no idea…"

"And you didn't find a location? An IP address?" asked Luger.

"No," Ramsay replied. "Although if we can spike another programme by this coder, using a similar opening, then we will be free to discover everything about them."

"Presumably we need to do that while the hacking is in progress…" Rashid mused.

"Yes."

Luger frowned. "And how in the hell can we do that?"

"How indeed…?" Ramsay replied somewhat distantly.

Chapter Eight

Canary Islands

King sat down heavily. Dead was dead. There was no coming back from it. It was over. That had been the best he could translate from the mechanic, although his Spanish wasn't good. Poor, in fact. One of the mechanics was a Russian who had lived in Spain and the Canary Islands for twenty years, so between them, King with his passable Russian, and the Russian with his poor English and fluent Spanish, they surmised that the engine was dead. No doubt there were sailors who were capable of sailing yachts right up to the dock by wind power alone, but King had not seen one yet. In fact, with the reefs and shallow waters over volcanic rocks that they had navigated, and the complicated marinas and ports that they had had to negotiate, no engine meant that they were well and truly scuppered.

They had sailed into a storm eighty miles off the coast of

Mauritania, West Africa, and had not been able to either avoid or outrun it. Thirty-foot seas, double troughs taking some waves to sixty feet high, and horizontal rain had taken them to the brink, and they had taken onboard almost enough water to sink them. With the cabin and engine bay full of water, the engine flooded, while bailing out with pumps and buckets as they sailed the mountainous seas, they had considered abandoning ship in the inflatable survival raft, and then, as quickly as the storm had loomed down upon them, the seas noticeably subsided and the rain stopped, and the wind dropped. Sailing onwards, with King at the helm and Caroline pumping and bailing out, they had sailed into the port town of Meloneras, Gran Canaria with supplies depleted and most of their equipment either broken or water damaged.

"A new engine?" Caroline sighed. "How much?"

"Twenty grand."

"Oh, no..."

"I can cover it."

"Really? How?"

King shrugged. "Dirty money," he replied. "I got an assassin who was after me to... er... divert his fee..."

"You cunning git!" she smiled.

"He didn't need it anymore."

"This life..." she said, shaking her head. "It's surreal sometimes."

"Only sometimes?" King shook his head. "I've been in it for so long now, I don't know what else there is."

Caroline sipped from her bottle of *Orangina* and stared at the beautifully blue ocean under the cloudless sky. "There is more, you know..."

"I know," he replied. "We're doing it."

"I mean there's a lot more, if you want..."

"Like what?"

She shrugged. "People grow. They have friends, let those same friends go, have careers, give those careers up for children..."

"I know," King replied, staring at the same patch of ocean and reflecting how clear and bright the horizon seemed. "We've done that. Given up the career..."

"I don't mean that, I mean, maybe it's about time we thought about starting a fam..."

"Wow, what are the odds of finding you both here?"

Caroline stopped mid-sentence, and King turned around at the sound of the familiar voice. Big Dave sauntered over with his shirt open and untucked, blowing in the breeze. He wore cheap mirrored aviators from a gift shop and held a half-finished ice cream in his large hand. At six-feet-four and eighteen stone, the man ate incessantly, but carried barely any fat on his muscled frame.

"Has Ramsay got trackers on us, or what?" Caroline asked accusingly, but she had a soft spot for the big Fijian and couldn't remain angry for long.

"I wouldn't put it past him," Big Dave replied lightly.

"Nor would I," King said gruffly as he nodded a greeting to his old friend.

Big Dave stared at the boats bobbing gently in the harbour as he tidied up the dripping ice cream cone with his tongue. "What's up with the boat?"

"Engine," replied King.

"Inboard?"

"Yes."

"Ouch."

"She's an older vessel, deep draft, so an outboard wasn't an option." King paused. "No offence, but what the fuck are you doing here?"

"Straight to the point..." Big Dave mocked.

King shrugged. "I mean, it's good to see you and all, but so soon?"

"None taken..." the Big Fijian smiled. "Ramsay wants to get the band back together."

"We're going solo," said King.

"Duo, surely?"

"You know what I mean."

"I think a coffee is in order," Caroline said lightly. She pointed to a café on the corner where the harbour met the road. "That looks as good a place as any."

They ordered their drinks and sat in the sun exchanging pleasantries until Big Dave said, "The two guys you brought in at the end of the last operation have been undergoing enhanced questioning in Scotland."

"And let me guess; one of them talked," King said heavily.

"Yes."

"The little Chinese bloke?" King ventured.

Big Dave frowned. "How did you guess that?"

King shrugged. "Fifty-fifty," he replied, but in truth, he had a feeling at the time. "He seemed the one to be more susceptible, I suppose."

The waitress arrived with two cappuccinos and breakfast tea for King. There was a tiny caramel-flavoured biscuit on the saucer beside the coffees, but not with the tea. King frowned, annoyed that he was not in the coffee club and unaware of the rules, or prejudice against tea drinkers. Big Dave ate his biscuit and eyed Caroline's with all the subtlety of a beagle. She rolled her eyes and handed it over much to King's annoyance.

"The Russian remains stoical to say the least," Big Dave commented.

"Let me at him with a hammer and a blowtorch and he'll sing soon enough," said King.

"The twentieth century called; it wants its agent back..." Caroline jeered.

King sipped some of his tea before placing it down and saying measuredly, "Times are changing, but the bad guys aren't. They still want the same things and will go to the same measures to attain them, but we grow ever softer in our pursuit of inclusivity, diversity, and political correctness. The Russians see this, and Iron Fist, too. That's why they tried to flood Europe with drugs to weaken our resolve. They were stopped, but for how long? The same plan would work again, it just needs our border security to miss the shipments this time."

Caroline did not respond. She knew that King was right, but that he was also finding it increasingly difficult to fit into this world, finding it frustrating how society was weakening and yet people like King would always be called upon to fight the threats. She knew, too, that she was on the borderline. Agreeing largely with the populace on current affairs and sociological outlook, and yet she had done untold things to keep her country safe, and suspected deep down that Western society was on a collision course with the same old enemy, who were no less tough or ruthless. The West was slowly and steadily handing themselves over on a plate.

"An E.L.E. was mentioned," said Big Dave. "An extinction level event."

"From Iron Fist?" King asked incredulously. "They're just a load of jealous misfits who neither want that, nor can agree with their own country's agenda." He scoffed. "They want what we have. They wouldn't risk their own lives to destroy it!"

"They want the status quo to change," said Caroline.

All the King's Men

"They're ideological and impatient. They have grown tired of their own countries and want to dominate the West, but I can't see them doing a big sacrifice Hail Mary of an attack where there are no winners. That's the threat of nuclear armament, and like it or not, that's what has kept the world largely in check for seventy years."

Big Dave nodded. "Ramsay thinks the same. However, he believes that something *is* wrong, and that there is a threat, possibly the largest and most lethal we have ever seen." He sipped some coffee and told them about the British Airways airliner and gruesome scene awaiting Jack Luger at Gatwick Airport.

King looked at his old friend incredulously. "They did all that remotely?"

"Yes," replied Big Dave. "I don't mind telling you I've just had the most unnerving three-and-a-half-hours of my life flying over here..." He shrugged. "Because you would know nothing about it, just nod off to sleep..."

Caroline shook her head. "And if they can take control of an aircraft from the ground, then they could change the course and fly the plane directly into any given target within fuel range. All they would need is the target's co-ordinates." She paused. "It would be so much more than simply another nine-eleven."

"Luger wondered whether nuclear powerplants could be targeted using aircraft as remote controlled missiles, but..."

"But the reactors are too strong," King interjected. "They would simply atomise upon impact. I believe they have been tested collisions with nuclear reactors using fighter jets strapped to railway lines and impacted at Mach One, and I think I remember a test where they flew a decommissioned airliner full of fuel into a nuclear reactor with no critical damage to the reactor's structure."

"This is next-level hacking, though. Could they use the same hackers to simply take control of nuclear powerplants and create a melt-down?" asked Caroline.

"Ramsay says no. Yes, a melt-down would be catastrophic, but even if you theoretically dropped a nuclear warhead on a nuclear power station, the damage and fallout would *only* be that of the nuclear warhead. I say, *only*, like it even matters..."

King sipped his tea and stared back out at the shimmering ocean, so peaceful and unthreatening. Unlike the storm that they had sailed through off West Africa. If ever there had been a time when he thought that his luck was up, it had been in those treacherous seas. The yearning to get back to life on the sea had diminished somewhat. "What if the interrogators misinterpreted the meaning of the E.L.E? What if Iron Fist want an extinction level event in terms of Western commerce?" King mused. "What if airplanes were taken control of and targeted at Wall Street, Canary Wharf, the Euronext in Paris, and the Frankfurt stock exchange. Every banking and financial centre in the West?" He paused. "That would be an extinction to our finances and infrastructure. We would be bankrupted and when the dust settles, it will be China and Russia and Asia that hold all the cards. Iran would rise as the dominant country in the Middle East. Especially if friendly Arab countries were targeted as well."

"That's a hell of a tangent to go on," Big Dave commented flatly. "I get it, though. And the confession would only be as good as the inference or translation."

"How many airliners are in the air at any one time?" Caroline asked.

"Around nine to ten thousand, with around a million and a half people in the air," Big Dave replied.

"What financial records and institutions remained would face a complete market crash," said King. "A million and a half deaths, further deaths on the ground, aviation companies ruined, banking collapsing, the stock market crashing..."

"It would be catastrophic," Caroline added.

"Well, this is depressing," said Big Dave sardonically. "I'm glad I tracked you both down, now." He paused. "I'm going to have to inform Ramsay of your gloom and doom theory," he said, taking out his phone. "So, are you coming back with me to have a look at this thing?"

Caroline shrugged, looking at King, but she could already see the change in him. His eyes were bright and alive, and he seemed taller somehow. *Rising to the occasion*, she mused. "I'll see the man and tell him to go ahead with the refit and let him know that we'll be away for a while." She paused to look back at King, but he hadn't heard and was already talking animatedly about his theory to Ramsay on Big Dave's phone.

Chapter Nine

Mid Pacific en route to Thailand

Hong Gil-dong was five vodkas in and had just buzzed the cabin crew for another. There were young children all around him and all he could do was think about the way those poor children would have died next to their mothers somewhere over Egypt on the ill-fated British Airways flight BA0106. Three hundred and two people. Dead. Because of him. The male air steward brought him his vodka and ice and he immediately asked for another. The steward frowned and Hong Gil-dong repeated his order firmly. The steward regarded him for a moment, weighing up whether he was the type to get rowdy and violent, or just the type to get morose. Morose won him over – Hong Gil-dong was already there – and he left to fetch the Korean another drink.

Hong Gil-dong closed his eyes as the vodka drained

from his glass and the ice clattered against his teeth. He could drink a hundred of these, drink and drink and drink until his heart gave out and he slumped in his seat and could no longer feel the anguish and torment inside. His family, his parents – not even knowing if they were still alive – he wanted to run away but he could not. His brother and sister would endure a living hell inside one of North Korea's many concentration camps. Rape and buggery was commonplace from the guards and there were stories of starvation and malnutrition from a diet of just half a portion of rice a day and nothing else. He remembered growing up how scarce food could sometimes be, how farmers had been instructed to use untreated human excrement for fertiliser because of sanctions and how he and his family had all suffered from tapeworms in their guts as a result. It had blown his mind when he had been chosen for a life serving the intelligence service, how the people in other countries had eaten and how much choice there had been. For years he had been grateful to serve his purpose because of the lifestyle it had afforded him. The visits from the RGB thugs had become less and less frequent, and he had achieved a sense of personal freedom. However, after years of training and working in the technology industry, gleaning valuable knowledge from his colleagues and the various firms he had worked for, the bell had tolled and he had been reminded of why he was living a life in the West, and what would happen if he did not fulfil North Korea's investment.

That reminder had presented himself shortly after take-off when the fasten seatbelt signs were switched off and the cacophony of unclipping buckles sounded in unison and people headed for the lavatories, or just ignored keeping their belts on during the flight. Hong Gil-dong had stared a moment too long, and the man had said everything with his eyes. Around halfway into the flight west, over the International Date Line, the man had approached silently from behind, clasping his shoulder and greeting him like an old friend, but he had whispered in his ear and it had been enough for Hong Gil-dong to know that he would never be free and he could neither live a life like this, nor run away and leave his family to their fate. However, there may be another way. He had left a breadcrumb for someone to follow, and as he looked at the back of the RGB agent's head, now seated seven rows in front of him, he wondered who would find the breadcrumb and whether they would find another. A foreign intelligence agency could prove to be his salvation, for he no longer cared whether he lived or died, just wanted an end to the senseless killing and his part in it. But if the RGB found his breadcrumb, and thought it intentional, then his family would be killed, and his own life would not be worth living.

Chapter Ten

London

Ramsay had chosen a non-descript office in Whitehall in which to meet the AAIB and Department of Transport minister. Nobody needed to know where his official office was, outside of the Prime Minister and their sister service MI6.

The Minister for Transport was seated at one end of the table, and Ramsay had expected no less from a politician who cared more for the title of the role than the sum of its parts. Lillia Bailey was seated in the middle with a more junior AAIB investigator on each side, while Jack Luger and Jim Kernow flanked Ramsay at the end opposite the minister. Ramsay had chosen Jim Kernow, his minder and driver, because of the man's photographic memory, and although the man had rebuffed Ramsay's attempts to have him take on more of an investigative role in his mid-fifties,

Ramsay was quietly persisting by making use of him in situations such as this. The Chief Constable of the Metropolitan Police Service and the Chief Constable of the British Transport Police took up the other side along with the Commander of Special Branch, the anti-terrorism branch of the police service.

Ramsay had been blindsided by the presence of three branches of the police service and assumed that the AAIB had requested that they attend.

"Good morning," he said as everyone settled down. "The Prime Minister granted my department…"

"Which is?" the Chief Constable of the Met sneered as he interrupted. "I must say, I have dealt with both you and your predecessors before with the Security Service, but I do not appreciate being kept out of the loop on matters of national security protocol."

"We are still the Security Service," Ramsay said matter-of-factly. "But we have a different remit. And that's all I will say on the matter at this point." He turned to Lillia Bailey and said, "I was under the impression that this was to be a meeting between my department and the AAIB…"

"This has been unprecedented," she replied. She had not looked at Jack Luger since entering the office, and still made a point not to. "The AAIB and the Department of Transport need to be granted access to investigate this travesty. Without further unnecessary delay."

Luger smiled. The only reason that she had left the restaurant last night was because of Harriet, and for her to have taken offence, to have felt uncomfortable, meant that she had feelings for him. The fact that she did not look at him now only cemented the fact. Or was she simply embarrassed at her behaviour, or perhaps annoyed with herself for going on a dinner date while she was still in a relationship?

And then Luger realised that nothing was cut and dry and there may be a dozen other reasons why she was reluctant to look at him, and he had no clue what they were. Girls had been the biggest puzzle to him when he was a teen, and he was certainly no closer to solving that puzzle fifteen years later now that they were women.

Ramsay nodded, taking a folded sheet of paper out from his inside jacket pocket. "I'm sorry that you feel this way," he said, then looked at the senior police officers and the Minister for Transport in turn. "And I'm sorry that you all had a wasted journey…"

"What do you mean?" the minster for transport asked indignantly.

Ramsay unfolded the sheet of paper and dropped it on the table in front of him. "That's a letter from the Prime Minister relinquishing all authority from the Department of Transport, the police service and the AAIB and placing both Ms Bailey and her team under my command for the duration of their investigation. The AAIB are subsequently under my command until further notice. Now, gentlemen…" he said, eyeing the three senior police officers and the minster of transport, "Good day to you…"

The Chief Constable of the Metropolitan Police Service swiped the letter and read it with a sneer before handing it unceremoniously to the commander of Special Branch beside him. "You won't get away with this, Ramsay," he seethed. "This is not how civilised, diplomatic countries operate."

The Chief Constable of the British Transport Police stood up and left, not bothering to tuck in his chair, and the minister, not usually at a loss for words, followed suit.

Jim Kernow got up and walked to the door, holding it

open for the remaining men and motioning them to leave. "This way, gentlemen..."

Lillia Bailey glanced at Luger, then averted her eyes when she caught him looking at her. Her number two beside her seemed perplexed. "So, we're working for you, now?"

"Not exactly," Ramsay replied as Kernow shut the door after the last of the men. "But you report your findings to me, and when I deem the investigation not to be a risk to national security, then the AAIB will be free to continue and publish its findings." He paused, handing her a card. "Call that number to have the black box delivered to you. A hangar at Gatwick Airport has been requisitioned for your investigation and the aircraft has been towed inside. You will find secure internet access, communications, and power to set up shop."

"Anything else?" she replied indignantly.

"Living quarters are being prepared for you and your team, and you will not be permitted to leave the site without running it by me first."

"You are joking!" she snapped.

"Jim will be on hand, and he will provide security for you as well."

"He'll be our jailer, more like..."

Ramsay shook his head. "A great deal of trouble was taken to kill those people on board. So, it's not out of the realms of possibility for whomever is behind this to see that we don't learn anything." He paused. "I believe that this was a test."

"A test of what?" Lillia asked somewhat dubiously.

"We do not yet know," he replied, then added, "And that is what scares me the most..."

Chapter Eleven

80 miles west of Pyongyang, Democratic People's Republic of Korea

The farmland surrounding the military base was largely scrub and dust. There had been no chemical or animal fertiliser for ten years and human excrement had poisoned the ground. Cattle and goats grazed the grassy tufts, bone-thin and slow-moving. There were no trees remaining in what had once been a forested valley because nobody had taken responsibility for replanting, the valley stripped for fuel and meagre industry. But all was well. The Supreme Leader told the people so.

General Cho watched the men and women of the North Korean SOF training on the dusty parade ground. They were the best of the best. Highly trained, well-fed and well-equipped. They were known as 'Torpedoes' by the navy, 'Invincibles' by the air force, and a slightly less catchy 'Human Bombs Protecting the Centre of the Revolution' by the army. Today, they were practising unarmed combat. All were black belts in taekwondo and kyeok sul do – karate style martial arts that incorporated strikes, kicks and throws, with an emphasis on acrobatic, often completely airborne kicks. They trained with knives and axes and many soldiers were routinely injured in training.

One man stood out from the others. He was a combat sergeant named Su Ji-ho, and he could leap further and higher than his counterparts and General Cho had just watched the man dispatch seven attackers in a flurry of punches and kicks. He was tall for a North Korean at five-foot-eight or nine and the best food in the North Korean military, and constant training had given him a twelve-stone, wedge-shaped frame with large biceps and powerful legs. Earlier in the day the General had witnessed his weapon handling skills with the Baek Du San pistol – a copy of the CZ-75 9mm – directly after a ten-mile run. The SOF soldiers had then used the Type-88 carbine – a copy of the Russian-made AK-105. All soldiers were expected to score bulls and v-bulls at fifty, one-hundred and two-hundred metres with eight out of ten rounds, and seven out of ten rounds at three-hundred metres. Su Ji-ho had scored highest with both weapons. He had been the fastest over the ten-mile run, too.

"Bring him to my quarters after the assault course," General Cho told the major standing beside him. "He has killed before?"

The major nodded. It was always a problem for North Korea to test its troops, and in particular the special agents of the country's special forces and operations command. North Korea was not a country at war, not in the true sense of the word at least, and nor had it been since 1953. There had been special forces incursions and skirmishes on the demarcation line and within the demilitarised zone, but that had been a rare occurrence and denied on both sides. "Dissidents and enemies of the Supreme Leader," the major replied. In other words, prisoners of the DPRK.

General Cho nodded, remembering the time his commanding officer had ordered him to execute the young farm labourer who had been captured swimming the river to China. He had held the pistol to the girl's neck and fired, never feeling so powerful as when she had dropped lifelessly to the ground. Since then, he had killed twice more for his Supreme Leader, and he would gladly do so again. "He will need an assistant, a decoy. Someone who can help him blend in. Your best female soldier today was an attractive creature. Have her brought to my quarters, too."

"As you wish, General..." the major bowed.

An hour later General Cho was drinking cheap Chinese whiskey in his quarters. The room was sparse but for an ornate chaise longue on which he regularly tested the resolve and political willingness of female recruits. He was close to key members of the politburo and to refuse his advances could mean being sent to a concentration camp for political correction. Other than the 'chair of passion' as he fondly referred to it, a mahogany desk and leather chair and a shelf full of books were the only creature comforts. The furniture had been gifted to him by the Supreme Leader. Lining the shelves were various biographies of Stalin, Hitler, Roosevelt, Churchill and Napoleon, as well as various editions of The Art of War by Sun Tzu. More modern tomes included biographies of tech billionaires and inspirational coaching books in business and sociology. General Cho had made it his life's work to know his country's enemies and the society they inhabited. Only by knowing one's enemy could you truly defeat them.

He looked up as a solid knock sounded twice upon the door and he called in his guests.

"Su Ji-ho and Eun-Ji," the major introduced the two soldiers, and they stepped into the General's quarters, took two paces forwards and stood to attention with a rigid salute.

General Cho stood unsteadily and returned the salute. He had consumed more whiskey than he had intended. "You have both been chosen for a mission," he explained, struggling to focus on them. "You will look like a handsome couple."

Su Ji-ho glanced at the woman beside him, then looked back at the General and frowned. "Forgive me, General. I do not understand."

"You will serve the Supreme Leader well, will you not?"

"Always," he replied.

"You have killed before?"

The woman shook her head but Su Ji-ho said, "Twice, General."

The general rested his elbows on the desk. "And how did that make you feel?"

"I was pleased to serve the Supreme Leader. The deaths of political dissidents meant nothing to me."

"Indeed," General Cho nodded somewhat ponderously. "You will pose as a South Korean couple," he said, his tone one of disdain for their disputed neighbour. "Can you act convincingly as a couple?"

They replied that they could in unison.

General Cho looked past them and dismissed the major, then when he had closed the door behind him, said. "Take off your clothes... both of you."

Eun-Ji tentatively unbuttoned her tunic, and Su Ji-ho slowly followed suit. When they had finished, both stood naked in front of the General. Eun-Ji's right hand hovered over her pudenda and the General motioned for her to move her hand with a wave of his own. She stood vulnerable before him, the tuft of jet-black pubic hair and her own black pageboy bob accentuating her white, almost translucent porcelain skin. Beside her, completely hairless apart from a tiny thatch of black pubic hair and a grade one military buzz cut, Su Ji-ho stood vulnerable, despite his rippling muscles and physical capabilities.

The General motioned to the chaise longue. "Make love to each other," he said quite dispassionately. "As a young couple in love would do…"

Eun-Ji stared up into Su Ji-ho's dark eyes, her body trembling. Fear, trepidation, anticipation of the unknown. She did not want to do this degrading thing, but to refuse an order was incomprehensible. Simply questioning the General's orders would see her inside a concentration camp, maybe worse, if that was a possibility. At least death was final. Su Ji-ho took her in his arms and kissed her tenderly and together they made their way to the chaise longue, where Eun-Ji sat down and swung her legs up onto the cushion, Su Ji-ho climbed on top of her, holding his chest off her, his sinewed arms comfortably taking his weight. He was becoming aroused; such was her beauty. Both glanced at the general, as if to see how far this should be taken, and the old man gestured impatiently for them to continue, as he sat behind his desk hiding his arousal. The look that the two young soldiers shared between them mirrored each other's feelings – fear, uncertainty, awkwardness, shame – but as Su Ji-ho positioned himself, Eun-Ji caressed his back and sides and let out a short, sharp moan as he entered her.

When he had finished, Su Ji-ho offered her a hand and she gratefully accepted it and pulled herself to her feet.

They both dressed hurriedly, awkwardly as the general watched them voyeuristically, until they were smartly attired and stood before him once more, flushed and glowing. The general seemed pleased with the performance.

"You have been chosen for a vital mission to protect our beloved country and our all-powerful Supreme Leader," the general told them. "You will tell nobody that you were here. You will tell nobody of this mission."

"I will obey your orders, General," Su Ji-ho said sharply.

"I will do as you command," Eun-Ji agreed with the same sentiment.

"Good. You must understand that you serve the Supreme Leader with this mission. You will first see to it that there are no loose threads."

"General?" Eun-Ji frowned.

"The major is a loose thread. If loose threads are pulled, then everything unravels. You will make it look like an accident. The Supreme Leader appreciates his sacrifice."

Su Ji-ho nodded. "We will do as you order, General." He paused. "If I may, General, what is the mission? What will you have us do?" he asked valiantly.

And so General Cho told them.

Chapter Twelve

L ondon

Ramsay looked up from his desk expectantly and with a sense of irritation. It was quite unlike Mae not to knock as he always needed time to prepare himself before interacting with people. When people interrupted him, or gave him information without warning, they never got the best of him.

"Sir, the nuclear power station outside Lyon, part of the Chinese owned Eternal Life Energy Group has entered second stage meltdown..." she said somewhat more calmly than her expression belied. "Mass evacuations are in progress and the French government have declared a national emergency."

"Dear god!"

"A COBRA meeting has been called immediately; all

parties are to make their way to the cabinet office briefing rooms. I've called Jim and he's bringing the car round..."

"Get me the chief of police in Lyon, the director of the DGSE and the most senior person at the power plant," he replied curtly. "A three-way conference call."

"Sir, there's an evacuation underway!"

"Now!" he wheeled himself around his desk and said, "I'll be downstairs with Charlotte and the rest of the analysts..."

Mae bustled out to her desk, ignoring his outburst, or at least not taking offence at it. She started dialling using the vital contact sheet as Ramsay wheeled himself past her and into the lift. When he came out on the floor below, Jim was breathlessly reaching the top of the stairs.

"The Jag's ready, boss," he said.

"Change of plan," he said. "Stay with me in case the plan changes again. It's fluid at best..."

In the computer suite there were six people at desks, and all looked up as their boss crashed through the doors. Only Charlotte got up from her desk and met Ramsay at the terminal and desk that he kept for himself.

"It looks like you're here for more than a Jammie Dodger and a catch-up," she said expectantly.

"Three-way conference call coming in. The French nuclear power plant outside Lyon, part of the Chinese Eternal Life Energy Group is in meltdown. I have the chief of police in Leon, the French secret service director and the general manager of the plant. He's a Brit, if memory serves me well."

"That's vexing..."

"That he's a Brit?"

"No, Neil. Because a nuclear power plant is melting down on our doorstep."

"Right," he nodded. "It is indeed vexing."

"Do you suspect enemy action?" she asked, not waiting for his reply. She logged onto Ramsay's computer and pulled a chair over for herself. "Our demonic air traffic controller?"

"It's just a hunch..."

"And thankfully more than a few of those have panned out," she commented. Ramsay did not know, but the attractive middle-aged women beside him had loved him for almost twenty years. A self-confessed sapiosexual, she found intelligence far more attractive than looks, physical attributes or humour. Ramsay had probably not thought too much about it, but despite being married and having two daughters, the woman beside him was probably his soulmate. "If you're thinking that the person behind the hacking of the airplane is behind the meltdown of this power station, then there is the distinct possibility that they have made the same mistake in their firewall."

"Not a mistake," Ramsay said sharply. "I think they have left a way in. Either for their collaborators or for somebody else to find."

"That's madness," Charlotte said, tapping on the screen and opening the line of the conference call system with Mae's desk upstairs. She sidelined the communications tab and sat poised with her fingers hovering over the keys.

"I have Director General Bernard Lerner of the DGSE, General Directorate of the National Police, Pierre Molineux and William Boyd, site manager of Saint Monica One, the nuclear power station currently in second stage meltdown." Mae's voice drifted over the speaker.

"Sirs, good morning. I won't waste any time. I want access to Saint Monica One's mainframe as I believe the hacker to be pertinent to an ongoing investigation with my department and I further believe that I can gain access through the hacker's own firewall," said Ramsay.

"Good morning, Neil, this is Bernard Lerner. In the interest of the nation's security, the DGSE has no qualms about your request, and would advise that the representative of the Saint Monica One powerplant grant you access immediately, unless of course, they have the situation in control."

"I have to speak to the directors first," William Boyd replied, his accent clearly that of a Yorkshireman.

"You will be reminded that in France's policy of energy security, that the French government are equal shareholders, and that Chinese Eternal Life Energy Group are minor shareholders, despite the fact they built the powerplant," Bernard Lerner said pointedly.

"If Mr Ramsay feels that he can halt this catastrophe, as Director General of the national police service, I would wholeheartedly agree with my DGSE counterpart. A full meltdown must be avoided at all costs..." Pierre Molineux urged.

"Even so, I can't allow our cyber security systems to be breached without proper consideration..."

"Mr Boyd, it is almost a certainty that your cyber security system has been hacked," Charlotte interrupted. "When Chernobyl melted down in nineteen eight six it formed the most dangerous substance on earth. You will, no doubt, be aware that the mound of corium known as the elephant's foot formed when the reactor melted will also remain the most hazardous substance ever to have existed for the next one hundred thousand years. This could happen right now, in the middle of central Europe. Chernobyl was not a densely populated area. This is about as bad for our countries as it can get."

There was a long pause and then Boyd came back on

the line and gave the IP address, followed by a series of numbers and letters. Ramsay started to type on the keyboard, the screen flicking from display to display almost too quickly to register. Charlotte seemed to understand what was happening, and Jim Kernow stared at the monitor looking utterly lost. While Ramsay typed, Charlotte scrolled through her tablet and brought up an intricate display of fault codes and diagrams. She slipped on a pair of glasses and studied the screen with the glasses resting on the tip of her nose. The rest of the staff in the suite had gathered round either to learn, witness or add something to the process. Ramsay stopped typing, reached into his inside jacket pocket and retrieved a small notepad which he flicked through, then wedged it open holding it in place with the bottom of the keyboard. He started typing a series of code, with Charlotte checking the code as he typed. She did not have to be asked to verify. They had done this sort of thing for hours on end in the old days at Thames House. Charlotte suddenly clutched his arm, her eyes wide and bright as she smiled.

"It's the same," he announced somewhat underwhelmed given the enormity of the event. "The same programmer who worked on sabotaging the BA flight also worked on this. It has their signature all over it, and once again, a gateway has been left open. I'm in."

Charlotte studied the screen and verified the next string of code that Ramsay typed. "Could it be a trap this time?" she asked. "Tease you with the aircraft flight information, then set you up with this? An electronic stalking horse."

"Possibly," he replied. "A Trojan horse... beware of Greeks bearing gifts..." he mused quietly. "But what are the chances that the same person, the same department even, would work on this?" Ramsay paused. "The nuclear plant is in another country. The gateway has been left open as a cry for help. The programmer *wants* to be found..."

Charlotte held up the screen of the tablet for Ramsay to see and he tentatively instructed the failed cooling system and heat sensors to go back online. To the right of the screen a series of bar charts indicated the tolerances, and they were at the top end, in the red and flashing. Which wasn't good. The air was tangible, the tension all encompassing. Nobody said anything, they were barely breathing. After what seemed an age, the bars stopped flashing. Charlotte glanced at Ramsay, but the man's eyes remained transfixed on the screen, his reflection showing nothing but steely determination. A collective gasp emanated from the other technicians as three bars dropped an increment. Within a minute, all the bars had dropped another three increments, and the system was well on the way to normal. Ramsay pushed himself back from the desk and sighed heavily.

"Is it done?" Jim Kernow asked tentatively.

"Yes," Ramsay replied. The bars retracted further, and he returned to the conference call. "Gentlemen, it would appear that we have just averted disaster."

"Can you confirm, Monsieur Boyd?" the police chief asked expectantly.

"I can," Boyd replied. *"But I'm nervous about this. Seventy percent of France's energy comes from fifty-six nuclear reactors across eighteen sites. If Saint Monica One can be hacked, then so can the others."*

"Agreed," replied Ramsay. "I am going to attend a COBRA meeting now and will recommend that my technicians meet with their French counterparts forthwith. We will, of course, share our findings freely with the French government."

"That was close," Jim Kernow commented. "Can I ask you something, Neil?"

"Of course," Ramsay replied.

"Could you sort out the settings on my iPhone?"

Several of the technicians laughed, but Ramsay had failed to recognise the man's humour. Instead, he told Kernow to let him have a look at it after the COBRA meeting.

Chapter Thirteen

Bangkok, Thailand

Hong Gil-dong stared at the screen in front of him, the ceiling fan above him doing little to stir the stale air, which was so thick, hot and humid that it was almost tangible. He had breathed a sigh of relief when the nuclear power plant had returned to normal, but he knew that the next attack would have to succeed, or he would be under suspicion and the goons from the RGB would be bundling him back to the DPRK. He scoffed at his country's name. There was nothing 'democratic' about the Democratic People's Republic of Korea.

There was little more to do now than sacrifice many to save himself and the lives of his family. He had chosen the target well. The security systems in place were virtually non-existent to anything other than financial hacking. He opened the tab and checked the schedule. Another ten minutes and he would enter the company's system. He had already been inside, penetrated the firewalls and knew what he had to do.

The knock at the door made him start. Something ominous, powerful about the tattoo. Not something housekeeping would do, especially by the tiny Thai and Pilipino women slap-slapping down the hall in flipflops as they pushed their housekeeping trolleys and chatted loudly to each other in their 'singsong' accents. The knock was powerful, meaningful and he already knew what would be waiting for him on the other side.

There was no spyhole in the door, so he left the chain on, opened the door and peered outside. Two hard-looking Korean men wearing black suits, white shirts and black ties stood before him, dark sunglasses hiding their expressions, but if the tightly set jaws and lack of smiles were anything to go by, he knew that their visit was not a good sign. He closed the door and took a deep breath. Had he not known firsthand how ruthless these people could be, he would have found their appearance almost comical, like a *Men in Black* comic strip, and certainly far from secretive and discreet as undercover agents should be. Hong Gil-dong closed the door, unlatched the chain with trepidation, resigned to his fate, and opened the door tentatively. The two men stepped inside and one of the men walked through the room and checked the bathroom and wardrobe while the other man removed his sunglasses and stared hard at the frightened Korean.

"Your last *project* failed..."

Hong Gil-dong dared not re-enter the system for Saint Monica One, nor the other French nuclear power stations whose systems he had studied and tested. Not for fear of being caught by the intelligence services of the West, but for the risk it would pose if it was noticed by his handlers. "I do not know how it could have failed," he replied indignantly. He did not know either of the agents' names, RGB agents did not have that sort of repartee with their assets. Hong Gil-dong knew that the next time the Supreme Leader's henchmen came visiting, it would likely be different agents, and every time after that. For as much as Hong Gil-dong knew it was to unsettle him, the Supreme Leader did not trust his agents not to strike up a relationship with their assets. There were no friends in the DPRK. Likewise, the Supreme Leader and the politburo did not want the rank and file experiencing too much of a good thing, so visits abroad were limited and the RGB agents would be viewed suspiciously until they had proved themselves utterly loyal to the regime. Tests would be undertaken to see if they had been turned by the trappings of the West.

"Can you be trusted?" the agent asked.

The second agent returned from his security checks and said, "No, I do not think he can be. Perhaps he needs a reminder of the precarious situation of his sister, his brother and their parents?"

"I can be trusted! I have done good work for the Supreme Leader and the DPRK!" Hong Gil-dong objected vehemently.

"Then why did the nuclear power plant fail to meltdown?" the first agent sneered. "The Supreme Leader is most disappointed."

"This, like the British Airways airliner, was meant to be the test for a full-scale cyber-attack. Thousands of airplanes, hundreds of nuclear power stations, nuclear missile silos, the complete annihilation of the West," the second agent said coldly.

"And it *will* happen," Hong Gil-dong protested. "But

like all technology, it takes time to test and make corrections to the programming."

"Then show us your next test," the first agent suggested. "Let us witness your work and see the effects of your labours. Give us something to go back to Pyongyang with and tell them that your family should be left alone and that you are loyal to the Supreme Leader and the Democratic People's Republic of Korea, and to be trusted."

Hong Gil-dong tried not to show either a sense of relief or disappointment. He knew that he had to make the next cyber-attack convincing, and he knew that people would die, but he could have chosen the time and the location. With these two goons looking over his shoulder, despite not being the most intelligent of creatures, they would be able to work out the point where the most damage would be done, and the most lives would be lost. He felt his hands start to shake as he returned to his chair in front of the desk and logged onto the remote server and the portal that would give him both the processing power and anonymity he would need. The remote server was powered by hundreds of processors, and miles of wiring and water-cooling pipes, and was a new set-up in Belarus after their facility in Turkey that had been planned for a major cyber-attack had been destroyed by enemy agents.

Hong Gil-dong's fingers glided across the keyboard. He had been close to getting past the company's firewalls when the two agents had interrupted him, but with them hovering over his shoulder like two evil spectres, he knew that the next few minutes would not only be difficult but would set him on a course to kill hundreds, if not a thousand or more people. As he worked, the seconds turning to minutes and then an hour, the two agents did not move. They filmed with their phones and occasionally whispered to one another, and as off-putting as it was to be monitored in such blatant fashion, Hong Gil-dong eventually found his way in and sat back in his chair as the screen in front of him brought up the control system of the target.

"It's ready," he said, his manner subdued. He had been trusted for fifteen years

– educated and sent around the world to learn his craft - and even though he was betraying his country by leaving clues in the coding and gaps in the firewalls, the presence of the agents and their accusing, suspicious manner had left him feeling affronted. What the hell did the dinosaurs surrounding the Supreme Leader expect? He had seen the world with fresh eyes, seen his country for what it was, had experienced a certain amount of freedom and the trappings that freedom and free commerce came with. How could he possibly go back? He knew that it was the same with the agents of the RGB, and why every time he was checked up on, it was someone different. The dictatorship of the DPRK would not risk giving their agents a long leash and the opportunities that luxury presented.

"Too soon," the first agent replied. He moved for the first time and perched on the edge of the desk while he scrolled on his phone.

"It's perfect!" Hong Gil-dong protested. "The longer we wait, the more time there is for a systems operator to discover that they've been hacked."

"We wait..." the second agent said sharply, all the while keeping his eyes on the screen. "For a man whose family is in *kwalliso* you are strangely belligerent towards representatives of the Supreme Leader. Perhaps you have been infected by your time in the West? Should we suggest a period of re-education inside a kwalliso to our superiors?"

Hong Gil-dong bowed his head. "No, that will not be necessary…"

"I thought not," he replied. "Your sister is pretty," he said. "Not as pretty as before she went into kwalliso, but still a tempting proposition, nonetheless. I want you to remember that, Hong Gil-dong…"

"I serve the Supreme Leader and the Democratic People's Republic of Korea," Hong Gil-dong answered emphatically. "My family should be free, and I should be trusted, because I have served the Supreme Leader well, and I have succeeded in my endeavours."

"Until recently."

"I am not infallible. Nobody is."

"The Supreme Leader is infallible!" the agent quickly chastised him. "As are the all-supreme and all-honourable Kim family…"

Hong Gil-dong closed his eyes momentarily. He knew that they were baiting him, and he knew that he had to be careful. These agents were machines, automatons. There was very little humanity left inside them after so much indoctrination. He opened his eyes and started clicking through the operating system. "I'm programming now," he said. "Enough time has passed since disembarkation."

The agent beside him checked his phone, studied the company's schedules and latest news, then said, "Alright. Do it."

Hong Gil-dong typed on the keyboard. The instructions had been sent, and he could see from the system board in front of him that the process had been initiated. He got up and stepped away from the desk, switching on the television with the remote and bringing up the *Sky News* channel.

"No, CNN," said the first agent.

Hong Gil-dong shook his head. "It's a British target, so

we should watch a British news network. CNN will get there late, and they'll be reporting already reported facts. In some American states, not even make the news, maybe not even make the tickertape banner on the bottom of the screen." He tossed the remote control onto the bed and slumped heavily in the chair. He had a bottle of duty-free vodka in his travel bag and as soon as these goons left him alone then he would take the head and shoulders off the bottle, and lament on how many lives he had taken as he set about finishing it.

Chapter Fourteen

L ondon

"How many," asked King.

"One thousand, two hundred and eighty-nine confirmed dead. Four hundred and seventy-two rescued and two-hundred and twenty-seven still missing." Ramsay paused. "Of the rescued, fifty-six are in a critical condition."

"Jesus wept..." Caroline said, watching the television and the Sky News report. The deaths and rescued figures were changing regularly on the tickertape banner. "And you suspect the same hacker?"

"We've confirmed it," said Ramsay. "The same modus operandi, the same hacker's signature, the same gaps in the firewalls, which I now suspect were chiselled out by other hackers from different locations."

King watched the news footage, somewhat voyeuristically pulled in by the images. The upturned cross-channel ferry, the coastguard and RNLI rescue boats and a flotilla of fishing and pleasure craft that had headed out from Dover to help the stricken vessel two miles out in the English Channel. Almost a thousand vehicles and two-thousand people had been onboard when the prow loading doors had opened and the operating system failed to be overridden. With strong winds and choppy waves of almost two metres high, the equivalent of a thousand Olympic-sized swimming pools had flooded inside the vehicle bays within seconds and destabilised the ship, causing the prow to plunge downwards and the vessel to overturn. The sea conditions were being reported as challenging for rescue teams and several pleasure craft had been swamped and required assistance. Vessels from the Royal Navy were en route, and Coastguard and Royal Navy helicopters had been air lifting the survivors to shore in Dover.

"Someone did this with the click of a button?" King asked, his eyes still transfixed on the macabre scene.

"Yes, well technically. Fifty keys, possibly."

King ignored Ramsay's pedantism. "Can we find him?" he asked, turning in his seat and staring at Ramsay.

"I think we already have."

"Then send me to kill him."

"Why are you assuming it's a man?" asked Caroline.

"Take it as a compliment," King said. "But women don't generally do this sort of thing."

"I remember a woman who was one of the worst people we've ever been up against."

King shrugged. "No argument there..."

Ramsay glanced at his watch. "King, you're booked on the next flight to Bangkok. Check-in is in two hours."

"And that's where he... *she*, is?" King asked.

"The hacker is leaving breadcrumbs for our analysts to

follow." Ramsay paused. "So, I believe so, yes. But it may not be as simple as that."

"Why?" Caroline asked.

Ramsay brought down the volume on the television with the remote and stared at them now that he had their undivided attention. "The hacking of the British Airways airliner was done from California." Caroline stiffened. Her last mission had taken her stateside and she wasn't looking to go back anytime soon. It would take a long time for the dust to settle. Perhaps it never would. "But France's nuclear power station was hacked from Bangkok, as was the ferry."

King shrugged. "Well, that's going to be a wild goose chase because I guarantee that the next cyber-attack will come from somewhere else." He paused. "It's like a sniper taking a shot from the same hide. I'm surprised that two attacks came from the same location."

"So am I," Ramsay agreed. "So, I wonder whether our hacker's hand was forced."

"You seriously think they're an unwilling combative?" Caroline frowned.

"It makes no sense," Ramsay replied. "The ingenuity of this hacker is incredible; their skills are world class. However, they have made mistakes that are so downright ridiculous that they can only be a cry for help. Whomever this hacker is, I believe that they operate through fear and intimidation."

"Give me what you've got, and I'll put a stop to this," King told him.

Ramsay nodded, passing a file across his desk. "But only if that *stop* means bringing them back here..."

"What?" King bristled.

"If our enemies have trained and invested in a hacker who operates at this level, then we have something to learn from them." Ramsay paused. "Talking with our analysts and tech specialists, we are all in agreement that we would not have stopped the nuclear meltdown in time, had we not found the way in that the hacker left for us."

"You want him arrested?" King asked incredulously. He had snatched people before, and it wasn't an easy thing to do across international borders.

"For want of a better term, yes."

"And we're leaving now?" Caroline asked.

"No. I want King to go out first." He paused. "You will go out afterwards with some help. I don't want unfriendly forces spotting the entire team."

"You think they could suspect us of countering their attack?"

Ramsay sighed. "Well, by now they will know that an intelligence agency has stopped at least one attack, but it's not that..." He paused. "It's the breadcrumbs. Because as much as we found them and followed them, they could have been set for an entirely different reason. This *could* all be a trap."

Chapter Fifteen

The River House
(MI6 Headquarters)

"He's brought back the brute in a suit... except he doesn't wear a bloody suit... Lord knows what goes on across the river," Devonshire said, still staring over the Thames in the general direction of Ramsay's new premises. "Which means a death sentence for someone..."

"We have no proof of that," Harriet replied. "And I can't find anything on the man in our files."

Devonshire scoffed. "He was unofficial. He was trained by that bloody Scottish dinosaur Peter Stewart." He paused, noticing her expression. "He was a real butcher. A functioning alcoholic, a psychopath to boot. Before your time, my dear," he said rather patronisingly. "Part of the old guard. Got himself killed up in Lapland, or Finland... someplace bloody cold. He was retired by then but found himself pulled back in for a bit of asset shepherding. However, the defection went tits up, the submarine sent to pick up the asset was lost, and Stewart ended up catching a bullet. But in his day, he was a tough old bastard, and he ran the special projects wing. All SAS types, but the man we know as King was a different sort. Some say he was a prisoner turned good, or bad, if the stories were true. Most of the old guard died around the same time as King left our employment."

"A coincidence?"

"Hardly. But who am I to speculate?" He shrugged. "But what I *do* know, is Stewart was the only one of the old guard who did not meet a terrible accident, and he retired soon afterwards. But not, I assume, without losing every detail we had on King. So, all we have is speculation and whispers from some of the people who were here at the same time as Stewart and the scruffy, thuggish ex-boxer type we know as Alex King."

"I wouldn't say he looks thuggish," Harriet mused. "Rugged, perhaps. And he's not *that* scruffy, just doesn't appear to own a suit…"

Devonshire sighed. "But he's trouble. And with Ramsay all over the COBRA meeting having successfully prevented a nuclear meltdown catastrophe, then calling in this King fellow means that his little band of merry men are onto something." Devonshire paused. "Which seriously diminishes our stock."

Harriet subconsciously fiddled with her pearl necklace, trying not to smile. Devonshire had a background in the city and still to all intents and purposes, looked like a bond trader. However, regardless of the analogy, with MI5 taking a somewhat sidelined role, there was no time like the present for MI6 to shine, but Ramsay's new MI5 department with its frustratingly vague and shadowy remit, was picking up the baton and keeping hold of it. "They got lucky, that's all," she replied, trying to belay his fears. "Ramsay's a geek and he took many geeks away from Thames House when he was reassigned. They all study their puzzles and coding, and simply got lucky."

"We need to know what *they* know," Devonshire mused. "You got on with that lad of theirs, didn't you? The one whose aunt made a big cock up with that defector and got herself killed..." he added, almost ambivalent that the late Stella Fox had been the Director General of the Security Service.

Typical of the man to be so equivocally dismissive, thought Harriet. She also wondered how much the man knew about her own dalliance with Jack Luger. "We had dinner," she replied offhandedly.

"That's nice," he replied sceptically. "Nice that a married woman can have dinner with a younger, handsome man and it not be considered a threat to her husband. Or her marriage. How is Raef, by the way?"

"Busy."

"I haven't seen him in years. Not since my stock exchange days. I must catch up with him soon..."

"I planted surveillance equipment at his flat. I told you that much," she said tersely. "How the hell do you think I got the devices in place? And now you want to threaten me with telling my husband?"

"Well, when you say it like that..." Devonshire said quietly, his eyes still on a spot somewhere across the river. She wasn't sure if even so much as a roof tile could be spotted on Ramsay's building from here, but the thought of how close his competition was geographically seemed to be eating him inside. "Would you meet with him again?"

Harriet thought of the young intelligence officer and felt

a flush run through her. She uncrossed and recrossed her legs, elegantly seated in the leather tub chair, but feeling the tiny waves of passion washing through her. *Yes. Yes, she could meet with the young man again...*

Chapter Sixteen

Gatwick Airport

The hangar swallowed the Boeing 787 Dreamliner with room to spare, and much of the aircraft had been dismantled by mechanics and engineers, and labelled and stacked by technicians in neatly taped-off sectors. Workstations had been organised and laptops ran programmes as their operators input the data. The flight computer had been removed and plugged into diagnostic equipment, and the black box – resplendent in orange – was plugged into several devices and undergoing much scrutiny. In charge of it all, Lillia Bailey sat at a workstation of her own, pensive and oblivious to Jack Luger as he stepped inside.

He carried pastries and coffee and placed them on Lillia's desk before pulling out a chair. "Good morning," he said lightly.

"Morning..." she replied, barely looking up. She caught

sight of the black labrador on a leather lead and her eyes lit up. "Oh my god! You really did keep the dog!"

"Meet Fido."

"Original..." she said as she bent down to stroke the dog on the top of his head. The tail started up ten to the dozen and when she stopped, he sat and held up a paw. "Ah... he's gorgeous..."

"He seems to like it." Luger paused. "The name, that is."

"He will have a name," she said. "It'll be in the cargo manifest. I'll get round to that later, just concentrating on *people* for the moment."

"You don't have a boyfriend, do you?" he stated rather than asked the question. She looked up and frowned, but he shook his head, his expression telling her that it did not matter either way. "I came on strong, and you're still grieving for your fiancé. I'm sorry if I was being pushy... It was a bit of an act, anyway. *Mr Confident...*" he said, somewhat abashed. "It's not really me, to be honest."

"She was a lover, wasn't she?" she said, stroking the dog once more. Dogs were a great distraction in awkward moments.

He thought about Harriet and her act at The Ivy. There was no point in lying to her. "Yes," he said. "A fling, nothing more."

"She had a large diamond engagement ring and a rather nice-looking wedding band," Lillia commented. "An eternity ring as well. That usually indicates a long marriage. She looks exactly the type to play games..."

"Perhaps," he replied, but he already knew the answer. "Anyway, you left me sitting there, and I suppose I deserved it. You didn't have to pay, though. I would always have taken care of that."

"Oh, I'm pretty sure that I did have to," she replied curtly. "I don't date and feel beholden to someone's perceived generosity. It always has a price."

Luger smiled and said, "Well, maybe I could return the compliment one day?"

Lillia shrugged. "We'll see," she said noncommittedly, visibly relaxing. "But in answer to your previous gambit, no I do not have a boyfriend, but I *still* do, if that makes sense?"

"It does. It makes perfect sense," he replied, handing her over a coffee. "I got you a cappuccino," he said. "Every coffee drinker can drink a cappuccino." He sipped some of his own extra-large, long black coffee and said, "If you were thinking about getting back onto the dating scene, tentatively after losing someone, then the last thing you needed was a cocky so and so playing the confident game." He shrugged, pushing the bag of pastries towards her. "Danishes and chocolate croissants, you can't go wrong with those, either."

She smiled, opened the pack and retrieved a sticky Danish pastry. "I'm starving," she smiled. "You're forgiven. But I don't think I'm ready to date, just yet." Fido had started to drool, and his paw made it to her knee as he eyed the Danish pastry. Lillia smiled and fed him a piece of doughy pastry without the icing.

"I got that," he smiled.

"I don't know what I was thinking, really."

"Thanks…"

"Not you!" she grinned. "Just, well, I thought perhaps it was time, and then when that beautiful married woman came over to our table and was all over you, well I knew then that I wasn't going to give heart, or perhaps more, to a player."

Luger felt rather foolish. In truth, he'd had a recent run

of good luck in the romance and sex department and had felt invincible. Lillia smacking him down was likely to be the best thing for him, but it hadn't felt like that at the time. "Let's draw a line under it and concentrate on how we can stop this..." He waved a hand around the cavernous hangar. "... from happening again."

"That sounds like a plan," she replied.

"So, how far have you got with this?"

"You're kidding, right?"

Luger shrugged. "Nope."

"All I can say is that hacking isn't something that we are equipped for. To control the computers in such a way, with such impunity, it's not something that aircraft manufacturers, travel companies or aviation safety and investigation authorities have considered, either. There are fail safes, of course. But that takes us back thirty years and it could be as simple as pulling a fuse, but aviation companies can't just pull the fuse to the air recirculation, or oxygen supply as a prevention method. It would compromise safety. And for something as vital as the air on board, this could take months, probably more realistically years to implement."

"Really? That long?"

"Air travel is big business," she replied with a shrug. "What you need to ascertain is whether this was an isolated incident, or something that's going to happen again."

"That's easier said than done."

"Well, hopefully you'll come up with another solution."

"Not any easier."

"You're a secret agent, aren't you?"

"Intelligence officer," he corrected her.

"I'm sticking with secret agent," she said. "And secret agents take people out, don't they?"

"Like I did with you for dinner?"

"I didn't mean that," she replied impatiently. "I meant... *take people out*... as in; kill them." Still, Luger gave away nothing, said nothing. "Okay, so you won't commit. But all I can say is that if the person who hacked this plane did what they did so easily, then the only way to stop catastrophe after catastrophe is to see that they can never hack an aircraft's system again or are left alive long enough to talk about it."

Chapter Seventeen

Jack Luger checked his phone as he stopped in slow-moving traffic in Berkley Square. The Bentley showroom to his left had featured on his daily commutes recently (sometimes he even went out of his way to pass the showroom) and it was becoming no less tempting as he stared past the gold-coloured lions beneath the highly polished 'JB' logo of the door handles and concentrated on the glistering vehicles within. He had a large legacy left to him by his aunt, and the suddenness and manner in which she had been taken had left him feeling that life did not wait for a rainy day, and perhaps he shouldn't, either. Especially now his work demanded more of him. He might not even live long enough for that rainy day. He liked the coupe, the Continental V8, and he could see himself behind the wheel on an open country road in Hampshire or taking the south coast roads through seaside towns and the New Forest. He imagined a woman like Lillia sitting elegantly beside him as they laughed and joked and loved their way through his daydream. The traffic started to move, and he pulled away, still no closer to stepping into the brightly lit showroom and realising his dream.

The text message had been from Harriet, and he was ashamed to admit to himself that he was excited as much as intrigued. He knew that he was being played, but Rashid and Jo had planted surveillance devices in her properties and now they were playing her, too. He thought about the woman's scent, the warmth of her breath as she had leaned in and kissed him on the cheek in the restaurant. There was something so physical about Harriet, so compellingly sexual. Her soft skin, firm tone and softness where it mattered. He had never known a woman like her, and even with the sting of rejection from Lillia still raw, and the fact that he knew Harriet to be disingenuous, he could think of little more than wanting to be with her again. Was this how male black widow spiders felt? Knowing that they could be consumed after mating, but still willing to try? There was no good that would come from meeting with Harriet, but he found himself justifying that they had bugged her, so surely it would pay to keep tabs on the woman. It was in the team's interest for him to remain close to her, perhaps even cultivate a relationship. Of course it wasn't, but like the tiny male spider, he found himself justifying anything to get to the female and the dangers lurking within her mind.

Chapter Eighteen

Bangkok, Thailand

Hong Gil-dong had done everything he could to leave a trail. All he wanted was a future. He did not want to abandon his parents and his brother and sister, but he could no longer live a half-life. Teased with the freedom and trappings of the West, forever looking over his shoulder for the agents of the RGB and under the constant fear of being forced to return to the DPRK. He knew that his skills, if they could not be utilised, would be seen as a threat. And threats to the DPRK and the Supreme Leader were only treated one way. What he knew would get him killed.

The RGB goons had left him alone, satisfied that the death toll of the cross-channel ferry disaster was suitably high, and he had hacked the vessel's ballast system and automatic loading doors skilfully. The RGB agents had told him that they would speak highly of him back in

Pyongyang, but he did not believe a word of it. In North Korea, nobody praised another. Not even families spoke highly of its members for fear of reprisals. There was no stock in praising others and the route to one's survival was to take the credit for other's work. By the time the two RGB agents finished their report, the operation would only have gone ahead because of their involvement, and Hong Gil-dong would be someone to keep a close eye on. What Hong Gil-dong did not know was that for the past four years, the various agents that appeared to keep tabs on him were not RGB agents from the DPRK, but North Korean defectors working for Iron Fist. The Supreme Leader had no knowledge of his involvement in the recent terrorist events and like many people from the DPRK who had travelled abroad, it was assumed that he had defected, and his family had been punished accordingly. Both his parents had been repeatedly run over with armoured personnel carriers until nothing recognisable as human remained. Afterwards, the mess that had been left had been ploughed into fields for fertiliser. His sister had been raped by an entire regiment of soldiers until she had died from her injuries on the second day. She had later been put on public display for treachery and after a week in the sun, she had been ploughed into the ground along with a dozen other dissidents. Hong Gil-dong's brother had been presented to the army for testing snipers on the one-thousand metre range. He too, had been ploughed into the fields so that crops could flourish.

Hong Gil-dong looked around the room. He had left nothing behind. No physical breadcrumbs for someone to follow. The goons that he thought to be from the RGB could come back after he checked out of the hotel and do a thorough shakedown. If he left a clue, however small, it would be a noose around his neck. He had been ordered to clean his fingerprints from all the hard surfaces and use some spray bleach to wipe out his DNA. He had deliberated on this, but if they checked and he had failed to do so, then he would have as good as handed the noose to the hangman.

Chapter Nineteen

Bangkok, Thailand

There was air-conditioning in the taxi, but it was broken. King didn't believe the driver and other than having an aversion to cool air, couldn't see why the man would lie with the thermometer nudging 40c and the humidity so close that it was practically touching him. It wasn't like it saved money keeping it switched off because the taxi driver's fuel economy would have been shot to pieces in the hustle and bustle and general chaos of Bangkok, but still King perspired, his shirt looking like he'd jumped into a swimming pool just twenty minutes earlier.

"You want girl? Quickie in alleyway just one thousand baht! That just twenty dollar!" the driver beamed a smile interrupted by two gold teeth and a sizeable gap. "Or ten thousand baht for longtime, all night long. Come as many time as want. She my sister, clean girl, no con you or steal from you..."

"I'm ok, thanks."

"You gay? I get you ladyboy. Perhaps two for five thousand baht. Or one hundred fifty dollar! I take dollar, too."

King frowned at the liberty the man was taking with maths and shook his head. "No."

"Drugs?" the man beamed a smile of yellowed teeth, gold caps and the gap. "I get what you want. Smoke, speed, blow, ice... I get you everything to party with. Maybe drugs, girls *and* ladyboy for good time?"

"A gun?" King shrugged.

The man took his eyes off the road for too long to stare at him and clipped two girls riding a scooter. King watched the two girls sprawl in the road, the scooter sliding under a crowded bus. The man didn't so much as blink. "I get you gun. What gun you want? Kalashnikov? You go out to jungle and play soldiers?" He paused. "I know man with goats and donkey. He let you shoot them for ten thousand baht..."

"A pistol," King replied. "And some ammunition."

The man nodded. "I drop you at hotel, then come back to foyer in one hour."

"That easy?"

The man laughed. "Nothing is hard in Bangkok," the man replied, then burst out laughing. "Apart from cock! Cock always hard in Bangkok!" He paused thoughtfully. "You need something to make cock hard? I get you that too!"

King had been glad to get out of the taxi, leave the driver behind him and step into the blissful air conditioning of the hotel. Between the chaos of the traffic, the heat and humidity and the driver selling his wares, the cool air conditioning, slow-turning ceiling fans and open sides to reception that allowed a gentle breeze, the hotel was a sanctuary. He wondered whether he was getting old. Of course he was. There was no slowing that, but he had never felt this way before. Retirement, semi-retirement, or whatever the hell he had been doing on the yacht with Caroline was, it was making him soft. He thought back to his first mission in Africa, in Angola and the Congo. Heat, thirst, hunger and harsh terrain, but he took it all in his stride and it merely glanced off the armour of youth. Years later, on operations in Iraq and Indonesia, he was only affected by the people he was up against, never the conditions. He had thought nothing of heat and the chaos around him, nothing of the uncomfortable travel and inevitable lack of sleep. He'd heard that Jack Luger had spent some time with the SAS recruits on selection, beasted and tested and brought to the edge of exhaustion. He remembered when Peter Stewart had sent him for the same week or two of hell, a couple of times a year, sometimes more. He had not learned soldiering or the skills that would see him kill for his country; it had been all about fitness and resilience. He decided that when he got back to England, when this was all over, then he would get Ramsay to arrange some time for him up at Hereford so he could test himself against soldiers almost half his age.

After showering and resting naked on the bed for half an hour under the respite of the ceiling fan, King got dressed in cargo shorts and a loose cotton shirt. He slipped on a pair of canvas deck shoes and checked himself in the mirror as he downed a bottle of water. He would fit right in on the streets of Bangkok, or the beaches of Ko Samui. His tan helped. He didn't look like he was straight off the plane and ripe to fleece. Gap year students and mid-life breakouts would arrive pasty of skin and green in the ways of Asia and were easily targeted to con, steal from or assault. A few weeks or months travelling around Thailand, the ubiquitous Golden Triangle and the islands in the south and they returned to Bangkok, sage old hands who knew their way around and were hardly worth bothering with.

In the garden a group of local children used whole peanuts to tease a tethered monkey, but it was fast and agile and swiped the nuts to screams and fits of laughter and climbed to the lower branches of a tree, its leash straining and stopping it from climbing any higher. The monkey picked through the shells and ate the nuts, tossing the pieces of shell at the children to more laughter. Two swarthy-looking men with long, greasy hair, wispy beards, tattered clothes and worn flip-flops were squatting on their haunches and smoking, the ash from their cigarettes dropping onto their bare toes. One looked up at King and made a steering wheel motion and shrugged when King declined. They were obviously resident taxi drivers and got the gig by agreeing not to hassle the guests. The front of house staff would be on a commission, and they would recommend the men to every guest. In Southeast Asia everybody had a side hustle and made money from everybody else.

The reception desk was long and manned by three young women in traditional Thai dress with lots of orange and flecks of gold embroidered into the material. King couldn't quite decide if they were saris or something else. He took a seat at a low table and waited. Guests came and went, the drivers miming their steering impression, the receptionists checking in people and giving out replacement keycards. The fans turned the warm air, and the open sides allowed some breeze in. The air conditioning ran continuously, blasting the entrance in arctic drifts, only to waft out the open sides of the reception building.

King's driver stopped and chatted to a lacklustre security guard in a soaked shirt, a baton hanging from his belt. The driver pressed his palms together and bowed his head and the security guard reciprocated. The gesture was the traditional Thai greeting, used frequently and quickly and given as either a hello or goodbye. The driver looked around the reception area, then hurried over when he saw King. He gave King the greeting, and King simply nodded in return.

"You have something for me?" asked King.

"In car," he said. "Come... come..."

King got up and followed the man to his vehicle, which he had parked way back from the hotel under a cluster of trees. King looked around him as the man opened the boot. Warm air greeted King in the face, along with the smell of oil. An open sports bag revealed several guns, and King pulled a few out and rested them on the carpeted surface. An old Colt 1911 .45 that could well have come across from Vietnam more than fifty years ago. King liked the weapon, but it was heavy and limited to just seven rounds. He discarded a couple of revolvers for the same reason. He preferred not to use wheel guns, unless it was specifically the Smith & Wesson model 60 snub nose. That weapon made sense because of its pocket size. He would also need to tuck the pistol into his waistband and revolvers did not tend to hold securely when carried in such fashion. He had once felt a heavy Colt .357 slide down his backside and halfway down a trouser leg and he vowed for that to never happen again. The Ruger LCP caught his eye. A compact semi-auto in .380 (sometimes known as 9mm short) that packed ten rounds into its magazine. It was a true pocket pistol, which negated the waistband carry, and he also decided it was the newest firearm there by thirty years. He liked the .380 round as well, less recoil than a 9mm from its slightly shorter case yet still good on ballistic performance, which allowed for accurate rapid fire.

"I'll take the Ruger," King said. He searched for another magazine, but there wasn't one. He found the .380 ammunition, twenty-rounds in a box that once contained fifty. "Is this gun clean?" he asked.

"Yes, just oiled," the driver replied.

"No, I meant has it been used in a crime?"

The driver laughed. "Many!" he replied. "All used many times." He shrugged. "You want clean, get Thailand residency, join gun club and apply for licence!" he wailed with laughter.

King pocketed the tiny pistol and tipped the twenty rounds into his left pocket, then took out his wallet. "How much?"

"Five hundred dollar."

King didn't argue. He peeled off five one-hundred-dollar bills and handed them to the man.

"You still want woman?"

"No, I don't," King replied. "Nor ladyboys or goats or donkeys or drugs." He turned and made his way back into the lobby. The children were still teasing the monkey and the two drivers, ash now covering their feet, continued to smoke and chat.

Back inside his room, King stripped the tiny pistol down and checked the firing pin. He loaded ten rounds into the magazine and set it down on the table while he reassembled the piece. He inserted the magazine into the butt, worked the slide, then repeatedly worked the slice back and forwards ejecting the bullets onto the bed. He reloaded the magazine a second time, then loaded the weapon and made it ready. It fitted into his pocket well, and the baggy cargo shorts hid any bulge. King then checked his phone. Ramsay had the location of the Genesis server – the server where their hacker had first signed in. Ramsay suspected a defection, and this was ground zero for King's search. Just an infinitesimally minute unit of time, three-hundredths of a second between logging onto the Wi-Fi and being routed to a dedicated server that bounced between a thousand IP addresses, all without their operators knowing that their systems were piggy-backing hostile intent, but those three-hundredths of a second had put the hacker in a hotel in Bangkok just minutes before the doors to the ferry had opened to disaster.

Chapter Twenty

Long Beach, California

Rashid stared at the CCTV footage. His task was akin to searching for a needle in a haystack, but Ramsay had insisted that he make the journey and get what they needed. His MI5 identification carried no weight here, but five-thousand dollars had been enough to bribe the head of security and allow him access to the call logs, security camera database and the room booking software. At the time of the three-hundredths of a second that the hotel's server showed up, there had been twenty-two signatures online. The reception desk, dining room and security office took care of three of those signatures. Seven more accounted for movie channels of various taste with three that would show as 'specialised entertainment' on the customer bills. That left eleven signatures who were browsing the internet and one who was controlling a 787 Dreamliner from the comfort of their hotel room.

Rashid had the list of names and contact details and all he could do for now was to photograph them and email them to Ramsay, where the techs on the floor below would start finding out everything about them.

Chapter Twenty-One

Bangkok, Thailand

At the same moment that Rashid was now driving north towards Silicon Valley on the gloriously scenic Pacific Highway, King was paying the hotel manager at the Rama Gardens Hotel in Bangkok a substantial sum of money to give him access to the hotel computer. Not as large a number as Rashid had paid the security manager in Long Beach, but certainly a third of a year's salary, which in real terms, was usually the figure to tempt people to look the other way over everything except life and death.

King had the list of guests in front of him and he sent a photo of it to Ramsay, but unlike Rashid's search, there had only been ten digital signatures, three belonging to hotel departments. One-hundred and eight-eight delegates had been spread across three function rooms in the hotel's business suite, and King discounted these because of the hacker's unlikeliness to blend in and do what would be required at a laptop, even if they were doing it by proxy through a server most likely on another continent. Which left four guests had been logged on for almost half a second around the time of the ferry disaster. King briefly wondered whether four bullets could prevent further loss. It was extreme, but... *No, too extreme,* he thought. He checked the front of house software and saw that one of the names had just checked out, and he leapt up and ran around to the lobby and reception desk. The two drivers had left their spot and the children had stopped tormenting the monkey, but other than an old couple checking in, the foyer was empty. King darted outside, stopped on the damp cobbles and looked both ways. The gardens were rich in that scent you only seem to get in tropical streets and the jungle – soil, leaves and decay, all permeated by excessive heat and humidity. King hadn't even noticed the torrential rain shower while he had been in the manager's office, but everything was now soaked and steaming in the sun. The humidity was intense, making the cobbles steam, but through the distortion he saw a slightly built Asian man getting into the rear of a white saloon with a petite, attractive Asian woman. The name on the check-out had been Hong. Korean was King's best reckoning, and the woman certainly looked Korean. He wondered whether this could be it – Iron Fist caught in the act of evacuating from their operating base. He stared long enough for the slightly built man to stare fleetingly back at him, then the woman shoved him inside, giving King a cursory glare. That was all King needed to see. He sprinted towards them, but the vehicle sped forwards, its front wheels spinning briefly on the wet cobblestones. King followed the vehicle through the gardened grounds and into the tarmacked carpark. The car was a Toyota Corolla, the ubiquitous rental car in Southeast Asia, and a popular taxi, Uber and private hire car. Once it got out onto the streets, he would likely lose it in the traffic unless he could get a vehicle. A car would be pointless because it was doubtful that he would be able to overtake the traffic, and he could already hear the traffic noises of revving engines and sounding horns, a melee of chaos that remained constant but had been drowned out by the hotel's walled gardens.

King saw a young Asian man stepping off his motorcycle, undoing his helmet. The man had found a good place to secure the bike to with a chain, but he had not yet done it. King leapt onto the machine and the man stood stunned for long enough for King to turn the key in the ignition and press the start button. The man snapped to his senses and caught hold of King's arm, but there was something in King's eyes, the determination, a cruelness even, and the man hesitated a moment too long and it was enough for King to stamp the gears down into first and accelerate out onto the street. He saw the Toyota, or at least he thought he did, there was another identical vehicle coming towards him and another pulling out of a turning three vehicles ahead of him. King wound on the throttle and changed up through the gears, but the motorcycle was low on power, and he pulled back into the traffic having only overtaken two cars. The Toyota turned off into a side street and King undertook the row of vehicles in front of him and took the turning sharply, dropping his knee to the ground then levelling up as he accelerated. The street was narrow with overfilled rubbish bins lining the pavement and children played close to their doorsteps while mothers pinned out washing after the rainstorm and swept in front of their houses. They all looked up as King powered through their lives on the motorcycle. This wasn't a thoroughfare, and as he looked ahead, he could see why. The Toyota was reversing towards him and swung into a J-turn, the vehicle swinging around amid tyre smoke on the hot, drying tarmac, the sound of protesting tyres and high engine revs clearly audible over the whine and rattle of King's somewhat underpowered machine. King looked for an out, but there wasn't one. He was only going twenty miles per hour, but the Toyota was accelerating hard, and the two vehicles were going to meet head on with a closing speed of close to seventy miles per hour. He came off the throttle, reached for the pistol and fired five shots in quick succession. The windscreen spiderwebbed but the vehicle continued to advance, gaining speed the entire time. With nowhere to go, King dropped the pistol and hit the brakes, leaping from the footpegs just a split second before the Toyota crashed into the front wheel of the motorcycle. King was airborne, the sound of crushing metal below him sounding like gunfire. He landed heavily on his feet just behind the car and chose to roll out the impact in a paratrooper roll. The road surface was unforgiving, but motion was lotion, the movement and momentum taking the sting out of the impact. He turned and looked back at the vehicle, its brake lights on, its bonnet dipped and rear bumper riding high as the driver stamped on the brake pedal. King would have reversed back to finish the job, and he limped to the curb, his eyes frantically searching the ground and wreckage of the motorcycle for the pistol. He was breathing heavily, both from exertion and the winding that the impact had left him with, and as he reached the curb, he saw the driver's window lower, and the toughlooking features of a Korean man leaned out of the window. The man raised his middle finger and smiled, then brought his arm back inside the vehicle, only for it to return with a mini-Uzi 9mm machine pistol in his clasp. King sprinted for his life, his bruised limbs screaming in protest, and he felt like he was running in slow motion as the gunshots rattled off behind him. He flung himself behind a cluster of rubbish bins, the bullets clattering into the metal as he scrambled on his front like a threatened crocodile on a muddy riverbank trying to get back into the water. King found himself under a stoop that was dusty and filled with insects and spiders. He crawled on his belly, hearing the clatter of automatic gunfire and the impacting bullets behind him. The beams above his head were low and he scraped his back against the wood but made it to the end of the building and punched out the siding, both splintering the rotten wood and pushing entire boards free of the nails. He scrambled onto his feet and ran down the side of the building. Should he engage his enemy, or retreat? He didn't often ask such questions, but the man meant business and King had lost his weapon. He also felt battered and bruised. As usual, he had a knife on him, this time a Leatherman and he opened the razor-sharp blade and kept it in his right hand. "Fuck it…" he said quietly, then tore down the side of the house towards his foe. He pumped his legs hard, sprinting at full pace. If he could surprise the man by running right into him and slash his neck with the blade, then he would stand a chance. If he couldn't, well, then he would die trying.

The Toyota had gone. The motorcycle was a wreck in two halves with fuel and fluids leaking into the gutter, and the playing children and mothers doing chores had vanished. King found the pistol, gave it a cursory check, then released the magazine, pocketed the weapon and reloaded the magazine from the loose rounds in his pocket as he walked back towards the busy street. He was silently cursing himself, cursing the loss of what was clearly the asset, and vowing to kill the man with the machine gun. Over everything else, he wanted another chance at the cocky Korean, but as he thought about the man's arrogant stare and his middle finger, he couldn't help chuckling to himself as he walked. He had an opponent not only with a fine set of skills, but with some attitude and spark. He was going to enjoy this.

Chapter Twenty-Two

Lambeth Pier, London

Jack Luger stood when Harriet crossed the pavement and stepped down the three stone steps to his table. She reached over the table and kissed him on both cheeks. Her lips soft, her scent and feel sending all the wrong signals to his primal, carnal senses.

"I'm not sure what to make of this," she said, glancing at the menu written in chalk on a blackboard. "Sausage, egg and chips? It's hardly The Ivy, *dahhling*..."

"Wait until you see the chicken nuggets or the pizza." He paused, returning to his seat with his back against the wall of the hut. "Although the pizza looks pretty good, to be fair."

"I'll take your word for that," she replied. "It's a bit touristy, isn't it?"

"With one of the best settings in town," he said,

sweeping a hand towards the river, which their seats were partially suspended over. There were boats moored to the pier behind the café and sightseeing vessels motoring up the Thames to his left. "It does good coffee and is just far enough away from the London Eye and the aquarium for the tourists to pass. They've already flooded the eateries and ice cream shops down there, so most walk on by." He nodded his head past the beautiful tree-lined walk, in front of St. Thomas's Hospital and the Covid memorial wall. Opposite which, on the other bank of the river, Big Ben and the Palace of Westminster reminded people that they were in the beating heart of London.

"So..." she said. "What's new with you?"

Luger shrugged. "I've got a dog."

"A dog? Hardly seems the thing for a man about town. Although I suppose *Alfie* had one at the end of the film. Quite fitting, really."

"Man about town?" he asked, somewhat irked by her comment. He'd seen the film. Both versions, and the reality hit him hard. He had already had to explain his behaviour to Lillia, and now he was being judged as a womaniser by a woman that he felt had seduced him. "It was just a work thing," he added defensively, though not entirely honestly.

"That girl was pretty," Harriet commented guardedly. "If you like that kind of thing..."

"Kind of thing?"

"Obvious beauty," she replied. "A model, a bit of an airhead."

"She's an air crash investigator," he said pointedly, instantly wishing that he hadn't.

"Really..." Harriet smiled.

The Turkish waiter came out offering no conversation and they ordered their drinks. Harriet was tempted by a piece of cake but changed her mind mid-order. Luger knew her figure could only have been attained by hard work in the gym and discipline in the kitchen. They made stunted, somewhat awkward small talk, then thankfully the coffees arrived and gave them both a prop. Luger had opted for a large Americano and Harriet had a skimmed milk latte. They sipped them gratefully, then Luger said, "Shall we stop beating around the bush?"

She smiled, a little coquettishly. "Already?" She paused, rubbing the two largest pearls on her necklace subconsciously. "At least give me chance to drink my coffee, you naughty boy…" she giggled.

That wasn't what he meant, but short of asking her why she had bugged his flat, he would have to play along. Luger studied her. He was usually good at reading people but was at a loss with her. She was clever, that was for sure. She had already got him to tell her about Lillia, simply by belittling the woman and waiting for his sense of fairness to come to her defence. Did she know that her two properties had been wired for video and sound? As he studied her, he could not decide. But he did know that he was almost certainly out of his league with the MI6 officer. "What are you up to?"

She propped both elbows on the metal table and leaned her chin on her elegant hands. "What do you mean?" she asked.

Luger shrugged. "I mean at Legoland," he replied, referring to MI6's obscure looking headquarters. Both an architectural triumph and utter eyesore, depending on your taste.

"Busy times," she replied. "How about you?"

"Always busy."

"Russia?"

"Always."

"Currently?"

"Someone will be on their case, but not me. Not at the moment." Luger shrugged and sipped some of his coffee. "How about you?"

"I like this game," Harriet said lightly. "How about we play two truths and a lie?"

"I would ask how you play, but it sounds fairly obvious," he commented.

"Alright, I'll go first." She coughed rather dramatically, and Luger got an insight into her right then. She liked to be the centre of attention. He imagined her holding court with her circle of friends or reading out the questions to a family game at Christmas, waiting for hushed tones before she started. "Number one: SIS are close to discovering the identity of the hacker who has been rather busy lately. Number two: I really enjoyed our little fling and would like to start something a little more regular. Number three: the PM was recently caught by an aide wearing stockings and suspenders in his office in the early hours after a conference call to the American president…"

Luger laughed, almost spitting out some coffee. He shook his head, but as he stared at her, he couldn't read a damn thing. "Well, I would like to think that you enjoyed our time together as much as I did, and for all your abilities and expertise over at the River House, I still don't think you have a clue who is behind the hacking, so that leaves the PM…" He paused, still none the wiser. They could be all lies for all he knew, his ego had taken a battering lately, so he wasn't too confident about her view of their time together. But they could be all truths. He doubted anything she said. "Let me see… a politician with deviances, it wouldn't be the first time… I couldn't say I'd be surprised by anything I heard about Westminster, but the new PM seems a decent sort of bloke." Luger smiled at her. "I think you got the game wrong. I think there's at least two lies in there instead of two truths. Unless you didn't enjoy our little tryst, and you're not really looking for something more."

Harriet looked at him coyly. She had the expression down. He could feel himself stirring. "I never said anything about looking for something more," she said breathily. "Just that I'd like to start something more regular..."

"That indicates something more to me," he replied, still no more able to read her face than a blind man.

"More of the same, perhaps. But not more in anything other than the physical sense."

He shrugged. "If only I earned a big city salary..."

She laughed, throwing her head back and showing her large, perfectly straight and white teeth. "Oh, lord no! Money has nothing to do with it. I love my husband dearly."

"Enough to cheat on him?"

"You're way off," she told him, still looking at him intently, and still quite unreadable. "It's physical. Foreplay, sex, orgasms, the afterglow... it's like going to the gym for your..." She glanced downwards, then looked back at him and smiled. "... well, that's what it's about. My husband has never been remotely adequate in that part of our relationship, so..."

"So, you look elsewhere," Luger finished it for her. "Should I be flattered?"

"Yes," she replied. "You're only the fourth man I have been with since marrying. I have to *really* like somebody first."

"Right..."

"Oh, don't be a prude!" she laughed and sipped a mouthful of her coffee. "We're all adults."

"All, or both?"

"All. My husband doesn't ask, and I don't tell."

"So, I'm what? The gardener in Lady Chatterley's Lover?" he asked, somewhat miffed. Harriet laughed, but she didn't answer the question. They finished their coffees and Luger nodded towards the river. "Shall we walk?"

"Why not..."

The sunlight was being kind to the Thames, and it glistened briefly until a patch of low cloud scudded across the sky and reminded them how dark and silky the river could look in the city. Tourists posed for their social media, taking selfies and not much interest in society or their surroundings. Luger thought, as he so often did lately, how society was sleepwalking into a new era that didn't look too appealing to him.

They walked under the trees, the Covid memorial wall to their right. The thousands of names and hearts inscribed a testament to a time of uncertainty, insecurity and death. Some people denied it ever really happened, lodged in conspiracy theories and insecurities around government and big pharma, while for others it was all too real, loved ones lost and to be remembered.

"Did you contract it?" Harriet asked sullenly.

"I think everybody did, didn't they? Some didn't know, others had a mild cold. I had some aches and tiredness for a few days then was ok."

"Same," she said with a shrug. "But my husband lost his sister and cousin, and I lost an aunt. All three seemed healthy before they contracted it."

"Luck of the draw..."

"The big one is coming," she said. "Something that will truly test us all. And we're no more prepared than we were before."

"Undoubtedly."

"It spread from Wuhan. One of my early rapid testing

kits was from Wuhan and predated the outbreak." Harriet shrugged. "I work at SIS and still don't know what to bloody believe!"

Luger stopped and looked at three swans gliding across the river. They'd been joined by a Canada goose, who was either way off course or just visiting friends. Together, the four fowl reached the middle of the river where one of the smaller tourist boats slowed while passengers tossed in sandwich crusts. "It's frightening what's real, what's hoax and what is a deadly threat in this game," he said heavily.

"Like the hacker?"

"Yes."

"What have you got so far?" she asked, staring at the swans and their dinner guest.

"I thought SIS had information?" He paused. "Quite close, you said. Or was that the lie?"

"They might have been *all* true."

"And they might all be lies. When dealing with MI6, one can never tell. Either way, I'll never look at the PM in the same way again..."

She laughed and started to walk again. "And is that all it is? Dealing with MI6? I thought you were interested in me, for me," she said over her shoulder. Luger followed then drew alongside her and she felt for his hand. Her skin was soft and warm, and he could feel his heart beat faster as their hands entwined. He squeezed her hand, knowing that he was playing with fire. For as much as he didn't trust her, he wanted her all the same. It was like the male black widow spider again. He had started to think of her as the black widow but shook the infantile notion from his thoughts as they walked. It took two, and he was the one throwing caution to the wind and being reckless.

"I am," he said. "But why do I get the impression we're

in a preamble for deals, rather than in the middle of something more intimate?"

Harriet shrugged, her hand still in his own. "This is thrilling," she said. "Walking with you, chancing seeing someone who knows me..."

"Risky," he commented flatly. "For you, that is."

"I told you that my husband doesn't ask questions."

"But others might. That could be awkward."

"And that's why it feels so utterly thrilling."

Luger stopped walking and pulled her back to him. He kissed her firmly on the lips and she hesitated for a moment before responding greedily. Luger pulled away and said, "That should feel more thrilling, am I right?"

"Yes..." she replied. "I took the liberty of booking us a room."

"Really?" Luger replied a little too excitedly.

She touched the tip of his nose with her index finger and said, "Of course, silly..."

"My flat is..."

"Too far away and anyway, somewhere more neutral might be more appropriate." She paused. "For all I know there could be a young lady at your place waiting for you to get home."

Luger knew full well that she didn't think that. She had left surveillance equipment there, had probably been monitoring it closely. He was so used to acting normally, he sometimes forgot all about the fact that he was being watched. He had been using a room at headquarters for times when he needed to relax and catch up on some sleep in private. "Do you live far away?" he asked, knowing that her Notting Hill flat was just five miles up the road.

"Quite far," she replied. She caught hold of his hand

and said, "Let's get a taxi. Have you heard of the Fleming Hotel?"

"No."

"It's delightful," she told him as they climbed the steps. "Five-star furnishings and service, champagne waiting on ice, so much nicer than many of the more *famous* London hotels. It has a wonderful room service menu as well."

"Sounds lovely," he said, flagging down a taxi near the hospital entrance. "I had you figured for a large mansion on the King's Road."

"Oh, dear god, no," she scoffed. "Just a flat in town," she said, not mentioning the country retreat in Berkshire. Luger had searched the internet and found it valued at six million, with her Notting Hill flat nudging two million. Impressive, if not highly dubious for a mid-ranking civil servant, had it not been for her broker husband, who was a big name on Canary Wharf.

Luger nodded, torn between the passion and the subterfuge, heading ever closer to the spider's web.

Chapter Twenty-Three

Bangkok, Thailand

King had nothing. He'd lost them. There was no CCTV on the street, and he couldn't even find any on the busy main street. There were security cameras inside a few of the shops and restaurants, but nothing that could capture a view of the street. It had a long shot. King had grown tired of searching, still wary that he was a target. He had hoped to return the motorcycle that he had stolen, perhaps with enough baht to ease the inconvenience for the young man, but the machine was totalled. He hoped that the man had been insured, but he doubted it. Anyway, he had more to worry about. The hacker had disappeared, and what's more, it looked like he had either a couple of minders and really was working against his will, or a foreign agency had abducted him, and that meant that they had competition.

King took a tuk-tuk back to the hotel. There was barely

room for him in the back of the three-wheeled motorcycle taxi, and what would have normally been a highlight for any tourist on their travels passed by with him barely noticing the chaotic traffic and suicidal pedestrians with Buddha on their side. His mind was on the man who had flipped him the bird, and the tiny Korean woman who had bundled a man half her size again into the back of a car with great skill and without any exertion. She had been trained well, and so had the cocky Korean with the machine pistol. South Korea wasn't a threat to anyone, so these two had to be agents of the DPRK or Iron Fist. He cursed himself as he paid the tuk-tuk driver and limped his way up the steps to the hotel.

He found the manager, who groaned when he saw King, thinking that he had earned some money and the risk of getting caught had gone. He edged to the end of the reception desk and said quietly, "Welcome to The Rama Gardens Hotel, again, sir..."

"The Korean who just checked out, I want everything you have on him," King told him bluntly.

The man seemed to consider this for a second, then said, "Ok, sir. Follow me..." King followed the man into the back office where he said, "Will the same fee be acceptable?"

King shrugged. "Yes," he replied irritably.

The man smiled. "There were two gentlemen meeting with your guest yesterday. They were Korean, also. The guest who you are inquiring about is travelling on an American passport, but he is Korean, too. I am certain of it. The name is Korean for sure."

"And what is his name?"

"Hong Gil-dong," the man chuckled.

"What's so funny," King asked tersely.

The man shrugged. "It is Korean for John Doe, like the nameless bodies in American cop dramas."

"Can you get me a picture of him?" King asked. "You will have photocopied his passport on check in..."

The man did so, and King left with a snapshot of the two visiting Koreans, as well. They looked tough and stupid, but King knew that looks could be deceptive.

He took another tuk-tuk back to his own hotel, the journey flashing by in a blur. He was no longer interested or excited by the bedlam of Bangkok. A dozen years ago, maybe. Now it was just an inconvenience as he sought to make out his report and send it to Ramsay. He had a name, and he had a picture of Hong Gil-dong, which he doubted was his real name, but it was a start. He also had photographs of two Koreans who looked very much like enforcers to King. It was a lot more than he had when he had stepped off the plane just a few hours previously.

The icy air-conditioning of the hotel foyer hit him like a sheet of ice and he both welcomed it, and found it irritating, chilling his sweat and making the hairs on the nape of his neck stand on end. He made his way to the bar and asked for a glass of water with lots of ice, and when he'd quickly finished it, he ordered a beer and asked for another to be sent up to his room in half an hour along with his food order. He left with the frosted glass of beer and took the lift to the third floor. Inside his room, he swigged down half the beer and ran a cold shower while he ordered room service. Stepping into the cold spray, he washed all over with soap, taking care to rub the lather into the many cuts and grazes left by the crash. The wounds stung, but he bore it, using it as a lesson. He had been seen tailing them, and the Korean man had acted swiftly and decisively. He would not allow that to happen again. The cool spray washed the soap away, and with it, some of the pain from the bruising. He stepped out of the shower and studied himself in the mirror. He was toned and fit, and the tan from sunning himself and working on the yacht had brought out his scars. One scar looked like a shark had bitten his torso and spat him back out. A complicated extraction of a soft-nosed bullet which had clipped his liver. His first job for MI5 under the command of Charles Forrester. He had put a lot of miles on the clock since then, had a bit of wear and tear, but he was still here, and he was still a formidable opponent. He took a deep breath. One small defeat wasn't the end of the war. But it could mean worse things for the enemy, because the Koreans would be confident. Overconfident. And that could work in King's favour.

He changed into clean boxers and slipped on a T-shirt while he let the waiter in, and the man set down the tray, grateful for the tip handed to him at the door. King never took the tray from service staff, not because it was beneath him but because he never wanted to be caught off guard with his hands full. He'd been there before at a hotel in Angola and vowed never again to be so vulnerable.

Lifting the silver cloches on the plates of the classic Pad Thai and Gaeng Daeng dishes filled the room with the aroma of chillies, ginger, garlic and lemongrass. King hadn't had a good Thai meal in years, and he was aware that hotels were the last place to experience this, but it still smelled and looked pretty good to him. He sat on the single chair and ate the prawn and noodles and red curried chicken at the vanity table, sipping his second beer between mouthfuls. There was nothing to be gained in going out in Bangkok at night. Not for him, at least. As for finding the hacker and the two Korean agents, the chances were slim to none. He had no hope whatsoever. Better to eat and rest and see whether the hacker had left another digital signature that Ramsay and his technicians on the floor below in their new headquarters could intercept.

King finished his meal, replaced the cloches and sat back on the bed with a copy of Three Men in a Boat. The story had started out amusing enough, but he was now halfway through and deciding whether it would be worth the effort. He found that few things had changed for men in the hundred and sixty years since it had first been published, and the preparation for the trip had reminded him of entertaining car shows where the presenters are simply inept. He started nodding his head, slipping into nanoseconds of sleep, but kept going, using the book to put him to sleep proper. It was still early, but his internal clock was struggling, and he expected to wake in a few hours, and he would clean the spices and garlic from his mouth and switch the lights off when he woke up. Eyes bleary from the tiny text in the book in front of him, he enjoyed the sensation knowing that soon he would drop off and leave the bitterness of his defeat for a few hours at least.

Chapter Twenty-Four

San Jose, California

As assignments went, it wasn't the worst job he'd ever had. Driving up sun-kissed California's coastal route with the surf on his left and the cliffs, mountains and forest on his right, motoring over impressive bridges through places like Big Sur and Monterey Bay, Rashid had donned his sunglasses and dropped the roof of his hired Mustang, taking an upgrade from the premium compact vehicle that Mae had booked for him in London – he'd have to argue that one out later – he had thoroughly enjoyed the six-hundred mile drive, eating in diners and staying a night in a motel in the picturesque town of Carmel-by-the-sea.

Most people knew that Silicon Valley was the centre for technological design and development but were probably unaware that the valley just south of San Francisco was in fact a loose term for several valleys and within those, the cities of Sunnyvale, Mountain View, Palo Alto and Menlo Park were all cited as the birthplace of Silicon Valley. San Jose is Silicon Valley's largest city, the third largest in California, and the twelfth most populous in the United States. Other major Silicon Valley cities include Santa Clara, Redwood City and Cupertino. The valleys were home to many of the world's largest high-tech corporations, including the headquarters of more than thirty businesses in the Fortune 1000, and thousands of startup companies who had placed themselves within reach of the beating heart of technology. Rashid could see that he had come to a wealthy place. The houses and vehicles were grander than even what he had seen in the monied areas of Los Angeles.

"What kind of man is he?" Rashid asked.

Tom Greensboro was personnel director of Microsoft in Redmond, and his office overlooked a neatly kept park with striped cut-grass lawns and a large tree-fringed lake in the distance. Smartly dressed in dark blue business suit and a light blue open neck shirt without a tie, his air-conditioned office was large, minimalistic and the windows made up an entire glass wall over fifty-feet wide and a dozen feet high. Rashid thought the man would look just as at home selling flashy cars and weighty finance deals as much as seated behind the desk of one of the world's largest, most prestigious software and development companies.

Greensboro steepled his fingers, elbows on the glass desktop. "In what way?"

"Just to get an idea of the man, what he's like to work with, what makes him tick. Friends, relationships, sporting interests, whether he mixed well or if he was reclusive."

Greensboro didn't have to tell him anything. Rashid had appealed to the man's better nature. Unless he went down the route of reading the FBI or CIA into the investigation -

and that meant dealing with the US State Department and both the UK Home Office and the Foreign Office - then the man was not obliged to say anything. But Rashid had worded it carefully, and eager not to have anything stick to the world's leading software company, Greensboro decided to have an initial meeting with him. Beside the man, an attractive blonde from 'legal' crossed her legs, then leaned in and whispered into Greensboro's ear. Rashid smiled and the woman eyed him as she whispered.

"This *is* off the record?" Greensboro asked when she had finished advising him.

"Absolutely," Rashid replied as if it went without question, but he promised nothing. He wasn't a reporter going off the record, he was an intelligence officer and was prepared to do anything to find the truth. "I appreciate your time and assistance with my investigation."

The woman from legal leaned into Greensboro again and whispered. When he had listened to what she had to say, he said, "What are we talking here? I mean, fraud, plagiarism?" He paused, glancing at the blonde woman. "Or something more sinister?"

"It's classified, of course. However, we are more concerned with the company Hong Gil-dong has become associated with."

"Apple?" Greensboro laughed, glancing at his attractive, but somewhat po-faced colleague at the inside joke.

"Not quite," Rashid replied humourlessly. "More like the personal company he kept."

"Are we talking terrorism here?"

Rashid narrowed his eyes. He wasn't saying anything, but his expression said everything. "Was he a loner, Mr Greensboro?"

America had a big problem with loners. They walked

into crowded places more than six-hundred times a year and shot innocent people. These were not bank robbers, drive-by gang shootings or road rage incidents, which happened daily. These were the school and shopping mall active shooters. Nobody wanted to be associated with these maladjusted murderers and the blonde woman from legal was whispering again, and Rashid could see this going one of two ways. They were going to go into clam mode. They were going to shut tight, or open wide. There was no in between. As it turned out, the legal from the software company wanted to be out in front.

"He was a quiet man when he worked for the company." Greensboro paused. "But due to the nature of his work, he tended to work alone, or in small, dedicated specialist teams."

"And what was the nature of his work?"

"He headed up our AI section. And for eight years before that, he was one of our most prominent cyber security specialists."

"With somebody who had a record like that, I'm surprised that you let him go…"

Time for legal to whisper into the personnel director's ear again. "While Hong Gil-dong's work was extraordinary, and as much as it pained us at first, we were happy with the way it worked out. As a company, we provide valuable, some would say essential, products and operating systems and even though we are huge, we still feel as if we are a family. Hong Gil-dong was not a team player." He paused. "He failed to make a single friend at Microsoft, and in a dozen years with what the company has to offer, that's an unusual event. Frankly, once we covered his work, on a personnel level at least, it was like he was never here."

"An on a technical level?" Rashid persisted.

Greensboro shrugged. "The man was a genius. He took us in directions that we barely believed possible. We have people who have followed his work and taken it to another level. That's just how the technology industry works."

"We don't have to tell you that Hong Gil-dong does not represent the company in any way," the woman from legal spoke for the first time without whispering. "In fact, such was Hong Gil-dong's anonymity within the company, he sat under our radar for years." She paused. "And because of this rare anomaly, the company has implemented plans for group interaction in the form of team building and social events, making at least two of these a year mandatory and part of the working week. All paid for at a rate of holiday plus one. We feel that social interaction, especially in the wake of the Covid lockdowns, is of the utmost importance of our organisation."

Rashid nodded. He wasn't interested in whether this had been implemented, or whether the woman from legal was making this up on the spot. He wasn't a journalist. He had come to learn some background on the Korean. Ramsay had already ascertained that from the information they had already collated, they were dealing with a thirty-eight-year-old male on a South Korean passport and visa under the name Hong Gil-dong. Ramsay had almost broken character and laughed when he had the name translated as John Doe. Hong Gil-dong was a shadow. An enigma. But you would not get odds against better, that he was from the DPRK and now under the umbrella of Iron Fist.

Chapter Twenty-Five

Bangkok, Thailand

King awoke with a start, the hairs on the nape of his neck standing on end, gently touching the soft cotton of the pillowcase. His eyes were dry and bleary, and he was thick-headed, but it had nothing to do with the flight and the time difference and the effects it had had on his body-clock. It was as if he was coming round from an anaesthetic. Groggy, thirsty, and confused. But he did not have the luxury of drifting between sleep and consciousness. His instincts told him to wake and wake now. He felt the pressure upon his left ankle, something touching him – as softly, yet directly as any lover – teasing at his calf and knee. Suddenly, he had never felt so awake, so alert as he did right now in the humid void of the dead of night. The ceiling fan turned slowly, the open blind rippling in the faint breeze as the sticky night came out of the doldrums and started to offer brief respite to the tangible air.

King felt the weight of the snake, the movement of its smooth, great belly as it made its way higher up his leg, sliding easily over his damp skin. The tongue tested the air, occasionally tickling his flesh. Was it aware that he was another creature? The reptile would no doubt feel the blood surging through his veins, pumping through his arteries, his own core body temperature and the touch of his hot skin feeding information to its primeval brain. The snake made its way higher, to his pubic hair, its tongue tasting his skin, so gently, almost sensually. Its tail caught his ankle, such was the size of the creature, and with its head now sliding over King's rippled stomach, his muscles tensed in both fear and anticipation. The reptile's head was recognisable through the single cotton sheet, and it stopped and tasted his skin, the gentle tongue tickling the hairs on King's chest. The tongue continued to probe, and King was sure that the creature was drinking his salty sweat, before it eased its head out under the sheet and finally stared into King's face. King recognised it as a Malayan pit viper, its diamond pattern just about visible in the dim light, its square head and forward positioned eyes made it clear that it was a killing machine that could strike in fractions of a second and deliver deadly venom through its hypodermic fangs. King knew that these creatures could strike automatically, simply by detecting movement through infrared sensors and doing what nature had programmed it to do over millions of years. People had even been fatally bitten by the heads of decapitated vipers. King barely breathed, his lungs aching, his muscles screaming in protest having been clenched for so long. Slowly, the rest of its body caught up with its upper third, and the animal lay coiled on King's chest, moving infinitesimally with the rise and fall of King's thwarted breathing.

Perspiration seeped from every pore like mountain springs, and he could feel that he was drenched with sweat, the soft cotton sheet beneath him sticky and cool against his skin. On the bedside table beside him, the compact Ruger .380 pistol rested tantalisingly, yet somewhat depressingly out of reach. Just as useless was the lock knife underneath his pillow. Both could save his life, and both were equally as useless because he would never be able to reach them fast enough, nor slowly enough if he tried. King desperately needed to take a deep breath, his lungs aching, his body starting to shake. He knew that he was close to snatching a breath and had felt the same way several times before as he had swum from deep water to the surface, desperately trying to avoid inhaling mouthfuls of water. But striking for the surface drew one ever closer, but here, he was going nowhere. Just ever closer to moving involuntarily and being bitten by the deadly viper as a result. Slowly, carefully, he moved his right hand and gathered some sheet in his hand. The snake tensed, its head rising from King's chest, and he could feel its tail stiffening against his leg. The weight of the snake shifted, too, and he was able to take in some air, but the snake moved its head back again, its tongue rapidly flicking in and out, tasting the humid air and King's terrified scent. King eased his hand further down the bed, gathering more of the damp material in his hand. He now had what equated to a crumbled shirt in terms of size in his hand. The viper tensed, its head rising higher, and the area just below its head flattening significantly. Its soulless eyes, just about visible in the gloom, looked angrier now, if that was possible. King knew that he had barely seconds before the creature struck. With his hand gripped around the sheet, he thrust his arm in the air and spread his palm out flat. The viper struck the wad of sheet, and with his left hand, King snatched the snake's tail and flung it with all the strength and speed he could muster away from the bed. He was up on his knees as the snake hit the far wall and dropped to the floor. Swinging himself over the bed, he landed softly on his feet and slammed his fist against the light switch. He could see the snake writhing on the floor, and he grabbed the knife from under his pillow and picked up a chair from beside the table. Stunned, but quickly coming to terms with its own mortality, the snake stopped writhing and spinning and twisting and slithered towards the bed, no doubt spotting a place to hide. King darted across the room and dropped the chair onto the snake, pinning it in place with the backrest of the chair. The snake fought to get free, sliding out towards the bed, but King lifted the chair slightly and pinned it down again, this time just leaving its head and two inches of body free. King whipped open the blade and pressed it down against the animal's neck with the backrest between the snake's head and the blade. He pressed harder and drew the knife backwards. The head separated and the body went into wild spasms as he lifted the chair and allowed it to play out its death throes. He wouldn't be going near the head anytime soon, either.

King swapped the knife for the gun and pulled on a pair of boxer shorts. He checked the open window, but the flyscreen was in place and locked from the inside. So, however the snake had got in, it certainly hadn't been through the window. The ceilings were high and vaulted, the ceiling fan anchored in the centre on a wooden beam. No, he was in the tropics, these things happened. The snake must have got inside of its own volition. Hunting a rat or mouse from the grounds. He was feeling paranoid. But paranoia had kept him alive. How could housekeeping have missed the snake? The room was uncluttered so there were not many places, bar underneath the bed, where it could have hidden. King thought back to when he had gone back to his room. Recently cleaned, fresh towels and soap in the bathroom. The Thai housekeeper had... Had she been Thai? He frowned at the notion. He had travelled enough to know how different people across the Asian continent could look – the woman had looked distinctly Korean. Certainly not Thai. The Japanese had a longer and wider face, easy to differentiate from Koreans as their faces tended to have higher more prominent cheekbones, and a stronger jaw line. Thais had rounder faces with less prominent jaws and eyelids that were softer in appearance. Could she had been an agent of the RGB or Iron Fist? As he pondered upon this, he was suddenly utterly convinced. The build, the movement. She had been the same woman who had bundled the hacker into the back of the Toyota outside The Rana Gardens Hotel.

King checked the door. The security chain wasn't in place, but he remembered putting the chain on after the man from room service had left with his tip. He ran a hand down the edge of the door, then allowed the tips of his fingers to glide over the surface six inches above the security chain and over the area six to eight inches from the edge of the door. There was a slight stickiness on the wood. So that's how they had done it. A simple break in and entry technique using a hairband and a rectangle of duct tape. King had used the method many times. Place the rectangle through the hairband, reach around the door and hook the hairband on the bolt of the chain. Stretch your arm as far as it would go and press the duct tape firmly on the door. All you needed to do then was close the door and the bolt and chain would pull clear. Slim arms worked best, but the woman was lithe and with practice, the technique could be done in the first few attempts. Now it made sense. It wasn't the travel and the toils of Three Men in a Boat that had sent him to sleep. He had been drugged. Room service. A stupid mistake on his part, and he had underestimated the opposition a second time. There were certainly easier ways to have tried to kill him, but accidental death was cautious on their side, and it showed a professionalism that was quite haunting.

King pulled on his trousers and loose cotton shirt and padded barefoot down the stairs to reception. He pocketed the compact Ruger pistol almost as an afterthought when he reached the bottom of the staircases. The man at the reception desk looked bored and tired and stood warily as King walked towards him. He did not look like he wanted to open the bar or rustle up a bowl of noodles or a club sandwich for the man who looked like a boxer readying for a fight.

"Good evening, sir..." he said expectantly.

"Evening... Your housekeeping staff... do you have any Korean women working for you?"

"No, sir," the man replied, puzzled at such a question at three-thirty in the morning. "But Thai ladies are very good in bed, you want me to make a call?"

"No," King replied tersely. "She was working when I went up to my room after dinner. She almost certainly had Korean features."

The man shook his head. "No sir. Housekeeping finish at six. If a guest requires something after that time, then reception staff will see to it." He paused. "What would you like me to get you, sir?"

"Nothing," King replied gruffly. "So, if she wasn't from housekeeping, then who was she?"

"We have no Koreans working here, sir. Just Thai ladies and Filipino workers do housekeeping duties." He frowned. "And nobody from housekeeping was on duty at dinner service, sir."

"She had a trolley with housekeeping supplies on it..." King paused irritably, looking around the foyer where he spotted a camera. "Can I see your CCTV?"

The man looked perplexed. "Hotel policy would not..."

King dropped four US fifty-dollar-bills on the desk. Around a month to a month and a half's salary for a hotel front of house worker. It was enough to do the trick. This man wasn't a manager, and he knew that tips like this did not come along often. If at all. The man beckoned King into the rear office, checking his watch and looking around him, suddenly feeling guilty and nervous, and now expecting someone to catch him in the act, but at this time in the morning he was going to be ok.

"Which floor, sir?"

"The third."

"And the time?"

"Eight."

The receptionist typed in the time and King saw himself on the screen. As he walked past her the 'housekeeper' turned away from him, but in doing so she exposed her face to the camera. The receptionist paused the screen, still looking around him a good two hours before the next member of staff came on shift. King took a picture of the woman's image with his phone, then maximised the image and took a screenshot.

"Where did she go after this?" King asked.

The receptionist tracked her down the corridor and to the lift then using another camera found her on the ground floor. He tracked her with different cameras, and she had lost the housekeeping trolley on the way. In the lift, no doubt. He then found the woman again outside, stepping into a white Toyota. King could see that the vehicle was undamaged, so they had changed their vehicle, but white Toyota Corollas were the standard hire car in Thailand.

"Pause it!" King told him. "Back a frame. There!" King took another photo, maximised the image again and took another screenshot. It was the man with the mini-Uzi. He was certain of it. He would never forget him, never forget the casual, confident way he had flipped him off, then sprayed a hail of lead all around him. King thanked the receptionist and made his way back to his room, sending a message and both images to Ramsay before he reached his door.

Chapter Twenty-Six

L ondon

"One facial recognition ping. The Thai authorities don't have a thorough CCTV traffic system. Not a great deal of point with tuk-tuks and horse-drawn carts riding alongside tour buses, and a ten-to-one-ratio of mopeds to cars, but they're getting there." She paused. "It's chaos times ten. Remember, I did a tour of the Golden Triangle, temples, canals and beaches a few years ago with Kerry from personnel?"

"No."

"I brought you back a wooden elephant..."

"Still no." He shrugged, then asked, "Was this *ping* on one of the main highways?" asked Ramsay.

Charlotte nodded. "The software picked him up again, but we've lost him heading towards the airport." She paused. "You really don't remember the wooden elephant?"

"The airport..." Ramsay sighed heavily. "And no, I don't remember any wooden elephant."

Charlotte shrugged. "So, I contacted the Thai NIA, spoke to Deputy Director Kiet Sukhum and he has granted me access to their CCTV link for Bangkok airport. He was willing to provide intelligence operatives and speak to the police, if necessary, but I told him not for now."

"Very wise," he replied. "Have you found him yet?"

"No. But if he shows up at the airport, then he's as good as ours."

"And what if he doesn't take our hacker through the airport?"

"Then we're back to square one," she said matter-of-factly. She held up a tea plate filled with biscuits, not taking her eyes off the screen in front of her. "Jammie Dodger?"

"Thank you," said Ramsay, taking two and slipping one into his pocket before biting the other in half."

"Got one for Ron?"

"Yes."

She smiled. When they worked together at Thames House, Ramsay would always take one for himself, and one for 'Ron' - or *later on*. "Any news on our man, Hong Gil-dong?"

"Nothing more," Ramsay replied. "We have a name and thanks to Rashid's investigation in California, we have a series of photographs from his Microsoft ID, and his work record. Rashid also has copies of his California driving licence, which was used for the rental of properties in Long Beach and San Jose, as well as the finance agreements on a series of vehicles, most recently a BMW purchased from a dealership in Santa Monica. Thanks to King we can corroborate Hong Gil-dong being in Thailand, and we have photographs of his minders, or the agents who have abducted him. We are not sure yet, but it's certainly more than we had twenty-four hours ago."

"A name and a photograph," Charlotte commented. "He's as good as ours..."

"But a John Doe," Ramsay chided. "We could do with finding out who the man really is."

"Fifteen years in the States under the name Hong Gil-dong and his real name is almost superfluous." Charlotte paused. "I doubt we'll ever know the man's real name."

"Perhaps. But there's always something more that's worth knowing. If he's from the DPRK, then he may well have had enough of the political ideals of a lunatic." Ramsay paused, helping himself to another Jammie Dodger for himself, and another for Ron. "Which means that he's either leaving breadcrumbs for us to find him as a cry for help, or he's setting a trap for us to walk into."

Chapter Twenty-Seven

Fleming's Hotel, Mayfair

Luger stepped into the room with trepidation. The male black widow, about to risk it all for his own desires. Harriet had been quite correct; Fleming's was understated class. Pure luxury personified, yet devoid of all pretentiousness. He looked at Harriet as she smoothed down her skirt, drawing his attention to her shapely hips. He would take the lead this time. Let her see the dominance in him, the man on the fringe of the boy. For that was how she made him feel. Like Dustin Hoffman in *The Graduate*.

She looked up at him as she sat down on the bed. "Bravo, by the way."

"For what?" he asked incredulously.

"For bugging my flat," she replied. "I don't know how you did it, but..."

"I don't know anything about that," he replied.

"Play poker?"

"No."

"Well, you should. Only, I know you're lying. Ok, maybe not you, but one of your band of renegades most certainly did bug my flat."

"Funny you should say that..."

She held up her hands. "Guilty as charged."

"Was that your only reason for sleeping with me?" he asked, somewhat disgruntled and not particularly wanting to hear the answer.

"No!" she glared at him. "Certainly not."

"But it certainly helped when I took a shower."

She shrugged. "Well, yes."

"So, what is this about?" he asked, casting a hand around the room.

"Neutral territory," she said pointedly. "Somewhere where we can talk freely."

"Talk?" he scoffed. "We could have done that safely enough walking along the Thames."

"Parabolic microphones, agents masquerading as passer's-by, I don't have to point out tradecraft to you, do I?"

"No." he replied acerbically.

"Sorry about the false pretences," she said. "But I didn't just bring you here for some afternoon delight."

Luger took a comfortable tub chair. The leather was distressed, and the brass tack heads were worn, the ones on the arms bright and polished from use, the ones out of the way of wear and tear looked tarnished and dull. "Then why?" he asked.

"My boss wants to take Neil Ramsay down." She paused. "And that means, all of you."

"Why? We're all on the same side."

"We are dear boy. But ambition and territory will always be the main driving force for some people."

"You set me up to fail in Russia…"

"Yes. That was regrettable. I hear you had fun and games getting back over the border." She smiled. "Real Evel Knievel stuff, or so I hear."

"Who?"

"Evel Knievel, famous motorbike stunt rider…"

"Never heard of her."

"Him."

"Right."

"Oh. You must have heard of him! Tried to jump the Grand Canyon."

"No."

"He was huge in the seventies and eighties."

Luger shrugged. "Well, you are so much older than I am," he said, irked at her casual attitude to his escape.

"Ouch…" she said, crestfallen.

He had regretted his snide remark as soon as he had said it, but he still wasn't letting her off the hook. "You also set up a foreign office employee to take the fall. You tried to have the man run over…"

"I know nothing about that," she said lightly. "However, my boss, Devonshire, is flagging a few issues up for me. I believe he's in deep with something, and I believe that your department is investigating the affair. It's got Devonshire rattled. Hence the bugging of your flat." She shrugged. "And your little tit-for-tat, of course."

"What's your suspicion?"

She sighed. "SIS have been running an asset inside the DPRK…"

"Really?"

She nodded. "Believe me, it wasn't easy. For years we've

had to be extremely careful that we hadn't just created a double agent who was feeding us lies. However, the information has always been spot-on."

"It could be a play," he ventured. "Giving you real information for you to get sucked in."

"Yes. That's what we thought at first." She paused. "The asset is golden, though."

"Sounds perfect. So, where do I come in?" Luger shrugged. "What are we doing here?"

"Our asset reports that two special forces soldiers have been dispatched from the DPRK on a mission. However, after snooping around, the asset can't find any evidence of this coming from anyone but a General Cho. It would appear to be Cho's personal mission." She paused. "But I caught Devonshire attempting to bury this fact, and he has not divulged it to anyone."

Luger frowned. "Why would he do that?"

"Exactly."

Luger looked at her. Her divulgence had been a passion-killer, but he was getting over that. There was something so sexual about her, even in a business suit. Or perhaps maybe because of it. It was tight in all the desired places, without making her look cheap. He hated to admit it, but he was still falling foul to the black widow factor. "Could he have a remit that you are unaware of?"

"It's a possibility," she replied. "But I work with him and have worked with him for years."

"For him."

"What?"

"You work *for* him."

"That's right. However, there are plenty of people like me. In offices around the world. That person who makes their line manager look good, and without whom, they wouldn't get a damn thing done." Harriet paused, pulling out her hairclip and releasing her tresses, before running a hand through her hair. "He's in his position because of me, and even he knows that he'd be finished without me. That's why I'm privy to everything he does. But not this. Devonshire is handling something on his own, for his own end and I just don't like the fact it involves agents of the DPRK, or worse, Iron Fist. Because that's what this looks like to me. So, why would Devonshire omit reporting these two special forces agents to the proper channels?" She paused, looking at him earnestly. "And why the hell would he try and hide the communique and not tell me?"

Luger thought on this as he watched her undress. Standing before him in nothing but a camisole, she laid back on the bed and beckoned him over. Soon, he was the male spider again. Answering the mating call, ever aware that he could be walking right into a trap.

Chapter Twenty-Eight

B angkok, Thailand

A series of texts from Ramsay had taken King to the airport. Outside the airport, the usual throng of tourists, scamming locals, pickpocketing children, blatant prostitutes in various states of undress, vocal taxi drivers and street vendors made for a melee of chaos and noise. Fumes from vehicles long overdue services or scrapping filled the thick air with both noxious smoke and noise alike, a cacophony that was truly an assault on the senses. King had left his luggage at the hotel, but it was nothing that he couldn't replace. He always carried his passport, cards and cash, but he had to ditch the pistol and the knife in a nearby rubbish bin. He shrugged it off. If Hong Gil-dong and his escort were going to the airport, then it would only be to catch a flight, and King would not get past the security checks with weapons.

Ramsay's messages had padded things out somewhat.

Through separate investigations they had a name. King had confirmed it. Now they had a work history and more importantly, they had his date of birth. They also had the man's first visa, which had been at the age of twenty-two, when Hong Gil-dong had entered America on a South Korean passport that was now regarded as almost certainly fake. The man also had American citizenship after ten years of official US residency. Hong Gil-dong was an artificial intelligence and cyber security specialist - an innovator, by all accounts - and Ramsay and his technicians on the floor below his office agreed that if Hong Gil-dong had not wanted to be found then they would not have found his breadcrumbs to follow. Everybody made mistakes, and that's what usually led to their downfall, but these little breadcrumbs of code were a cry for help. If they had not been, then the French nuclear power station would have had a catastrophic reactor meltdown. Which meant that the hacker had not been given a choice in the matter of the cross-channel ferry disaster, and for him to be assigned two special forces agents, then whoever was controlling him was worried about his level of commitment, and other agencies getting to him.

King snatched a baseball cap and a pair of sunglasses off a trader's stand and handed the man too much money, not waiting for change. Donning both, he stepped through the automatic glass doors and found a money exchange which he sidled up to for cover as he studied the crowd. Standing in the middle of the check-in area would attract attention if Hong Gil-dong's minders were on the lookout for him.

King scanned the people looking for features. Short to medium height, black hair. Two men and a woman. Once he found his groove - skimming over the white and black people, the tall and the stout, the blondes and the gingers –

he found the Asian and Oriental people easy to identify. And there they were. The woman who had bundled Hong Gil-dong into the rear of the vehicle was at the Qantas check-in desk. King looked at the destination and flight time. Brisbane. He checked his vintage Rolex to confirm the time. Three hours from now. Hong Gil-dong was next up, with the man who had shot at King standing directly behind him. King tensed, wanting nothing more than to kill the cocky Korean. But he couldn't do it here. An airport security guard shouted at the Korean, pointing at the yellow line on the floor, which he was a good foot over. The man stepped back quite unhurriedly, staring hostilely at the security guard. The guard looked away, uncomfortable at the exchange, but at least the man had stepped back behind the line. The guard hadn't lost face.

King watched as Hong Gil-dong walked away from the desk, met by the Korean woman. Together they waited for the young man, but they looked uncomfortable together. King thought them inexperienced in fieldcraft. Close quarter combat was one thing, but acting naturally under pressure was something else. Did Hong Gil-dong look under duress? King wasn't so sure. Neither of his minders could carry a weapon in here, so Hong Gil-dong had every opportunity to create a scene or call for security. There were airport security guards all over the place, with armed police on the exits. The two Koreans wouldn't be able to do much if the guards all came running.

King noticed the concierge service desk on the other side of the check-in desks and headed over, where the woman behind the counter looked bored, but her expression lit up when she saw King.

"Hello," he said.

"Hi, how can I help you?"

"I need a flight to Brisbane," said King. "And it must get in before the outgoing

Qantas flight." He glanced at his watch, knowing that Qantas flight QF508 would be boarding in three hours. "It's a medical emergency. I have no luggage, either."

"You are ill?" she asked, somewhat concerned. "Do you need a doctor."

"No, thanks. My partner has been involved in an accident and I must get to Brisbane as soon as possible."

The woman typed on her keyboard, her eyes transfixed on the screen in front of her. "There is a Thai Airways flight that has been undersold," she said. "It's boarding in fifteen minutes, but as you have no luggage, I can get an escort to take you through to departures. All part of our concierge service."

King handed her his credit card and passport without questioning her. He could see that the concierge tariff quoted a twenty-percent commission on all purchases. Ramsay could deal with that aspect later, but King was already sending him a text message informing him of his plan, as the woman started typing his details onto the screen.

Chapter Twenty-Nine

Brisbane, Australia

As it turned out the last-minute flight to Brisbane had been in first class and King had made good use of the larger lavatory cubicle and the complimentary grooming kit. A strip wash, shave and the mini toothbrush and single portion of toothpaste had left him feeling fresh as he disembarked the aircraft and made his way towards customs and immigration, reading the series of texts that awaited him when he switched his phone back on. With no luggage to claim he was the first through and once clear of immigration he made his way to the left luggage counter and claimed a bag with the reference that Ramsay had sent him, along with further instructions. Inside the bag were a change of clothes in his approximate size, toiletries and the keys and details to the hire car that had been left for him. Simply by feeling the weight of the bag he knew that there was a weapon and ammunition in there, too. The task would have been a break from the dull routine of the British embassy's resident spook, but the procurement of a weapon would have been the icing on the cake. Days like this did not happen often for embassy intelligence officers.

The Brisbane climate was more forgiving than Bangkok, but still hot. King was working up a sweat as he walked to the car. The vehicle was a Ford Everest. A large SUV that boasted a three-litre turbo-charged engine. King had never heard of the model and assumed that it must be unique to Australia. All he knew of Australia was that it was big and hot and virtually empty in the middle. To someone from the UK it seemed uncannily familiar because of the British heritage and lineage, but also the Americanisms were strong. The Ford Everest showed that, because King had never seen a car as large on British streets other than the latest full-sized Range Rover Vogue. King wondered whether the embassy spook could have found him a more noticeable vehicle, but at least the colour was a drab grey. He did, however, get the spook's reasoning. This was Australia and the terrain could get demanding once clear of the towns and cities. He had used the first class dedicated Wi-Fi and browser in his personal tv screen to do some hasty research on Brisbane and the surrounding area. Roads could go from world-class asphalt to dust in the space of fifty miles, and once on the lonely routes, a large, reliable vehicle was essential. King had also noted the bull bars that wrapped around the bonnet, which were recommended for rural and night driving in certain areas. King checked the vehicle over and discovered three large jerry cans in the rear, held firmly in place by webbing straps. Two of them were marked as diesel and a fuel nozzle was strapped to one of the handles, and the other was marked as drinking water.

All the King's Men

Beside the cans a comprehensive vehicle toolkit was strapped in place, along with two spare wheels, a coil of rope and a folding entrenching tool. King had set off on drives in Africa and Alaska with far less equipment, but he imagined that the embassy's resident spook was proving themselves. This wasn't a posting in Bogota or Lebanon. This would have been a quiet posting for a junior officer. A good word from Ramsay and their career could climb swiftly.

Next to the fuel, water and tools was a large canvas holdall. King opened it to find an expensive-looking paintball gun with a CO_2 cannister attached. It differed, however, from its adrenalin experience counterpart because it loaded a single .50 calibre rubber ball directly into the breech. King picked up a small plastic box and studied the six rubber balls. There was a note included with instructions and a QR code. He took out his phone and hovered it over the QR box, then smiled as the app installed automatically. "Clever," he said to himself somewhat impressed. "Very clever indeed..."

Chapter Thirty

Su Ji-ho and Eun-Ji had made love in the lavatory onboard the flight, smiling at one another afterwards after joining the 'mile high club'. Rather than resent General Cho's humiliating orders in his office on that renowned chaise longue where the general had forced himself on some of the female recruits, the pair had become lovers. Relationships in the DPRK were both difficult to initiate and maintain. Trust was one issue. A dating pool and places to meet the opposite sex was another. Many marriages were arranged, often by the state, and families merged not so much for status, but security. Punishments for crimes against the state (often as little as reading contraband books or viewing smuggled DVDs) were punishable by death, along with two further generations of the same family. This meant that people were less likely to choose a partner without being absolutely sure that they posed little risk. People who had committed crimes, served their time in a concentration camp and been released were often shunned altogether. Eun-Ji had not taken a lover before, and the act in front of General Cho had been her first time. Su

All the King's Men

Ji-ho had boasted of several lovers, but Eun-Ji doubted his truth, as men always needed to be seen to have more experience. For the pair, the freedoms and trappings of a 'free' country such as Thailand had opened their eyes. The vibrancy of Bangkok, the food stalls and restaurants - the technology, the music, the films and music videos playing in electronic shop windows, the freedom of talk and expression – all were alien to them, and all had been an experience that they did not want to ignore again.

Eun-Ji did not want to return to the DPRK. She had seen how free the women were in Bangkok. The female tourists with their clothes and mobile phones, their designer handbags. She had no idea that the handbags had cost those women five dollars in the market, or that their phones were three years old. She had no idea that these women were dressing down for their holiday touring the streets and markets. But they looked like fashion models to her, from what she had seen of smuggled magazines and DVDs. Su Ji-ho, by contrast, wanted to succeed on this mission. Yes, the trappings of what he now knew to be the 'free' world was something he wanted, but he also felt the need, after five years of training and reaching the rank of sergeant, to prove himself against the 'enemy'. But were they really the enemy? He had been led to believe that countries that did not stand with North Korea, and by that token, China and Russia, were on a constant high alert against them. That every country sanctioning the DPRK, and the Supreme Leader was ready to fight to the last drop of blood. That was why the people of the DPRK sacrificed many things in preparation of war. This was why military service was so important. Why he and his school friends had given their youth and the beginnings of their adult lives to serve in the military. In truth, he had forgotten that he had been given no choice, such was the strength and effect of the nation's indoctrination. However, all he had seen was freedom and a nonchalance in the people. The Thai people were certainly not on a war footing, and the people he had seen at the airport in Seoul, where they had flown from after breeching the border and demilitarised zone line, had seemed unconcerned that one of the world's largest standing armies was training constantly for invasion just a few short miles away.

Now back in his seat and enjoying another delightful inflight meal – so plentiful and delicious – he prepared to watch another film. He had seen no sign of political hate speech in the previous film that he had watched, and when he told Hong Gil-dong as much, the man had laughed like Su Ji-ho had been a fool. The hacker was now asleep beside him. He hadn't wanted his meal and Su Ji-ho had thought him mad. He had gratefully accepted it, because even though the DPRK fed its troops considerably more than the famished civilians, he could not ever remember feeling anything but hungry. On the other side of Hong Gil-dong, Eun-Ji looked happy as she studied her meal. She had tried wine for the first time and was now on her third Coca Cola. She seemed contented and he thought it was as much from the trappings of the West as what they had just done together in the lavatory at the rear of the plane.

Australia would be interesting. For Su Ji-ho, he would see what a country of predominantly white, westernised people valued most. He had heard that Australia was like the United Kingdom and the United States of America. He had been told that both countries were the same as one another and were filthy vermin to be culled and eradicated. He would see what war footing the Australians were on, and whether they feared the DPRK as much as he had been told.

Chapter Thirty-One

London

"You don't like things simple, do you..." Rashid commented.

Luger shrugged. "Where's the fun in that?" he replied, with more bravado than he had intended.

"Playing with fire, more like," said Caroline. "She seems a handful."

"We can't trust her," said Rashid. "We get an invite to the River House before our last operation, only to find out that MI6 were fishing, then they set Jack up, using him as bait in a double agent mole hunt. The woman bugged Jack's flat, then conveniently the embassy man in Estonia escapes an attempt on his life, taking the fall for MI6 and this Devonshire chap covering his back." He paused. "Now we're meant to believe that this woman is suspicious of her boss. It sounds as if she's merely getting out in front and covering herself."

"She must be dynamite in the sack," Big Dave commented.

Ramsay pulled a face, uncomfortable with such talk. He found intimacy difficult to talk about outside of his marriage. "We need someone on her. Two people, in fact, maybe more." He paused. "One to bring her in, and one to watch for what she does."

"Good cop; bad cop?" Jo asked.

"More like suspicious cop; invisible cop," Ramsay replied. "I want her monitored electronically, and organically. Eyes on at all times. Jack, you have the rapport with Harriet, and er... well, you *know* her better than anyone else here..."

"Doesn't he just..." Big Dave smiled.

"Yes, yes..." Ramsay said tersely. "Anyway, you bring her in. Slowly."

"Who's on the sly?" Caroline asked.

"You," he replied.

"Shouldn't I go to aid Alex?"

"No. I have that under control."

"But..."

Ramsay held up a hand. "You're a great judge of character," he said sharply. "One of the best people I know at reading somebody. I'm going to lend you Jim Kernow as well. He's got an incredible memory recall and he's an expert in surveillance. Carter has been holed up in a safe house since the incident in Estonia, so he can start to earn his keep."

Caroline shrugged. There was a time when she would have argued like cat and dog with Neil Ramsay, but those days were gone. She respected him as head of department and knew that the man was always thinking three or more moves ahead of the enemy. "We need to keep an eye on

Devonshire as well," Caroline commented flatly. "We've got to find out why he's kept this General Cho's involvement quiet."

"Indeed," Ramsay replied. "Together with Jo, the three of you should have Harriet covered, and Devonshire as well. Caroline, you are in charge," he said, glancing at Jo Blyth. "Jo, you were an anti-terrorism officer in the Met, so this will be right up your street." She nodded, and Ramsay mused. "We need to know more about this General Cho character." He shifted himself in his wheelchair using the desk as leverage and when he settled back into the chair, he looked relieved. The specialist had said that some nerve endings were responding well to physio, but the result meant that it sometimes became uncomfortable to sit for so long. Ironic, really, for somebody who could not stand. "And finding out about a military leader in the DPRK is easier said than done."

Big Dave chuckled. "For a moment, I thought you were going to suggest us going into the DPRK and bringing him back with us." He paused. "A closed nation with a lunatic dictator, a brainwashed population who inform on their own family and neighbours for survival, and a nation with no white or black citizens..."

"Actually, there are two-hundred Americans living in North Korea," Ramsay interrupted. "And ten-thousand Russians. Disaffected both, I am quite sure."

"Wow," Rashid commented. "Fancy living in Russia and thinking, wait, *I know somewhere even more shit where we could live...*"

"I know, right?" Big Dave said lightly. "Anyway, a black or a white face is going to stick out like a bulldog's bollocks. It's not somewhere foreign agents operate. Apart from the South Koreans, of course."

"It could be done though, couldn't it?" Ramsay pondered.

"It would be extremely difficult," Rashid concluded.

"But not impossible?" Ramsay asked.

"Well, they say nothing's impossible," Rashid replied.

"What would you need?"

"Seriously?" Caroline interjected.

Ramsay ignored her and looked at Rashid. "To get in, snatch General Cho and get him out... What would it take?"

"Planning, co-operation from the South Korean intelligence service, weapons, equipment, prior intelligence..." Rashid paused. "Inside information from someone who knows the compound or offices or wherever this General is based..."

"What else?"

Rashid shrugged. "King..."

Chapter Thirty-Two

Brisbane, Australia

King read the text and tossed the phone onto the seat beside him. The plan had changed, but some things were easier said than done. He had no back up – no help whatsoever. The Korean agent who had calmly flipped him off and emptied a machine gun in his direction wasn't a man to be underestimated. Could King kill him? Almost certainly. Could King snatch the hacker and the two Korean agents alive for interrogation? He doubted it. Not without his team around him. He checked his watch. Back-up wasn't coming for another thirty hours, and by then it would likely be too late.

King watched the exit and sat up when he saw Hong Gil-dong and the petit Korean woman walk out onto the pavement carrying just carry-on bags, with the hacker weighed down by two laptop cases hung over his shoulders.

King noted that they were crossed over his chest like bandoliers. Nobody was snatching these from him. The tough-looking Korean followed. He was slim and his height was tall for a Korean, but not overly for the West. King guessed around five-eight or five-nine. He had a few inches on the man, and at least three stone of muscle. He already knew that the man would be an expert in martial arts, but that had never worried him too much. King had boxed both semi-professionally, and unlicensed. There was no better fighting system up close and for a swift ending. He had been taught judo and ju-jitsu, but he had practised relentlessly for years on end with no desire or goal of gaining a belt. When Krav Maga had been introduced into MI6 special operations training, King had learned from the best Israeli Mossad instructors, one of whom had been an original student of the fighting system created for the Israeli commandos. His old mentor Peter Stewart had formulated an amalgamation of all these disciplines and made it his own. The man had often run full-contact sessions where for practical reasons only eye-gouging was off limits, in training at least. Everything else was fair game, and King was confident that his training was more than enough to take on any man walking.

King crawled forwards, the big SUV surprisingly quiet given the size of its engine. He already knew where the car rental companies were located and that was on a dead-end road, so he did not need to follow them all the way, but he at least would be ready and facing the right way when they emerged back onto the traffic thoroughfare. King glanced down at the weapon beside his left leg in the footwell. He would have to have a clean shot, and he would only get one. When he looked back at the trio, Hong Gil-dong was out in front, and the special forces agents were holding hands.

All the King's Men

King frowned as he watched, the woman pulled the man closer, and they kissed. It was only a shared moment, but as they pulled apart and followed the hacker there was a bounce in the woman's step, and a beaming smile upon her face. The man looked pleased, too. So, he'd found their weakness. The couple were smitten with one another. He found himself smiling, then wondered whether he had ever shown a weakness around Caroline. Although they had never shown public affection on assignment, the thought made his blood run cold. He hadn't intended to start something with someone he worked with, but these things didn't have a playbook. It just sort of happened. Like these two trained soldiers in front of him. Did they know that their feelings for each other was the chink in their armour? The two looked in the first flush of their relationship, it was doubtful that they would have given it so much as a second's thought. And like this couple, he wondered whether he could continue in this line of work for as long as he was with Caroline. They would forever be the other's Achilles' heel.

King waited. Hire cars stopped at the junction, then entered the steady flow of one-way traffic. He wound down both front windows, visually going through the procedures of hiring a car and imagining the Koreans filling in the forms and being shown around the vehicle. Would they have been familiar with the process? Had they left the DPRK before, or did the North Koreans have training camps like the Soviet KGB had for their agents in the fifties and sixties? Imitation nightclubs, replica hotel receptions based on Holiday Inns and Forte hotels, libraries and shops. KGB agents would use dollars or pounds – depending on where they were going to be deployed – and immerse themselves in Western culture like music, media, books and films. King had heard that the political elite in the DPRK had access to supermarkets stocking Western food brands and alcohol and he imagined their agents shopping in such places to get the practice.

The white Kia crossover gave way at the junction and King could see the male agent at the wheel and the woman in the passenger seat. The hacker was in the rear seat and staring at his mobile phone. King picked up the gun, shouldered it and aimed directly at the rear of the vehicle as it pulled out of the junction and headed away from him. He squeezed the trigger, and the weapon fired quietly, a distinct 'pop' as a jolt of compressed air propelled the .50 calibre rubber projectile rapidly over the sixty metres to the target at three-hundred feet per second, but slow enough for King to see its last few metres of travel as it impacted just above the numberplate. The gel squashed flat, sticking securely, the transmitter activating with the force of impact. King dropped the modified paintball gun into the passenger footwell and held his breath as he unlocked his mobile phone and opened the app. The red dot flashed intermittently, its direction of travel on the image of the map clearly visible. King pinched the screen with his thumb and forefinger, getting a larger overall image of the map. The notes in the bag informed him that the transmitter would work up to a range of five miles, which meant that he could follow the target without being seen. King pulled out into the traffic, glancing at the phone in the centre console to confirm the road that he should take at the large roundabout ahead.

He held back, keeping either on or just under the speed limit as he tracked the vehicle on the screen. In the door pocket beside him the 9mm Browning was made ready, but the text from Ramsay changing the plan meant that it would remain unfired, unless the plan went to pieces. King had been planning on killing the two agents and snatching the hacker when an opportunity presented itself, but now he had bigger problems. Now he had to snatch all three.

Chapter Thirty-Three

St. James' Park, London

Luger watched her walking towards him, annoyed that his heart fluttered as she drew closer. He'd started to think of her as The Black Widow now, and still he would succumb to her advances if she gave him the green light.

"You don't trust me enough to go to your headquarters?" she asked, somewhat indignantly, yet her eyes showed humour behind the comment. "What's the problem, embarrassed that your HQ doesn't have a bar?"

"MI6 make decisions over Scotch or champagne. MI5 make decisions over a cup of tea or coffee." Luger paused. "And therein lies the problem, some would say…"

She laughed, sweeping her hair away from her face. "MI6 takes most of its personnel from Oxford or Cambridge," she said pointedly. "While MI5 is happy with a two-two from former polytechnics."

"Ouch." Luger smiled. "So, the fact that I got a first from Cambridge might just disprove your theory."

"Really! You're an alumni?" She paused. "And we never met..."

"Well, you're quite a lot older than me," he chided. "Like that motorbike bloke."

"Ouch. Oh, touché, young man." Harriet paused, visibly irked. "Well, that's shifted my mood somewhat."

"It may be for the best."

"I'll decide what's for the best."

Luger shrugged and started to walk. For a moment he thought that Harriet may not follow, but she relented and joined him as they walked side by side. "You don't want me," he said. "I get it. So, perhaps it would be better if we forgot what happened between us, stopped pretending that it was for any other purpose than to bug my flat, and concentrated on what you think Devonshire is up to, and why he wouldn't share information regarding a North Korean spy." He looked at her, feeling a sudden weight lift inside him now that he had put it out there and called the 'relationship' what it was.

"It's complicated. Anyway, if I didn't want you, then why would we have done what we did at the Fleming Hotel?"

"To keep me onside?"

"I'm not like that," she replied, looking somewhat hurt and dejected. Luger wondered whether this was an act, but if it was the woman had lost her true calling. He had never been so convinced that she had been stung by his comments. "Like I said, my marriage is my business; something between my husband and me. And no, I didn't *just* sleep with you to plant those devices. Or to keep you onside at the hotel."

Luger wasn't sure that he would take her word for it, but there was nothing to be gained from a back and forth. "What about this asset of yours in the DPRK?" he asked, changing the delicate subject matter.

"We have two," she replied. "General Cho is a career sycophant of the Supreme Leader. We have been running him for eight years. He was recruited in China."

"Money or blackmail?"

"Both." She paused, reaching out discreetly and holding his hand. He found himself gripping back firmly, a spark of electricity between them. "General Cho is a pervert. Women, men, boys and girls. He's not fussy, and quite depraved, really. A film was made, but he was also sweetened with a Swiss bank account and fifty thousand pounds a year to feedback information back to us."

"I'm surprised the regime are bothered about some sexual indiscretion. They're not a wholesome bunch. Didn't the Supreme Leader execute his own uncle with an anti-aircraft gun?"

"That's right. Oh, they execute people in all manner of methods. The camps are rape hotspots as well. However, these girls and boys were very young and with the Supreme Leader's sister taking a more prominent role these days, well, there is a bit more female solidarity. Don't get me wrong, she's a bloody lunatic, just like her brother, but they're not perverts or child molesters. I'll give them that much." She paused. "But what Devonshire doesn't know, is that his predecessor, and my long-time mentor in the SIS already had a mole in the regime. Devonshire wasn't privee to this, as his predecessor wasn't exactly enthralled by his replacement. I never disclosed to Devonshire that we had another asset."

All the King's Men

"And it's this asset who reported that General Cho has initiated a mission against the West?"

"Yes," she replied pointedly. "And Devonshire has not disclosed this to anyone. My worry is, why?"

"Why indeed? And could this General Cho character be working with Iron Fist?" He stopped and looked at her, and she went to lean in and kiss him and he nodded towards the nearby park bench where Ramsay sat adjacent in his wheelchair and Rashid sat on the bench, his cotton shirt open to reveal a T-shirt and the glimpse of a Glock 19 inside a pancake holster. "He'll see you now..."

"Quite protective of the new digs, is he?" she said somewhat sharply. "Has his bodyguard got clearance from the Home Office for that weapon?"

"I wouldn't bank on it." Luger paused. "And he's not his bodyguard. But he won't hesitate to use it."

"That's a lot of paperwork and almost guaranteed to spark an inquest."

"Not if it's unregistered, previously unused and tossed in the Thames after using," he smiled. "That's how we do things."

"You lot really are a bunch of cowboys."

"We prefer, band of Merry Men."

"Pirates, more like."

Beside Ramsay a man had his back to them and when he turned around, Luger watched Harriet's expression. Nothing, not even a flicker. Someone had tried to kill the embassy's security man in Tallinn, Estonia on their last operation. Carter now stood in front of her, as bold as brass, and the woman did not bat an eyelid. Luger knew that the order had come from Devonshire, but now he was not so sure that Harriet had been in on it.

Luger grinned. "I must be going," he told her. "Things to do; places to be. You're in good hands..."

"You're not staying?"

Luger did not answer as he walked back across the park. He had already taken out his phone and texted to Caroline, *She's with him now...*

Chapter Thirty-Four

Sky News Report

"Seven deadly commercial airline flights have now been confirmed with Canada, the UK, France, Indonesia and the USA all affected. One thousand, nine-hundred and ninety-seven people have now been confirmed dead. The International Civil Aviation Organisation is calling for talks with airline and travel companies to discuss grounding flights and the militaries of more than thirty nations are making airfields available to accommodate grounded aircraft. Aircraft safety authorities are blaming faulty O_2 condensers and commercial airliner companies are taking measures to establish a link.

In further news, the death toll from the stricken ferries that went down in unrelated incidents in the Greek Islands has now risen to two-thousand and seventeen."

. . .

Front page of the Daily Mail

'Brexit Supply Bureaucracy Fuelled Airline Disasters'

Faulty oxygen cylinders have been suspected of poisoning the air in seven commercial airliners. Needless European bureaucratic delays are quite possibly to blame, as the UK is punished for Brexit and the will of the majority.

GB News

"Ten thousand illegal migrants have used the deaths of innocent tourists to slip past the Greek coastguard and police in the wake of two unrelated ferry disasters. The death toll has now reached two thousand, with many more still missing."

Front page of The Mirror

Holidays on Hold as Planes Grounded!

Chapter Thirty-Five

Palace of Westminster

The Prime Minister seldom took meetings regarding matters of either national or international security in Downing Street. His working office in the Houses of Parliament was better suited because the press were always camped out on Downing Street, and he did not want to raise concerns meeting his heads of intelligence, especially as nobody outside of MI5, MI6 and the cabinet had the faintest idea who Neil Ramsay was, or indeed the depth of his remit as head of a new 'department' under the umbrella of MI5.

The office of the Prime Minister was small, the carpet threadbare and the walls seemingly like that of a church. The two narrow windows were finished in a lattice of lead and looked down onto the murky waters of the Thames, with the terrace pavilion directly below.

"Where will this end!" the Prime Minister threw down the newspaper on the desk and stared at Ramsay. "I thought you had an ID on the hacker?"

Ramsay recognised when blame was heading his way. The Westminster two-step. Hold them close, then spin them out across the floor into the limelight. "We have." Ramsay paused. "But these recent attacks were coordinated simultaneously from different IP addresses, all hacked, and with no openings in the firewalls. This means that other hackers are behind these tragedies. So, we need to determine who is behind this, not just the man at the keyboard..."

"Apprehend this man now! This needs to stop!"

"As I just said, Prime Minister, it's not as simple as that." Ramsay reiterated. "These attacks happened within hours of each other, without the openings that we found in the first three hacking attempts. This is clearly somebody else, possibly multiple hackers."

"Better yet, I want the bastard dead!" the Prime Minister continued without listening. "Stop this man; stop the attacks!"

"The hacker has made a cry for help," Ramsay told him. "He is now known to us, and we have his employment records, US tax codes and previous addresses. He has weaved lines of coding into his work to show us his location. It is our belief that the DPRK trained him and sent him to the US as a deep sleeper. We are sure that through his DPRK handler, he has been set to work for Iron Fist. Before we can lift this hacker, we need to sever the link in the chain. Otherwise, other sleeper cells could be activated, and we will lose all leads to Iron Fist. What we have here, is essentially the chance to halt Iron Fist and limit the chances of further escalation."

The Prime Minister scoffed. "So, until then, we just sit back and allow people to be killed?"

"With respect Prime Minister, wars in the Middle East have cost civilians a hundred times these figures, and nobody in government seems to bat an eyelid when it's for oil or political cohesiveness."

"Don't presume to lecture me on the weight of war!"

"Sir, short of launching ballistic missiles on the DPRK to eliminate the high-ranking military officer working for Iron Fist, and that is never going to happen, my agents are the best chance we've got."

The Prime Minister nodded, seemingly hesitant to continue. Ramsay studied the man. Oxbridge, lawyer, early fifties, a multi-millionaire despite socialist pretensions. He wanted to believe that the man had what it took to lift the country and the general state of British politics, but he had yet to prove himself. He had a tell, of course. Ramsay doubted many had noticed it, but he knew that bad news was coming. A slight twitch of his left eye and busy fingers, despite the man's efforts to keep his hands from view at times like this. "There is talk in the intelligence community that my predecessor was wrong to hand you such a broad remit," he said. "Some people feel that with the Security Service's recent data and security breach, your department should be shut down and the Secret Intelligence Service should be given overall control. The two services were set up over a hundred years ago in wartime. It is time to bring security and intelligence into the fore and no longer lack transparency or suffer from failure to share information."

Ramsay nodded. "I believe you were at university together," he said, then added when he saw the man's expression, "With Devonshire, that is."

"I don't see what that has to do…"

"It has everything to do with the suggestion," Ramsay interrupted. "If I may, Prime Minister, you are new to the office. It would not be advised to bring friendships into the realm of intelligence and security. It never ends well for all those concerned, and it can cost people their lives..."

"Are you threatening me?"

"Certainly not," Ramsay replied. "But clouded judgement and conflicts of interest make for poor decisions." He paused solemnly. "And those poor decisions cost lives further down the line. It's what weighs on me most heavily... and what should weigh on our leaders..."

"Are you finished?"

"Sir, if I may?"

The Prime Minister shrugged. "If you must."

Ramsay sighed, then looked at the man squarely in the eyes. Not an easy task for someone as far along the autism spectrum as Ramsay, but he manged it, nonetheless. "You were voted into office on the back of the previous government's history of failure to understand the public's perception of self-serving cabinet members. Blatant disregard for laws, bona fide cases of corruption and business interests that gained government contracts and influence." He paused. "If I were you, I wouldn't stand by old friends or acquaintances who may find themselves of interest to my department. In fact, I would distance myself entirely."

The Prime Minister stared at him, his tell clear as day. "Thank you, Neil. That will be all..."

Chapter Thirty-Six

The South Bank, London

"It's a meet," said Kernow. "There's no other reason for her being here. I mean, she's not eating her lunch or checking her phone."

"Agreed," Caroline replied. "We just need to see who she's meeting with."

"And whether they're an interest to us."

"Is this chap Carter any good?" she asked.

"I reckon. He was an embassy spook, so he would have learned a lot along the way. MI6 was what Ramsay told me, then he had a misstep. Divorce, alcohol, money issues, but I gather he paid for it with shitty embassy posts in shitty little countries." He shrugged. "I don't think he'd be here unless Ramsay saw something in him."

Caroline nodded. Enough said. Harriet had left her meeting with Ramsey in St. James' Park and taken a devious route on foot through Westminster to Covent Garden, then taken two taxis and a stretch underground on the Northern Line. Another two taxis and she had walked the last half a mile. She had checked behind her for a tail using shop windows and changing direction regularly. She practised good fieldcraft, but she was no match for Carter, Caroline, Luger and Jim Kernow. Not when Luger followed on a motorcycle with a tinted helmet visor and Jim and Carter followed on foot. Caroline drove, heading for waypoints indicated by both Jim and Carter over texts, and by maintaining regular contact with Luger through his headset and mic. She was driving a London black cab with its taxi light switched off, which gave her use of taxi lanes as well as ninety percent of the bus lanes. Like all black cabs, the vehicle benefited from a one-hundred-and-eighty-degree front wheel lock, which made U-turns easy in narrow streets and vehicle lanes. Ramsay had purchased two such vehicles and they had undergone communication upgrades and been fitted with run-flat tyres, ballistic glass and Kevlar-lined door panels. They were almost invisible in the London traffic – hiding in plain sight.

"This looks promising," Caroline said before speaking into her mic, her voice activating the four-way conversation. "Carter, wait east. Luger, wait west."

"Have that," Carter replied.

"Got it," Luger responded.

With Carter and Luger each taking position east and west of them, there was no way of Harriet giving them the slip. They would wait before an exit to the south became clear, with north hemmed in by the Thames. Caroline watched as the man drew near. She took a picture of him and sent it to the number that they had been designated. When she looked back, the two of them embraced and greeted each other warmly. Harriet looked around her, then led the man over to a bench seat beside an ornate bronze statue of lion and overlooking the river.

Caroline checked her phone. The picture was of the same man but in an olive-coloured uniform. "Christ," she said. "His name is Igor Reznikov. He's Russian. A serving GRU officer wanted in connection with an assassination in Rome."

"Do we apprehend him?" Jim asked. As Ramsay's official bodyguard and former diplomatic protection officer with the Metropolitan Police Service, Jim Kernow had been afforded permission to carry a firearm and had a 9mm Glock 19 nestled in a pancake holster tucked inside his waistband.

"No," Caroline replied. "Not yet..."

"We could have done with a parabolic microphone," Jim commented.

"Carter, come back towards the target," said Caroline. "When they leave, I want you to stay on Harriet. Luger, you stay on the Russian. Jim and I will take the Russian, also. We need to see what he does next."

People walked past the man and the woman on the bench without knowing that one of them was a serving MI6 officer, and the other a Russian GRU agent. They had work on their minds, dates, sex, shopping, lunch, the argument with their partner that morning, their children's homework, money, debt – everything that filled the minds of people as they went about their day. The two spies enjoyed complete anonymity amid the mundane. Caroline watched them closely. Apart from the hug, there had been no further contact. No chance of slipping something into the other's pocket – unless that had been done from the off. She studied the body language, knew when they were done.

They both stood up and hugged again, but Caroline did not see anything suspicious as they did so. The Russian briefly embraced her, and she had placed her hands upon his shoulders. Almost at once, Harriet headed away from them and the Russian waited a good minute before walking in the same direction.

Caroline reached the road and got back behind the wheel of the taxi, ignoring a Japanese couple who wanted to get a lift to the London Eye. By the time she had pulled back into the road and travelled a hundred metres, Jim called in. *"He's on a number seventy-six bus. He's on the top deck, and I'm on the bottom."*

"Okay..." Caroline pulled a pained expression for nobody to see. If the Russian had noticed Jim Kernow and suspected being followed, then he'd sure as hell know for sure if he saw him again. But she knew that after leaving her the man would have had to make a split-second decision, and they'd all been there at some time or another.

"If you confirm when you have the bus in sight, then I'll get off at the next stop..." said Kernow.

She smiled. "Sounds good," she replied. "Seventy-six... alright, I have it."

"I've got the spare helmet," Luger entered the chat. *"I'll pick you up, Jim. Caroline, you hold for the time being. When the bus stops again, I'll drop Jim off in front of you and you can pick him up again."*

Good thinking, thought Caroline. "Have that," she replied.

Five minutes later the bus pulled in at the bus stop and a few passengers got off, the Russian amongst them. Several passengers got on and the bus pulled away. Caroline frowned, unable to see Jim Kernow. He must have had his exit blocked and kept his back to the target. She slammed the taxi up the curb and got out. "Jack, I'm on foot!"

"Have that," Jack Luger replied.

"Jim, get off at the next stop and wait for an update," she said curtly. She jogged down the steps and caught sight of the Russian GRU agent walking along the pavement beside the river. "Jim...?" There was no reply and she cursed under her breath at the comms failure. The Russian stopped walking and Caroline ducked beside a souvenir kiosk, fearing that he would turn around. When she chanced a look, the Russian was leaning on the ornate balustrade beneath another bronze statue of a rearing lion, one of ten thousand such statues scattered around the city. Beside him, a tall, slim man wearing a navy pinstriped suit had adopted a similar stance. "The target is with someone..." she said, waiting for him to turn before taking his picture. She caught a good side profile and sent it to the designated number. "Awaiting identification..." The text came back moments later, looping all four of them into the text.

"That's Devonshire!" Luger said before Caroline had chance to read the text.

Caroline had never met the man, but she had heard Big Dave's, Jack Luger's and Jim Kernow's accounts of him after their meeting at MI6 headquarters during their last operation, and none had been favourable. "What the hell are two SIS officers meeting separately with a Russian GRU agent for?" she mused, her eyes still on the two men beside the river. "Jim, are you receiving us?"

No reply.

"Where are you, Jack?" she asked.

"Parked up ahead of the bus at its next stop," he replied. *"I still haven't got eyes on Jim..."*

Caroline shivered. The breeze was warm, and even in

the shade it wasn't exactly cold, but the shiver that ran down her spine told her that something was wrong. She watched as Devonshire handed the Russian something which was slipped quickly into his pocket. Devonshire turned and walked away. Caroline's instinct told her to stay with the Russian and she climbed the steps to intercept him back on the street. When she reached the top, she waited, but the Russian didn't show. She cursed and said into her mic, "Jack, change of plan. The target is heading west on the river walk. Head him off and follow him. Do *not* lose sight of him..."

She turned around and gasped with surprise as she stared directly into Devonshire's face.

"Silly girl..." he said acidly. "Ramsay will play his little games, won't he..." She made to move around him, but he shoved her back against the wall. "You're in too deep. You have no idea what is at stake..."

Caroline stood her ground and said, "Meetings with Russian GRU agents don't tend to end well for British intelligence officers." She paused. "You're on film doing that, and so is your underling..."

Devonshire frowned. "Who?" Caroline tried to step around him, but he pushed her again. This time she tried to spin him around using a judo technique, but he jabbed her under her armpit with rigid fingers and she yelped, then suddenly felt faint. She knew that he had hit a sensitive pressure point, but what was more frightening was the expert way in which he had done it. "The next blow will be so severe it will make your fucking womb haemorrhage, so be *very* careful what you do next, silly girl..."

The coldness in his voice shocked her to her very core. She had never felt so helpless. Never one to rely on a man, and taking pride in the fact, she wished that King was here to strike this odious creature dead. "What the hell are you up to?" she asked, feeling the usual confidence gone in her voice. All she could think of now was getting away from this beast.

"Silly girl. Do you think we don't know who we're up against?"

"SIS?" she retorted. "We are not enemies..."

Devonshire looked around himself, then looked back at her. Caroline thought about the man's threat, not sure if he was going to strike her or share some snippet of information. Kill or be killed was the only instinct she listened to, and she jabbed the man in his eye with her fingernails and darted to the side, giving her some space away from the wall.

Devonshire hollered and cupped his right eye, as two passersby broke London code and hovered with concern. "Not SIS!" he laughed, not caring who overheard. "My god, you lot don't know anything..." Caroline's shoulders sagged in relief as Devonshire did an about turn and walked to the curb. She was shaking inside, but she had stood her ground. She couldn't help thinking that retirement had softened her, and she vowed to change that. Devonshire looked back at her in contempt, his right eye sore and watery. "You're out of your bloody depth, silly girl..."

Devonshire stepped out into the road and Caroline heard the engine before she saw it. A scream of pistons and gears and the growl of the exhaust note. Spinning tyres on the worn road surface. Devonshire turned towards the sound but was struck with tremendous force and spun in the air like a rag doll tossed from a crib. He sailed over the car and landed heavily on the ground. There were screams from pedestrians and the vehicle slammed on its brakes. Caroline watched as Devonshire lifted his head and tried to get up, but the car – a large Audi SUV – was slammed into reverse and shot backwards, reversing into Devonshire, his head striking the rear bumper and the vehicle driving right over him. There had been a heavy 'thud' as the man's head bore the brunt of the impact, followed by a sickening 'crunch' of breaking bones. Watching helplessly, Caroline heard a squelching sound as the vehicle pulled forwards over the broken, bloody mess that had once been a person, and accelerated down the road and into the traffic. Then, the sound of scraping metal and breaking glass told Caroline that the driver was using the vehicle as a battering ram to escape traffic further down the street.

Shaken and bewildered, Caroline looked away from the body and activated her mic. "Jack, Devonshire is down! He's dead! A hit and run driver in a black Audi SUV. Q, something... blacked out windows, two large exhausts... big alloys... drug dealer type..." She paused, fighting for breath although she had not exerted herself. Shock, fear, relief – all carried around her body by a flood of adrenalin. "Get after that car, Jack!" She hurried to the taxi and got inside. "Jack, are you there?"

"I'm here," he replied dejectedly. *"Caroline, Jim has been stabbed. It's bad..."*

"What?" she gasped.

"I'm on the bus," he told her. *"It's pulled over and police have detained some of the passengers for questioning. A lot of passengers have taken off... Jim was stabbed in the back and in his neck."* He paused heavily. *"There's a hell of a lot of blood. An ambulance is on its way..."*

"Jesus..." she replied quietly. "Was it Reznikov?"

"Jim can't talk, but I reckon so."

"Where is Igor Reznikov now?"

"I don't know. I've lost him..."

Chapter Thirty-Seven

Queensland, Australia

The property was a small holding, but not as King knew it. Over a hundred acres of waist-high pasture and sub-tropical forest over rolling hills and deep crags, a hundred miles inland from Surfer's Paradise. Rusted wire fences, long since trampled by feral cattle and wild deer marked the land out from nature, but it was a losing battle.

The farmhouse sat roughly in the middle of the plot. What was called a bungalow in the UK and a ranch house in the US, the building was low and long and topped with wooden tiles that had twisted and warped from relentless sun and the occasional deluge of rain. Propped up on three-foot-high struts, the sidings had crumbled, and the wrap-around veranda looked somewhat precarious from King's vantage point four-hundred metres due west, where he could keep the sun from his eyes and the shine of the binocular's lens from his quarry.

Whomever had chosen this place had chosen well. The property was on the electric grid, and there was a recently installed satellite dish behind the building, with a parabolic bowl at least three metres in diameter and a central feed horn jutting out more than a metre. King guessed that the newly built shed nearby would provide the dish with a backup generator, power inverter and battery supply. King could see a neighbouring property on the ridgeline a mile or so away, and the road that he had come in on was a dust and gravel affair compacted flat from lack of rain. Using Google Maps, King could see that the plateau played host to a dozen such plots, all around a hundred acres. Many of the houses looked derelict, but a few had held on and were in better repair and the land looked cared for. On the drive in, King had seen bank foreclosure signs at the end of overgrown driveways, and he assumed that the property had been chosen for this reason.

King had followed the Koreans from the airport and into the suburbs of Brisbane. At a cheap motel, he had parked close enough to observe them taking two rooms. The young couple clearly in love, or at least in the throes of a new relationship, and oblivious of their surroundings. After dark, and performing several anti-surveillance drills, to rule out the fact that he too could have been followed, King replaced the ingenious little paintball gel tracker with a magnetic one which he tucked under the vehicle's heat deflector, then made his way over to the reception building and took a room, starting a conversation with the desk clerk and noting that the party had taken two rooms under the name Woo. An American style motel block with designated parking spaces outside the rooms, the booking system was not computerised, and King suspected that cash would be welcomed. He paid cash and a tip, left a false name and mixed up two digits on his vehicle's numberplate. In his room, he showered and ordered a pizza delivery. Empty calories but satisfying. He drank tea from the complimentary tray, losing patience with the tiny, low wattage kettle and grimacing at the UHT milk sachets, and watched the news on a low volume, his pistol resting beside him on the bed. His phone was propped up on a pillow beside him, the app showing the doors to the Koreans' rooms and their vehicle parked outside. King had rigged the wireless camera to his window ledge, receiving the image via Bluetooth connectivity.

King had learned his lesson in Bangkok and had pulled out the bed and used the blade of his Leatherman to prise a sizeable piece of skirting board away from the wall and whittle it into a wedge. He had then kicked the wedge under the door and tested it. The door wasn't opening anytime soon, not without a battering ram or a sledgehammer, and he sat back on the bed and switched the light off. Just the quiet drone of the television and its blue light dancing across the walls. Sleep soon came to him, and with it dreams of Koreans with machine pistols, people screaming for help in choppy seas and pilotless airplanes falling from a clear blue sky. He dreamed of Caroline, but by the end of the dream she had turned into Jane, and he was standing beside her grave in the tiny graveyard in London that had been reserved for MI6 and MI5 officers who had died in service. He heard a noise and looked for it, then when he glanced back at the grave the ground had opened and a swirling void of flame and shadows beckoned him downwards, screams telling him that an afterlife down there was far from comfortable. When he awoke, he was drenched in sweat. He checked the image on the phone and showered. It had been four-forty-five AM, and he packed quickly, sipped tea with the disgusting UHT milk and headed out to his car to wait.

The Koreans had eaten breakfast at the roadside café opposite the motel, then driven directly to the farm. It was an eighty-mile drive in all, and King had followed solely using the tracking device and had not had to show himself even once. After parking in a copse of eucalyptus trees, King had made his way across the overgrown pasture and patches of woods, taking refuge in the trees on the ridge, and settling down to observe. He had a powerful pair of field glasses through which he could see right into the building through two windows. The pistol rested beside him, along with his phone.

King watched, his heart racing, as the young Korean man stepped out onto the veranda and started to perform some callisthenics. He looked fit, muscled and slim. The man leapt over the balustrade and landed softly on the ground, then started performing a series of what King recognised as martial arts katas. He did not know what the Koreans called their practice forms, but he did know that taekwondo was similar to karate, and it all looked the same to him. Punches, blocks, strikes, kicks and swift turns against an imaginary opponent, in a fixed choreographed sequence of attacks and counterattacks. The man then started with some drills of his own, and King noted that his routine was heavy with high roundhouse and spinning kicks, certainly acrobatic and good for keeping distance, but King knew that fights only ended once distance had been broken. He didn't plan on meeting the younger man head-on in hand-to-hand combat, but he already had a few ideas in that scenario.

All the King's Men

The woman stepped out onto the veranda and stretched, just wearing black bra and pants. There was little material covering her, and she was stick-thin with her ribs clearly visible and only the slightest curve at her hips. She too started with some katas and after she had warmed up, she smiled and said something to the man, and they set about sparring. King noted that she was a formidable opponent and there was little between them as they kicked and punched and countered one another, using control and semi-contact. They were not going to make each other bleed, but they weren't exactly being gentle. Then, quite bizarrely, they embraced, kissed and started to make love on the ground without an apparent care in the world. King put down the binoculars, quite bemused. The two were like teenagers who had just discovered themselves. There was no intimacy, just a raw need.

King concentrated on the building, catching sight of Hong Gil-dong watching the couple from the window. He wasn't sure what was more uncomfortable, watching the couple in full flow, or the weaselly-looking Korean taking pleasure in them taking pleasure. When the couple had finished, the hacker lowered the net curtain and stepped back away from the window.

King checked his phone as the couple went back inside the house. The text was from Ramsay and the orders had been quite specific about what King should do with the three Koreans after he had captured them. King suspected that Ramsay had been moving the chess pieces around in his mind, lining up each move and counter-move, giving Caroline, or Big Dave or Luger their tasks in conjunction with King's own. King responded to the text, confirming what had been asked of him. The phone signal hovered between one bar and none, and the text took a few attempts to send. King could not assume that the Koreans were not armed. Certainly, they had left the airport in Brisbane in a hire car, but weapons could have been left for them in the motel room, or indeed, in the house. Somebody had made the place available, installed the satellite and the power inverter. That same person would likely have left essentials and weapons in the property. Illegal weapons were easy to get hold of in Australia. They were brought in from Indonesia and Southeast Asia to the north or stolen from legitimate owners' years previously when gun ownership was less stringent. Weapons also made their way onto the black market from military bases that had become 'lost' before audits. He suspected the old, worn Browning Hi-Power model beside him had hit the streets via that route. The Embassy man who had left it for him had not anticipated King using it, as it came only with the thirteen 9mm rounds in the single magazine. He would have to use his wits and the element of surprise, because any weapon 'contact' would be over in seconds.

The text irked him. He had no help, and time was of the essence. Ramsay had made that clear. But with the hacker in sight, wouldn't that mean that the threat was contained? King thought so. First up, he would destroy the satellite and its control unit and power inverter. Next, he would take care of the two Korean soldiers. Or DPRK agents. Or Iron Fist terrorists... or whatever the hell they were. He wasn't sure how he would do that yet, because Ramsay had stated that he wanted them all alive, and King had not counted on that.

Chapter Thirty-Eight

B^{elarus}

There were two hundred monitors mounted to a gantry with two-thirds of the world's commercial aviation routes running in a livestream and fifty operators seated at computer terminals in five neat rows of ten. The enterprise occupied an entire aircraft hangar with the hangar directly next door housing the thousands of processors and miles of wiring, with the twenty Mitsubishi air-conditioners providing the cooling required for such processing power. The facility had been online for three months, set up in tandem with another in Istanbul that had been destroyed by British security services who uncovered the operation. That facility had been intended for AI attacks, but this one had a more specific remit. The satellite dishes spread in an array behind the two hangars were receiving information from both orbiting satellites and direct hacking of air traffic control centres throughout most of the northern hemisphere. It would also be from where the annihilation of the two largest NATO member states would meet their demise.

Pacing somewhat pensively around the room, an attractive Indian woman in her early thirties examined the work logs of the technicians seated in front of the monitors. He name was Sangita Raj, and she was a product of an expensive Swiss education followed by Oxford and MIT, and she was one of the finest computer programmers in the world, who had given up a mid-six-figure salary in Silicon Valley for ten-times the money and the knowledge that she was helping beat Western dominance of oppressed nations that were unfairly sanctioned because of their socio-political agenda. Her home nation of India did not sanction Russia, and nor did they support Ukraine. Business, commerce and society should not be affected by petty border squabbles.

Raj had set up the facility, overseen the installation of the processors and circuitry, pushed for the most efficient and quiet air-conditioners and pioneered the copper coils pumping saltwater – because saltwater did not freeze until -1.7c and the coils provided pads for each processor to sit on. She had insisted on the latest American satellite technology, rather than Russian military stock and had been instrumental in hand-picking the technicians alongside her Russian and Chinese paymasters who had vetted her technical choices for socio-political ideals, as well as substantial financial gain.

Mishkin, a former Belarus army general and now a kingpin in Iron Fist entered the hangar and walked over to her, accompanied as he always seemed to be by his bodyguard, Andreas Popov – a Greek-Russian hawk-like figure who had been rumoured to have served in the Russian GRU.

"Are we ready?" Mishkin asked, barely looking at her.

"Yes," she replied ambivalently. She did not care for the man. Did not care for the fact that he would have looked at her, shown her more respect if she were a man.

"Without Hong Gil-dong?"

"Of course," she scoffed. The Korean had been instrumental in the development of the AI coding, but she had been the one to take it over the line. If it wasn't for the North Korean contingent of Iron Fist, she would have advised that he be reassigned. The man had a poor work ethic, had become far too capitalist and swayed by consumerism during his time in the US, and from his internet search history that she had once seen, an overly keen interest in internet voyeuristic pornography. "We are ready to roll it out."

"Not yet. Not without Australasia and the South Pacific. Hong Gil-dong will be bringing that online soon." He paused. "I don't know why that could not be done from here, but this is not my expertise."

Raj shrugged. "We live on a globe. We don't have line of sight for communications in the Southern Hemisphere. The code we have designed..."

"That Hong Gil-dong designed..." Mishkin interrupted.

"That he designed, but *we* both developed," she continued. "As I was saying, the code that *we* developed will piggy-back off twenty-seven of the forty-six satellite earth stations spread across Australia. You see, Australia has a unique terrain and position for satellite receiver stations, and due to global warming, the ozone layer is thinner, too. We are looking at perfect conditions for the sending and receiving of the encoded data in the form of radio waves."

"When will he be ready?"

"Soon," she replied impatiently. "Now, General, if there is nothing else...?"

General Mishkin sneered at her. "Dismissed..." he said coldly.

Chapter Thirty-Nine

L ondon

There were no teas or coffees, nothing social about the gathering in Ramsay's office. Mae had not been at her desk, and they had let themselves into the room. Ramsay sat in his wheelchair, his back to them as he stared down at the Thames.

"He's in surgery now," Ramsay said heavily, his eyes not leaving the gently flowing water of the river. "It's not good. He was stabbed in the carotid artery. The stab wound to his back was close to the spine. Luckily, a nurse returning from her shift in A & E pinched the severed artery until paramedics arrived, but it's too soon to say…"

"Is there any news regarding Igor Reznikov?" Caroline asked.

Ramsay sighed. "No. The police are actively searching,

and the service's ports and airports division and UK Border Force have the man on a watch list."

Caroline nodded. "I can't get in contact with Carter either," she said. "So, we don't know where Harriet went after she met the Russian. I must say, I'm not really a fan of the man. Seems a bit of a wash-out..."

Ramsay wheeled himself around. "Carter's dead," he said matter-of-factly.

"Oh, my..." Caroline put a hand to her mouth. "Oh, God, I didn't mean..."

"A single, small calibre bullet to the heart," Ramsay said, not caring about making Caroline feel less uncomfortable after her tactless faux pas. "Broad daylight, no witnesses, no cameras. A complete blind spot in the city that can claim the most CCTV systems in the world."

"How...? Why...?" Caroline stumbled over her words.

"Scorch marks on his shirt, very little bleeding." Ramsay paused. "The lead forensic scientist said it was likely a point two-two pistol, pushed up closely, possibly touching. They won't know the calibre until they've done the postmortem."

"Not a floating barrel, then," Caroline mused, then when she say Ramsay's blank expression she added, "Most modern semi-automatic pistols will disengage the floating barrel if pressed against something. The system makes for more efficient cartridge feeds and less recoil, which makes successive shots more accurate."

"So, it was an old-fashioned gun?" Ramsay asked.

Caroline shrugged. "Typically. A small pocket pistol like a Beretta Bobcat or a baby Browning in point twenty-five, which surprisingly, isn't as powerful as point two-two, and would likely account for the lack of bleeding because there would not have been any over-penetration."

"I don't expect the pistol will ever be found. It's probably in the Thames or a canal by now. Probably in pieces," Ramsay mulled the thought over. "I can't help feeling responsible. I brought Carter into this after Jack worked with him, then later saved him in Estonia. It was highly likely that either Devonshire or Harriet put the hit on the man to mask their involvement in using Jack to flush out the mole in Russia. Getting rid of Carter would have covered one, or both their backs. Someone saw an opportunity."

"Anything else to go on?" asked Luger.

"Nothing," Ramsay replied. "Unless, of course, our assassin was wearing a string of pearls," he mused. "There were pearls around the area where Carter's body was found. Strange, really."

"Pearls?" Luger asked, picturing the string around Harriet's neck. She had made a habit of rubbing the largest between her thumb and forefinger. It had been her tell. Her eyes and expression gave nothing away, and it had taken him time to realise when the woman was lying. Or at least, telling half-truths.

"Yes. Does that mean anything to you, Jack?"

"No," he lied. "Nothing at all..."

Chapter Forty

Queensland, Australia

King had moved fast. Ramsay's text message hadn't given him much time or the opportunity to plan, but he had made a career out of acting on his instincts and surprise counted for hours of planning. He used the surrounding cover, watching his footsteps for snakes, but hopeful that he made enough vibrations for the snakes to flee into the bush. Australia was home to eight of the world's ten most venomous snakes, and countless others that could end his days out here. King wore a pair of leather desert boots, so he was afforded some protection, but as he stepped through the knee-high grass, it didn't fill him with confidence.

There was approximately fifty metres of ground to cover from his position in the overgrown remnants of what would have once been a cottage garden for fruits and vegetables but had since grown wild and been encroached upon by the bush. King watched the house for movement. He wondered whether the Korean couple would be making love again, and whether the hacker was peeping through a keyhole. The situation was quite bizarre. Whatever they were doing in there, they wouldn't be suspecting over fourteen stone of muscle barging through the heat-warped door with a 9mm Browning in their hand.

There was nothing to be gained from creeping across the open ground, so King darted out and sprinted across the dusty ground, just as the door opened and the young Korean man stepped out onto the veranda. There was no look of surprise, no fear, even. He simply leapt over the balustrade as King aimed the pistol, but he was confident that as he darted left and right, ducked low and sprung at King, that the sights of the pistol were never quite on him. And he would be right. King stopped dead and aimed at the man, just as his back jarred, almost threatening to break and the wind was pounded from his lungs. He fell forwards dropping the pistol, but as the man bent for it, he managed to swipe it away into the undergrowth. The man hesitated, annoyed, but smiled as King felt the full force of an axe kick between the shoulder blades. He sprawled forwards, poleaxed. Blood rushed around his ears, and he struggled to suck air through his teeth. Instinctively, he rolled aside onto his back as the woman's heel struck the ground with a blow that he realised could have killed him had it connected with the nape of his neck or his cranium. He was aware of a blur, the man's heel coming down like a guillotine, and he rolled just in time, lashing out with his foot and catching the woman on the side of her knee. She yelped and staggered back, but King still could not get to his feet as the man leaped high in the air, spun over and came down intending to land on his toes, knees and left palm, his right arm pulled back and ready to punch straight into King's face. It was an impressive move, but it gave King time to raise his knee, and the man connected with his sternum, and he did not manage to execute his punch as King punched upwards and caught the man in his throat. The woman screamed in rage and lined up a footballer's free kick with King's ribs, but King grabbed the man by both ears and wrenched him sideways, her kick catching her lover in the back of his head.

King rolled free and got to his feet. He was still reeling from the blow to his back, but he raised his hands and spread his feet and got ready for the woman's attack, which when it came was in a melee of kicks and punches, which King blocked and parried with, but ultimately it was a shockingly quick roundhouse kick that caught his temple and sent him to the ground where he cushioned his fall with nothing more than his own face. He could hear pounding towards him, and as he looked up, the woman leapt onto his back and got her arm around his throat in a choke hold. Unable to breathe and knowing that he did not have much time before he either lost consciousness, or she held on until he suffocated, King heaved himself to his feet. The woman's legs were wrapped so tightly around his waist that had he been able to suck precious air down his throat, he wouldn't have been able to breathe anyway. The man was getting to his feet and King staggered towards him, turned his back to him, and fell backwards, landing the middle of the woman's spine on the man's head. Both groaned, but so did he, the wind knocked out of him once more.

King broke free of the woman's limbs and coughed and spluttered to his feet. The woman was sobbing, and the man was trying to crawl free of her. King wasn't going to give him the chance to get to his feet, so he stepped forwards and stamped on the man's knee. The man rolled onto his side as he screamed, and King stamped again, this time with a resounding 'crack' as he dislodged the man's kneecap. At once, King dropped onto the woman, straddling her back. He pulled her right arm backwards until she grimaced and yelped, then he punched down onto her shoulder blade and dislocated her shoulder. Their screams echoed in unison as King stood back up, walked breathlessly to the undergrowth and found the pistol. He looked back at them, admiring their spirit. The woman had already got to her feet, and the man was desperately trying to do so. Ignoring the man, who wasn't going anywhere anytime soon, King aimed the pistol at the woman, watching her freeze like a deer in the headlights.

"Stop," he said firmly. "The first step you take, a bullet goes through lover-boy's head. The second step, well, I'll just let you guess where that's going..."

The woman frowned, easing weight onto her left foot, her eyes expressing anything but defeat.

"Stop!" a voice came from the veranda. There followed a gabble of Korean, with a sing-song timbre to it. "They do not speak English..."

King looked up at Hong Gil-dong, the pistol still aimed at the woman. This was a messy development, but King was still on top. What he needed to do now was maintain the status quo. Walking calmly up to the woman, he stamped his foot into her kneecap, and she dropped to the ground beside her lover a second after the 'snap'.

"Why did you do that!" Hong Gil-dong protested vehemently. "You animal!"

King had been called worse by his own mother. He adjusted his aim, putting the hacker firmly between his sights. "What's the plan?" he asked quietly.

"I..."

"You left threads of code that our analysts and technicians could find," said King. "I'm here to find out why."

The hacker stared at the two Koreans writhing on the ground, then looked up at King. "When I started this journey, I was a loyal citizen and a devout follower of the *Supreme Leader*," he said, a note of disgust in his tone. "And then I saw the world for what it was. The West is not perfect, but it is not the picture of evil painted by North Korea's politburo. But I was always shadowed by agents of the DPRK. They would sit down beside me on a bus, take a table beside my own at a restaurant. One time, my date turned out to be an agent. She dropped that bombshell as I settled the bill, then she walked away. They never left me alone for long."

"You want to defect?"

Hong Gil-dong nodded. "But I couldn't simply disobey orders. Not with them breathing down my neck..."

King frowned. "So, you killed everyone on board an airliner and a cross-channel ferry?" he asked incredulously.

"But I helped your people halt a nuclear meltdown..."

"From what I gather, to quote Wellington, it was a damned near-run thing..." King reasoned. "So, what about the other six airline disasters, and the two ferries in Greek waters?"

Hong Gil-dong shrugged. "There are other hackers," he said heavily. "Another hacking programme. They have already started, and it will only get worse."

"Where are these hackers?"

"All I know is that the servers and technicians are somewhere in Belarus," the Korean replied. "But the man who sent these two to see that I saw this operation through knows everything."

"General Cho?"

Hong Gil-dong looked surprised. "Yes…"

"What do you know about him?"

"Very little."

"Where is he based?"

"At a military compound used for training. It's about a hundred miles from the capital, towards the coast. That's all I know."

"That's it?"

The Korean shrugged. "These two are not essentially loyal to him. Not any longer. They are confused. They have had their eyes opened by the free world. What's more, they have fallen for one another." King did not mention that he knew. That he had seen them demonstrate that, and he had seen more besides. The hacker shrugged and continued, "They were sent here by General Cho. They know the man, and the military base. Reading between the lines, only fear of the regime keeps them here. That and the young man's desire to prove himself. Which I think maybe has waned since you broke his kneecap…"

"Interesting," King mused, glancing at them as they groaned and struggled on the ground.

"So, you won't kill them, then?"

Not yet, thought King. "No," he replied. A few hours ago, then he would have thought them as good as dead, but Ramsay wanted as much information on the North Korean camp as he could get, and that meant all three of the Koreans coming in for a debrief. Or enhanced questioning, or whatever the hell they called it nowadays. But certainly, there was now an opportunity here, and a way to close the gap on more hackers with a most deadly agenda.

Chapter Forty-One

The interior of the house was basic. The furnishings were typical of the late eighties, and it was doubtful whether anyone had decorated, or even given the place a touch-up with paint for over twenty years. Savagely hot summers had warped the woodwork, and the interior had a faint smell reminiscent of a Swedish pine sauna.

The injured Koreans were seated on the sofa nursing their knees with ice compresses, but only after King had checked the gaps in the sofa cushions for weapons. He had put Eun-Ji's shoulder back in, but there was little he could do for their damaged kneecaps, so he had started off the questioning by offering medical attention at a small hospital fifty miles away, or simply kicking them in the knee again and it was entirely down to them how it panned out.

Hong Gil-dong sat opposite King and between them, on the table King's phone recorded their conversation, which included translations from both Su Ji-ho and Eun-Ji on their mission and what they could tell him about the military base outside Pyongyang and their commander, General

Cho. King was seated in a deep armchair, the 9mm Browning resting in his lap, his hand on the grips, his finger on the trigger guard. The weapon's hammer was cocked, and the safety was off. There was nothing more unnerving than being unarmed when your enemy was not, and at this range, the Korean soldiers knew they had no hope of escape, and no choice but to cooperate.

"Belarus was chosen because of its proximity to both Russia and Ukraine, and the fact that being the most junior member of Iron Fist they could take all the risk and be pleased about it. The whipping boy, as you may say."

King didn't know where or how Hong Gil-dong got his grasp of English, but it was certainly something that King would say. He also noted that the man had an oddly dated tone and English accent. Like that of a newsreader in the forties or fifties. Although because of his time in California, the occasional twang crept in and sounded quite comical. The intelligence school in North Korea was clearly stuck in the past and with outdated preconceptions as they had taught him his fundamental English. "What can these two tell me about Iron Fist?" King asked.

"Nothing," Hong Gil-dong replied. "They think they are working for the politburo and the Supreme Leader. They don't know anything about Iron Fist."

"You're joking..."

"No. They've been played as much as anyone else."

King stared at them. Something about the man unnerved him. He had seemed a credible opponent, not one to retreat into himself so easily. He had a dislocated kneecap, but King had crawled miles on his stomach over rocks to escape capture with worse injuries in the past. He did not believe that the man was done just yet. "You understand English," he said, aiming the pistol at his stomach.

"Don't fuck with me; I know enough about body language and tells to read you..." He moved the pistol across to the woman, still staring the man in the eye. "Maybe you should start talking..." Nothing. King fired and the report of the pistol in the confines of the house was deafening. The woman screamed and the man sprung forwards and King lurched out of his chair and kicked the man in the stomach and he fell back down onto the sofa, grimacing both from the pain of the kick and the movement that had aggravated his knee. Hong Gil-dong had shouted something, but now sat with his hand over his mouth, staring at the blood soaking the woman's shoulder.

"What did you do that for?!" Hong Gil-dong shouted, then looking at the smoking gun in King's hand, sunk back into himself and stared back at Eun-Ji.

"Because he understands English," King replied coldly, then stared at the younger man. "You do, don't you..."

"You bastard..." Su Ji-ho spat at him, confirming King's suspicion, before turning to Eun-Ji and pressing the old, dusty cushion over the bullet wound.

"You're out of your depth, sunshine," King commented flatly. "You've been set up by General Cho. You are working for a terrorist organisation, and you will start a world war if you don't stand down. I'll give you one chance and one chance only. You tell me everything about the camp at Pyongyang and General Cho, and I will let you and your girlfriend live." He glanced at Hong Gil-dong and said, "You're coming with me, pal. But these two can stay and be Australia's problem. They've clearly fallen for each other and had their eyes opened by the free world. If they talk, then they'll live. Tell the girl."

Hong Gil-dong started speaking in rapid Korean, and Su Ji-ho interjected, all the time pressing the cushion to his lover's wound and occasionally scowling at King. Eun-Ji groaned in pain, nodded as she listened and occasionally added something to the three-way conversation, and all the while, Hong Gil-dong translated for the recording phone on the table in front of them. For all King knew they could be planning their escape, but he knew body language and tells, and he recognised people looking for an out when he saw it. King wasn't overly bothered about the gunshot wound, it had merely blown a chunk of flesh from the woman's delicate shoulder and there was still some meat underneath, not the white of bone. The wound would soon start to clot.

Chapter Forty-Two

King watched Rashid and Jo Blyth get out of the hired Hyundai SUV. Jo headed across the dusty ground carrying a supermarket carrier bag with a laptop bag over her shoulder while Rashid checked his surroundings. To King they both looked like people who had flown for twelve hours, spent an hour in a transfer lounge not knowing whether to eat breakfast or dinner, flown another fourteen hours then driven for another two. He smiled at the thought of his first-class flight, and the pair obviously experiencing the delights of Ramsay's expense budget and 'cattle-class' economy. He'd be sure to drop a few remarks in Rashid's ear before long.

"Kettle's on," King said to Jo. He did not know her well, but she seemed to have settled in well. "Did you bring teabags and milk?"

Jo smiled, holding up the carrier bag. "And some snacks," she said. "I'll get a brew going. White, one sugar, right?"

"Perfect." King stepped aside for her, and she headed

into the house. He looked at Rashid as he reached the steps and said, "You look like shit, mate…"

"Economy class at its worst," Rashid replied. "Twenty-seven bloody hours. I barely know which way is up."

"Down there in this hemisphere," he grinned, pointing to the ground. "I arrived by first class. Did you know that the meals come out on china plates?"

"Idiot," Rashid rolled his eyes. "Where are the hostiles?"

"Inside, taped up. The asset is secured as well. I'm not certain whether he's friend or foe."

"There are a couple of very nice women at the castle who will soon find out for us…" Rashid said, referring to the country house in Scotland that Ramsay had requisitioned for 'questioning' terrorists or foreign agents. "Actually, when I say nice, I don't mean it so much…"

King led the way inside. Both Su Ji-ho and Eun-Ji were seated at the table, ankles secured to the chair legs with duct tape, hands secured behind their backs with more tape with a wrap of tape running around their stomachs securing them to the chair rest. Hong Gil-dong had been afforded no niceties; he had been secured in the same manner with his back to the other two. King had cleaned and patched the woman's gunshot wound – a graze really – and he had wrenched their knees back in place to a lot of screaming, and then a whole lot of relief. They would be limping for a month or more but were no longer in agony.

Rashid nodded for King to follow him into the kitchen, where Jo had made some tea and coffee. King gratefully took the mug of tea from her, nodding a thanks before he sipped.

"Ramsay wants the hacker back ASAP. Jo is going to accompany him back to London," Rashid paused, looking at

Jo Blyth and said, "Sorry about that. You're going to feel like shit after another twenty-five hours in the air."

She shrugged as she sipped her tea. "In-flight movies, meals and drinks, it's not that tough, really." She paused. "The plane disasters make it a bit nerve-wracking though."

Rashid nodded. There wasn't much he could say to that. He had been glad to touch down in Brisbane. He looked at King and said, "You and I have another job on."

King nodded. "I can guess what that is..."

Jo frowned as she handed Rashid his mug. "What's that?"

"This General Cho character," said King. "He knows what *we* need to know. With more hackers out there working on this, then as far as we are concerned - no General Cho, then no hackers. We can't stop this without him."

King had sent the recording to Ramsay, and his team of analysts had checked the information, also employing a trusted translator to listen through the snippets of Korean spoken between the three of them. Hong Gil-dong had been tasked to hack into and then piggy-back the earth station satellites in Australia, whereby all Southern Hemisphere interference could be co-ordinated. That element had now been halted, but without General Cho, then they were no closer to discovering the location of the other hackers and servers.

"But he's in North Korea!" Jo said incredulously. "You can't just go in and get him!"

King smiled. "I think that's exactly what Ramsay will want us to do."

Chapter Forty-Three

Hong Gil-dong had translated the interview. Jo had sent transcripts back to London for confirmation of the content without the Korean hacker knowing. The translations were broadly accurate, but King noted a sense of drama with Hong Gil-dong's translation, but it was still passable enough. King suspected that Hong Gil-dong was not only desperate to be trusted and taken seriously, but eager to be seen as a valuable commodity with the chosen nation for his defection.

Su Ji-ho and Eun-Ji had bargained the best they could for two people indoctrinated by a dictatorship unlike any other. They did not have the experience of finances and commodities and material values. They had provided meticulous details of the military base where General Cho could be found, including shift changes, roll calls and worshipful appreciation of the Supreme Leader, which from what King could gather was flag waving and cheering to a static radio in front of statues of not only the Supreme Leader, but of the man's father and grandfather. They had details of military training, exercises and the locations of barracks, weaponry, mess halls and admin blocks. The transcripts had been checked with information already on file, as well as satellite imagery from both the CIA and GCHQ. Ramsay wasn't concerned with the information that these two soldiers held beyond the operation. It was clear that they had been duped into working for Iron Fist, but knew nothing of the terrorist organisation, and he wasn't interested in the inner workings of the DPRK. In the past North Korean defectors had not provided information beyond what the South Koreans already knew or could guess. South Korea, however, welcomed all defectors and Ramsay had arranged for them to be granted a meeting with the South Korean ambassador who was flying to Brisbane from Sydney along with plane tickets, temporary visas and single-use passports to Seoul. They would be flown business class as a sweetener and given every help starting a new life in the south of the country. The South Korean intelligence services would interview them separately and determine how useful the couple could be, but they were out of the regime and had a brighter future than they did yesterday. King suspected that they would soon be doing the PR for South Korea, which would filter back to their countrymen by the loudspeakers at the border and the balloon drops from twenty-thousand feet, scattering leaflets and shock-proof cartons containing pre-paid mobile phones to encourage insurrection in the north.

The mood in the car was tense. King had encouraged Hong Gil-dong to explain to the two soldiers what was happening, and they had seemed enthusiastic at first, but since they had got into the vehicle, there had been a growing tension between them. King had regretted releasing the tape restraints at their wrists. Now, with Su Ji-ho beside him in the front seat, and Eun-Ji in the rear he

All the King's Men

couldn't help catching glances between them, with Su Ji-ho using the vanity mirror in his sun visor to see her seated behind him.

Rashid and Jo Blyth had already left with Hong Gil-dong, but the two-car convoy had been broken up by two mighty road trains, and then an actual train at a level crossing that had been the longest train King had ever seen, its trucks laden high with coal and iron ore. The Koreans had been blown away by both sights but had now returned to their state of unease.

King turned down the long, straight road, which was a smooth ribbon of asphalt cutting through scrubland and sparse trees. There were kangaroos springing towards them, and King slowed in anticipation to them crossing a hundred metres ahead. The movement came in a flash. The woman looped the knotted shoelaces over King's head and the headrest and pulled back with all her strength. The result was instant choking, and the complete closure of his airway. His fingers instinctively reached for the cordage, but the man caught hold of both of King's wrists and pulled downwards. With just a few seconds remaining before he blacked out, King floored the accelerator and the big turbo-charged engine roared into life. He was already losing consciousness, barely able to focus on the horizon as the vehicle surged down the road. He could feel the man's grip on his wrists tightening, the woman's pull strengthening as they tried to finish him off. The last thing King remembered was shifting his knee against the steering wheel to veer off the straight road, and the woman's desperate screaming in his ear.

Chapter Forty-Four

King could hear the dripping of fluids and smell the acrid fuel long before he could muster the ability to open his eyes. His heart was pounding, his ears pulsing, and he could feel pressure in his neck and chin. He had no idea how long he had been unconscious, or how close he had been to the unfathomable void of death. And he had no idea that he was suspended from his seatbelt, upside down, his arms hanging loosely and blood dripping from his chin, over his face and off his forehead. He could see the blood pooling on the ceiling below him, soaking into the headlining, and he put his right hand in it to hold himself up as he unfastened the seatbelt with his left. His strength had left him, and he fell into a heap and had to twist and roll himself upright. The windscreen had shattered, but the woman's feet and ankles were on the roof. She had gone straight through the windscreen and her crumpled form lay on the dusty ground, the bonnet of the huge vehicle pinning her to the earth.

King crawled out through his shattered side-window and rolled onto the ground. The sun was setting, so he knew that he had been unconscious for at least a few hours. There was no sight of Su Ji-ho, and King checked his waistband for the Browning. He already knew from the lack of weight that it was not there, and it wasn't in the vehicle. King got up and staggered around the vehicle, where the boot lid was hanging off and the contents had scattered on the ground. King bent down and retrieved the entrenching tool, unscrewed the base and opened the shovel blade. One side was serrated, the other sharpened to act as a makeshift axe. When he screwed the collar tight, the tool was the ideal digging and camp tool to split kindling and even chop small logs. It also made one hell of a weapon. The Russian spetsnaz had made an artform of fighting with their entrenching tool, even throwing it with skilful effect.

Rounding the rear quarter of the vehicle, he saw Su Ji-ho stirring facedown on the ground, the Browning in his hand. King figured he had picked up the weapon and climbed out of the vehicle but had passed out shortly afterwards. As he drew nearer, King could see Eun-Ji and reckoned she would have been a great advert for a seatbelt campaign. The pretty young woman now had virtually no face left and was breathing shallowly, her remaining eye, wide open and terrified as she watched King approaching. He bent down and took the pistol from Su Ji-ho's grasp, checking the breech out of instinct. He turned and shot the woman in the head, then before the sound of the gunshot could jolt Su Ji-ho out of his semi-conscious state, he shot the man in the back of the neck. King then made the weapon safe and tucked it into his waistband and set out across the bush with the entrenching tool where he would dig a grave just large enough for two.

Chapter Forty-Five

It had taken six hours for King to get to Brisbane. His phone was first without signal, then ran out of charge. He had walked for two hours along the road, ignored by an oncoming vehicle, then fortunately picked up by a farmer whom King suspected of being several times over the drink-drive limit. The farmer had talked incessantly about the government and the monarchy and had not had much love for either. The pickup had rattled and whined, and King thought they had been lucky to make the drive but could not fault the man for going the extra ten miles out of his way to the airport. He had given the man fifty dollars for some fuel or beer, and suspected that the man would head straight to the off-licence.

Bruised and grazed, King had buried the two Koreans fifty metres from the site of the crash but had spent the entire time miffed about the attack. He supposed that they were loyal to their country and leaders and had simply bided their time to escape. Ultimately, he suspected they would have headed for the airport to either snatch Hong Gil-dong back from Rashid and Jo, or at the very least, kill the man that they had been sent to protect so that a foreign intelligence service did not gain an asset that could harm the DPRK. However, what if the hacker had not translated correctly? Could the man have an agenda different to what Ramsay and his analysts believed, or what he indeed had claimed? Could the breadcrumbs of data that had been discovered simply have been a trap, rather than a cry for help? King now suspected as much, but time had cost him dear. The farmer had not owned a mobile and with the sudden darkness that had fallen King had not noticed the houses set back from the road. At a petrol station when the farmer had stopped for a call of nature, King had asked to use the phone and caught only Rashid's voicemail. He had left a curt message. He had then dialled Ramsay's number and his call had been diverted to the night watch. The woman had promised to relay King's message, even agreeing to send someone to Ramsay's house personally. With that, he had to hedge his bets and head for the airport.

King had found Rashid waiting outside at the departure entrance.

"It's too late," he said as King limped towards him. "Jo's already on the plane with him..."

"Can we contact her?"

"Doubtful. She'll have put her phone in airplane mode. We can try, but..." he shrugged.

"We need to contact the pilot," said King. "And we can't do that without Ramsay's authority, because we'll simply get nowhere."

"Yeah, more likely arrested," Rashid agreed. "Ramsay will have to go through Aussie intelligence, or the police, and then the aviation authorities. What else can we do?"

King shrugged. "We wait," he said. "It's down to the

desk jockeys and diplomats now." He paused. "Where was the transfer?"

"Dubai," Rashid replied.

"Well, that's about fourteen hours," said King pointedly. "With another seven or eight hours to London. So, if Hong Gil-dong is up to something, then it'll be in the next fourteen hours because he won't want to risk being picked up in Dubai on the layover."

"That's fourteen long hours," Rashid commented flatly.

"You like her, don't you..." King stated rather than asked.

"Very much," Rashid replied. "I just didn't want to make a move, because of... well, you know..."

King knew indeed. Rashid had once had a work relationship with Marnie. Ultimately, she died because of a mistake King had made. It had almost cost them their friendship. Because of this, nobody so much as mentioned her name. An unjust remembrance of such a good person. "I know..." he said without looking him in the eye. Of all the people who had been lost along the way during his career, Marnie was the one he regretted the most. A lesson in overconfidence, that he thought about daily. The death of her parents had been on him, too. "Come on," he said. "Let's find somewhere better than this to try Ramsay again..."

Chapter Forty-Six

Big Dave had just stepped outside into the nighttime heat of Brisbane when he received the text from Ramsay. Hot, weary from travel and an unforgiving time zone, he had hailed a taxi and headed to the address in the text message. The thought of hopping onto another plane so soon wasn't the best prospect. Not until he had showered and eaten a decent plateful of food.

He found Rashid and King in the bar of the hotel. The two men had empty plates on the table and a beer in their hands. King saw Big Dave before he took another pace across the bar.

"Don't get too comfortable, lads," said the big Fijian. "We're on a plane in three hours."

"Where?" Rashid asked incredulously.

"Seoul."

"South Korea?"

"Unless there's another Seoul, that I don't know about..."

"Knob..." Rashid rolled his eyes and sipped his beer. "It's a bit sudden."

"No, I sort of figured it would be on the cards," said King. "But I don't know whether or not we can trust the source."

A waiter wandered over and asked if Big Dave wanted to order. He ordered two plates of steak and chips, a pint of Victoria Bitter and a pint of water. When the waiter came back with cutlery for two wrapped in a paper napkin, he handed one back and said it was just for him. The waiter laughed and put the second knife and fork down anyway before returning to the bar.

"Hungry?" asked King.

Big Dave shrugged. "Airplane food," he said, like it explained everything, which it probably did. "I won't get a room. But I'll take a shower in one of yours."

"But I like the little soaps," said King.

"And I like a fresh, dry towel..." Rashid chided. "And a dry bathmat."

Big Dave shook his head. "Dickheads," he said, then looked up as the waiter brought his beer and his water. He drank half the water, then sat back in his chair with the beer and rested the bottom of the glass on the arm of the chair.

"What's the objective, then?" Rashid asked.

"Snatch and run," he said. "I have the orders. They are being held on a dedicated webpage that we access. One of Ramsay's new initiatives. A bit like DocuSign. We can view them once we're in South Korea. Arrangements are being made for us out there as we speak."

King sipped his beer and wondered how good Hong Gil-dong's information was, or indeed, if the man could be trusted at all.

Chapter Forty-Seven

London

Jim Kernow was in an induced coma. His stats were low, but his condition had been described as stable. Ramsay watched from the doorway. He had grown close to the man, as close as he could come to calling someone his friend, at least. He had spoken to the on-duty doctor, and she had explained that it was imperative that the patient did not move after surgery, as the cauterisation and suturing was on the cusp of what the surgeon considered possible. An involuntary movement could rupture the artery, and he could die within minutes, so an induced coma was essential for the first few days at least.

"He's in a poor state," Caroline commented from beside him. Ramsay had not heard her enter, and he glanced up and nodded. "What's the news?"

"Induced coma, technical plastic surgery. He will recover from the wound to the neck, but it's too early to know if the stab to the spine has caused paralysis."

Caroline winced. It must have been raw for him, having lost the use of his legs because of an assassin's bullet. Instinctively, she placed a hand on his shoulder. "We'll just have to cross our fingers," she said. "Like we did for you…"

Ramsay touched her hand, a rare display of affection or emotion for him. But the gesture of appreciation was gone in an instant as he let go and wheeled around half a turn to face her. "The CCTV on the bus doesn't show who stabbed Jim, but it shows the Russian getting off. He didn't go near Jim on the bottom deck. So, if it wasn't the Russian…"

"It was Harriet," Caroline said adamantly. "It makes sense. She left with Carter following her. She killed him, then set about getting us off the Russian's tail. All she had to do was hop on the bus and stab Jim – she was already way ahead of the bus – then get off and pick up the hit and run vehicle. Jim wasn't discovered until after the next stop. She either had a vehicle waiting, or more likely, stole one." She paused, almost excitedly at the notion. "She's an SIS officer, and we don't know what wing she served in, or where her career has taken her. She could have been trained to steal cars and pick locks, just like we have been trained to do."

"There's no news on the Audi," Ramsay told her. "The police haven't found it, and nobody has reported it stolen."

She shrugged. "Well, it looked like a drug dealer's or wide boy's car. Those things are usually bought with cash from fellow criminals. Half the price, but off the radar of the DVLA and the police. They don't insure or tax them. After a few months using them, they ship them out to somewhere like Albania for cash and find something else to drive." Caroline shrugged. "If we find the Audi, I'd bet a month's salary that the number plates and documents don't match the VIN plates."

Ramsay nodded. "Where's Jack?"

"I don't know," she replied. "He's gone off radar. Must be a woman..."

Chapter Forty-Eight

Incheon, South Korea

"Does it float?"

"It's floating now, isn't it?"

"Does it run?"

"Just about."

King stared at the wooden boat deciding that despite previously owning two yachts he wasn't bringing any expertise into the equation. Maybe he would have known more if one hadn't been blown up and the other one's engine hadn't died on him off West Africa. "It's big," he said.

Big Dave laughed. "Well, I'm glad the expert is onboard..."

King ignored him. "What's the deal with the infiltration?" King paused, watching Rashid lifting crates up the gangplank and onto the deck. "North Korea aren't just going to let us sail in and get off the boat." He paused as

Flymo stepped out of the wheelhouse and took one of the crates from the Big Fijian. "Never mind, I'm all caught up…"

Big Dave smiled and King followed his gaze to the forward deck where a tarp covered what he had previously presumed from the shape was a stack of boxes. "A Huey. Old as fuck. The Yanks left it behind in Vietnam, the Vietnamese sold it to the Laos army, some guy from Thailand bought it for tourist trips in the nineties and then it found its way over to South Korea. Flymo has been onboard working on it for a week, overhauling it and trying to make up for sloppy servicing over the years."

"A week?"

King shook his head. "So, Ramsay was always going to have us do this…"

"It certainly looks that way."

"Don't helicopters have to be certified?"

Big Dave shrugged and rubbed his thumb and forefinger together. "Southeast Asia. Paperwork gets lost, while other, more valuable pieces of paper changes hands."

"North Korea has air defences. They have radar and sonar, too." King paused. "We don't know how cutting edge those systems will be, but we have to assume that Russian and Chinese influence has brought them into the twenty-first century."

"Yep."

"So, how?"

"This trawler was stolen from North Korea by South Korean commandos. They made it look like it had sunk. The crew were paid off and relocated to the south. Apparently, they jumped at the chance." Big Dave paused. "North Korea has a starvation and famine problem. Lack of modern farming skills, sanctions on fertiliser and chemicals and overdemand for domestic food production has left the ground infertile. China and Russia trade with them, but they have their own problems. Recently Russia and Iran have swapped food for missiles, so although depleting, North Korea obviously has a lot of weapons and ordnance stockpiled."

"Thanks for the National Geographic talk. Is this leading anywhere?"

"Jeez..."

"Jesus? Not some six-headed serpent fish, or something like that?"

"No, I save Jesus for when I'm being derogatory," Big Dave grinned. "Anyway, Fijian mythology and religion takes a bit of explaining..."

"Well, I'm not bothered either way."

"Come on, you've got to believe in something?"

King shook his head. "Why?"

"Because there has to be something else. What kind of life is it to know that when you're dead, you're dead?" the Big Fijian shrugged.

"Because that's what happens."

"Where's your proof?"

"I haven't got to prove it. I don't need it. I've just got to live with it." King paused. "My proof is about as certain as yours. Anyway, if there *is* a heaven with pearly gates or a paradise with seventy-two virgins, or even a big cave filled with flowers and seashells underneath Fiji or Polynesia, well, none of us are getting in anytime soon. Even beer-drinking, sausage-eating, promiscuous Muslims like him..." he nodded towards Rashid. "Not after the things we've done."

"Well, this has been nice. We must do it again," Big Dave commented sardonically. "Ok, so we were talking about the DPRK and their sonar, radar and air-defences." He paused. "South Korean intelligence informs us of plenty, but just how effective they are is not known."

"An old wooden tugboat like this, and a sixty-year-old utility chopper are not going to fool even obsolete radar systems," King retorted.

"And that brings us back to the famine and agriculture crisis. The North Korean government think that they have answered the fertiliser shortage with meal ground from the guts, scales and bones of fish, at the same time providing protein for the population. The North Koreans are fishing the hell out of the seas, often straying into South Korean, Russian and Chinese waters, and into Japanese waters off the east coast. In retaliation, those nations quite blatantly stray into North Korean waters. Fishing boats like this one are largely ignored in favour of large, steel-hulled factory ships. Especially as we will be flying a North Korean flag. The plan is we tap into our resident pilot's insane track record, and he gets us ashore by damn near skimming the water. Above sonar and under the air-defence warning system of two-hundred feet."

King considered this for a moment, then nodded. "But we still need intel on the camp, the layout and the location of this general." He paused. "Until then, we're just on a fishing trip carrying a helicopter. If a DPRK gunboat happens upon us, then we're in the shit."

"Up to here..." Big Dave held a hand to the top of his head, and it didn't go unnoticed by King that the 'shit level' was a good four inches above the top of his own head. "The intelligence is still very much linear. Thanks to the analysts we now have a photograph of General Cho..." He took a photograph out of his pocket. The paper was thin and the image grainy. "It's printed on rice paper," he explained, then added, "Just in case we're compromised, we can quickly eat it."

"Yeah, I figured that out…"

"All the intel has been printed on rice paper."

"Well, if we're caught, then I'm sure you can take care of it."

"It's better with jam on it."

King smiled. "So, by linear, you mean we still don't have all the details?"

"No." Big Dave said adamantly. "Not enough yet, but it won't take us five minutes to sail there, either."

"Well, to me it looks as if we have a boat, a chopper, and a face… but no idea of where the target is located."

"That's about right."

"That's not enough to warrant setting sail."

"Ramsay and his analysts are still going through the transcripts of the hacker and the two Korean agents."

"Those two agents jumped me," said King. "And I can't see why they would do that if Hong Gil-dong translated accurately."

Big Dave shrugged. "You can't always assume that people who live in a regime or dictatorship will betray their country for the trappings of the West. Maybe they went with the flow, saw their chance and took it." He paused. "That would put the hacker on the level."

"But that would still mean that the intel given by the two agents would likely be false."

"Not if they thought it could be checked. Perhaps in killing you, they thought they could get to Hong *dongdinga-long* and neutralise him…"

King looked at Rashid loading the crates. He knew that the man was sweet on Jo Blyth, but King did not want to say that what Hong Gil dong did next would decide whether he was to be trusted or not. He checked his watch. Their plane would land in ninety minutes. "Nothing much changes, does it?" he mused.

"Nope. Mushroom farming again - kept in the dark and fed on a load of shit..." Big Dave grinned. "I'm getting too old for this shit."

King shrugged. "Well, this plan is so sketchy, you may not get too much older..."

"Great..." Big Dave replied sardonically.

"Wishing you stayed in Fiji now?" King grinned.

"I was about to ask the same thing. Gran Canaria must look pretty good from here."

King nodded as he walked across the deck to the stack of crates. "Let's see what toys we've got," he said, and stepped down into the hold. The vessel no longer smelled of fish, but it did have a strong aroma of salty residue and seaweed. There were still coils of rope, buoys and netting in the hold, and King recognised the hemp rope and netting, and the glass buoys as decades old. He had once seen such equipment at the Maritime Museum in Falmouth when he lived part of the year in Cornwall. The equipment certainly pointed towards a country with no money or development, cut off from the outside world since the fifties.

King picked up a crowbar lying beside the wooden crates and jemmied one open. Inside were 9mm Sterling sub-machine guns with their coat hanger buttstocks and side-mounted, curved magazines. The boxes of ammunition were packed in dusty, brown cardboard that had spotted with mould at some time.

"Well, this is crap," King commented.

Big Dave took the crowbar from him and prised another crate open. Packed in musty-smelling straw were two Bren Guns and two Browning Automatic Rifles (BAR).

"This is a bloody nightmare," said King. "We've got submachine guns that were replaced by almost every country with cars instead of horse and carts in the seventies, World War Two spec Brens in three-oh-three and the American equivalent, and not as good as the Brens to be fair, in thirty-oh-six."

"Still better than the civil servant, though..." Rashid commented.

"Civil servant?" King asked.

"Yeah," he replied. "We called the SA-80 the *civil servant*, on account that it didn't work much and couldn't easily be fired. I was glad when I was badged in the regiment and never had to use one again..." Rashid jemmied open the other crate and started to laugh, holding up two handguns. "The Browning nine-mil is a fair weapon, but Enfield revolvers? Someone is taking the piss..."

"These were left for us by South Korean intelligence," said Rashid. "Surplus from the war. They're keen not to have any involvement, and that goes for the US, too. Ramsay spoke to the CIA man in Seoul, and he didn't want to supply any modern American weapons."

"What, they couldn't just find us some Kalashnikovs to use?" King asked as he hefted out one of the BARs. "Christ, that's heavy," he said. "And it only has a twenty-round magazine." He dropped it on top of one of the crates and picked up a Sterling sub-machine gun. "This feels like it's made from pressed sheet metal in about three minutes. Probably was..." He paused. "I've used one before and it's no better or worse than an Uzi or a Mac-10, but it ain't no Heckler and Koch..." He turned the weapon over in his hand. There was nowhere to mount a scope or suppressor, no picatinny rails for a red-dot or torch. It was simply a basic tool made in the fifties from Second World War technology. However, he did like the side-mounted magazine because you could lay down in the dirt and keep your head down when you fired.

The men stood around counting the weapons. None of them looked enthralled with the cache. One of the crates contained fragmentation grenades and another held a Lee Enfield rifle with a basic-looking scope attached.

"I'd better have that," said Rashid, the resident sniper. "We can zero the sights and test fire at sea."

"I'm not planning on getting out of the helicopter while it's still in one piece," said Flymo. "So, I'll take one of those ancient revolvers, leave the semi-autos for you guys…"

"We should take the Sterling sub-machine guns as our primary weapons, perhaps rig the BARs to the doors of the chopper, fashion some sort of magazine holder for rapid mag changes," said King. He looked at Flymo and said, "If I got you a welder, angle grinder and some wire. Perhaps even an electrical switch, could you rig those Bren guns to either side of the aircraft. With some clever cutting and welding I'm sure you could adapt the magazines to hold a hundred rounds. The top-mounted Bren magazines have gravity on their side as well as springs."

"I could do something," Flymo replied. "If you can get some four-inch tubing, I could fit an endcap and use a simple wire and pin to release. We could carefully pull the pin on the grenades and stack them behind each other. Pull the wire and a dozen or more grenades fall out of the tube and rain on the ground. There's enough grenades to rig four delivery systems. That's a lot of damage if I can drop them around fuel dumps, vehicles or on the barracks."

"Sounds good," said King.

"We could make petrol bombs, too," Big Dave suggested. "A butane blowtorch is a rapid way to light them.

Just as long as they are stored in decent crates to stop them spilling." He paused. "They could create a distraction as much as cause damage."

"There's a high probability that Flymo's flying will cause spillage," Rashid said seriously.

"Now I'm offended!" Flymo retorted. "Centrifugal force and motion, man! I fly smooth. I may fly hard, but I fly damned smooth. You load those Molotov cocktails, and I'll show you some real special shit, and I won't spill a drop..."

King smiled. They were coming together, and he had missed the camaraderie. They were up against impossible odds and had to work with what was available to them. It would not be ideal, but he had always thought that it was whose hands a weapon was in, not the weapon that counted. It was time to put that theory to the test.

Chapter Forty-Nine

**39,000 feet over The Arabian Sea
Midway between India and Dubai**

She had made light of the quick turnaround, but like most people on long haul flights Jo Blyth was tired. She didn't know which meal was her real breakfast and felt like she may fall asleep at any moment, but always snapped back awake. Beside her, resting his head against the window, Hong Gil-dong cat-napped, jolting awake with the periodic turbulence and change of engine tone. No sooner had the noise and movement passed, then he nodded back to his fitful slumber.

Ahead of her, the cabin crew were starting food service. This time it had to be breakfast, but she thought she could smell curried lamb and what she thought as Christmas spices – nutmeg, cinnamon, mace, cardamon and ginger. Standard international breakfast with an Arabian airline. *No bacon and eggs, or pancakes and syrup up here*, she thought. She gasped and jolted in her seat, in unison with the three hundred passengers onboard. The aircraft dropped for several seconds. Jo could feel herself lift out of her seat, her loosened seatbelt allowing her to hover momentarily as the parabola dive created zero-gravity. Other passengers and cabin crew were not so lucky and hit the ceiling in unison before falling heavily to the floor or onto seated passengers to screams and muted groans, and then suddenly, abject chaos.

The emergency oxygen system initiated, and the air masks dropped in unison, the plastic covers falling free. The cabin was filled with screams and people scrabbled to put on their masks, most ignoring the airline safety advice and fitting their children's first, panicked and desperate as they struggled with what should have been an easy task but in stark reality, was altogether more difficult. Jo grabbed her own, and Hong Gil-dong grabbed her arm and told her to wait. All around her, people breathed frantically through their masks, eyes wide in terror. Jo looked at him, and he shook his head. There was an empty seat next to her, but the family seated in the row of four seats across the aisle were all asleep. She watched the row in front, heads bowing slowly, but surely to rest. Almost at once the aircraft grew quiet. Eerily so.

"What have you done?" she said scrutinising the Korean.

The hacker shook his head. "It's not me," he said quietly, his voice barely audible above the rumble of the engines and the hiss of the oxygen masks. "They know I'm here," he told her. "They want to silence me before I tell you anything..."

"What do we do?" Jo asked, the frantic tone in her voice punctuated by the total silence of her fellow passengers.

All the King's Men

"Auto-land will be activated," he said. "We will arrive in Dubai safely…"

The aircraft pitch changed, and they banked hard, dropping in height dramatically. The engines whined and they were pinned back in their seats. The manoeuvre was unlike any they had experienced on an airliner, a turn more akin to acrobatic displays. The engines howled and the overhead lockers on their port side and the ones across the aisle from them unlatched and the contents spilled into the aisle and upon the unconscious passengers. Jo found herself looking at the ocean, almost on top of the Korean who was pinned to the fuselage.

"Oh my God! What can we do?" Jo yelled above the increasing engine noise. "We must be able to do something!"

Hong Gil-dong wasn't listening to her. His eyes seemed to glaze over, and he shook his head slowly from side to side, his expression one of condemnation, and then regret. He reached out and caught hold of the oxygen mask and attached it to himself, leaning back in his seat and closing his eyes. Jo watched him slowly nod, then relax, his chin slumping to his chest. She cried out in realisation of what was happening, of her fate. All around her the passengers moved in unison with the aircraft's inertia, a synchronised dance, macabre and unworldly. She could see only the sun and sky out of the portside window, the glistening Arabian Sea out of the window beside Hong Gil-dong's body. The water was getting ever closer, but even in her sense of dread, she could not help but think it beautiful. She reached out for her mask and attached it to her face, then focused on the ocean and the light and reflection of the mirrored surface. There were boats visible now, fishing boats, she thought. She had once been taken fishing by her father. Many years ago, now. She would have been twelve, no eleven. They had been camping in Norfolk and had taken a fishing trip from Lowestoft. She had caught a mackerel and had begged her father not to kill it, and they had watched it swim down to the ocean depths. Streaks of glistening silver and blue and black and then, gone. She closed her eyes. Just a little sleep. Nothing more to it than that. Darkness was coming now, closing in on her. It was comforting, really. The darkness seemed to hold her and tell her that it was going to be alright, before it went to an absolute void and there was nothing more to come, nothing else to remember.

Chapter Fifty

They had left their mobile phones, wallets and passports back in the hotel in Seoul. The rooms were paid in full for a week, but they hoped to be back in three days. King had a satphone on which he could communicate with Ramsay, and they each carried a two-way radio for the raid, set to the same frequency with a procedure of channel switches if one was lost or it became clear that their network had been compromised.

The conditions were favourable. A light wind, calm seas and clear skies. King, Big Dave and Flymo took turns at the helm, with Big Dave's experience growing up on the sea in Fiji evident, and King's recent yachting experience adding to the voyage. Rashid had discovered that he wasn't a good sailor and had spent a good deal of time leaning over the side and shouting for someone called 'Hugh!'. He was now finding his sea legs and dry retching whenever he saw Big Dave eating an extra-filled sandwich, which appeared to be hourly.

Other vessels were visible on the horizon, but they gave

them all a wide berth. They could not see land but knew that it was sixteen miles distant. That was the irony about sea distance. Just because you could not see land, it didn't mean that you could not be seen from land. The highest point on the boat gave them an elevation above sea-level of thirty-two feet, which meant that they could only see 6.9 miles. However, someone standing atop a three-hundred-foot cliff in North Korea could see 21.2 miles. Without elevation there was no such thing as seeing without being seen.

Flymo had bastardised the Bren gun magazines by cutting and welding three together to hold eighty-eight .303 rounds, losing two rounds to the cuts and welds, and they were now mounted on each side of the helicopter cockpit. Using the winch to turn the aircraft sideways, he had zeroed them in a forty-five-gallon drums at approximately one-hundred metres. The electric trigger switches and cabling was an untidy job, but they weren't going for ergonomics. The four lengths of drainpipes with capped ends would theoretically hold at least forty grenades, giving four drops of ten pieces of ordnance. They all agreed that would be one hell of a lot of firepower, but Big Dave had made twenty petrol bombs using a mixture of petrol, diesel, oil and sugar, which when combined gave a highly volatile fuel which melted the sugar and became a sticky mess with the diesel allowing it to burn long afterwards. Oiled rags had been stuffed into the necks, and a blowtorch tethered to a length of paracord secured the method of lighting to the crate where they were stored inside individual cuts of the same drainpipe that Flymo had used for the grenade launchers.

The two Browning Automatic Rifles had been fastened to a wooden frame and Flymo had bastardised the twenty-round magazines by cutting and welding and bonding the springs to hold thirty-five .30-06 rounds. The weapons were set at sixteen inches apart – which fitted each of Big Dave's shoulders - with dowel rod and wire linking the triggers. The system was harnessed with paracord and bungee and again, had been zeroed to one-hundred-metres on floating forty-five-gallon oil drums. The men had taken it in turns to test fire the Sterling sub-machine guns with their thirty-four round magazines, and the Browning pistols at targets set over the stern at distances of ten, twenty-five and fifty metres.

The three men were experienced enough to realise that the weapons were simply tools, and that they could get the job done as well with them as with the most cutting-edge technology. What mattered in battle could not easily be replicated on the firing range, and the pistol in King's hand that had been designed ninety years ago was no less effective than a modern polymer framed pistol with attachment rails to accommodate all sorts of technology that he would never choose to use. King holstered the weapon and checked the ringing satphone. It could only have been Ramsay, and King was eager for updates on the situation regarding both the credibility and trustworthiness of Hong Gil-dong.

"King..."

"King, bad news, I'm afraid..."

"Go on..." he said, checking that he was alone. He could see Flymo at the helm, with Rashid sipping coffee beside him.

"The flight didn't make it," he said heavily. *"Air traffic control lost tracking visuals. It came down in the Arabian Sea, midway between Mumbai and Oman. It was close to*

shipping lanes and there were plenty of fishing boats that witnessed the crash. So far, no survivors, and search and rescue have intimated that the status will not change. The plane was obliterated. A Maersk sea-captain described the aircraft as 'atomising upon impact'. His account describes no loss in speed from altitude to impact. And while there will certainly be pieces of debris that has not atomised, I understand the sea-captain's analogy," he said stiffly. *"Hong Gil-dong is dead, and tragically, Jo Blyth along with him. She's gone..."*

King cursed and sighed heavily. "I thought so," he replied.

"What do you mean?"

"I got to the airport too late. The two Koreans turned on me. They're both dead. I thought that Hong Gil-dong might have translated something else to them, that he was playing us. But the fact that his plane went down is too much of a coincidence. Iron Fist killed him to stop him talking to us, and they sacrificed Jo and an entire plane full of innocent people to do it."

"What about the raid?" Ramsay asked incredulously. *"The intelligence is likely to be flawed."*

"Hong Gil-dong was run by General Cho. But it now appears that he was on the level and wanted to defect. I think the two Korean agents filled in the gaps because they planned on killing me and seeing that the hacker never made the flight. If they played around with the details of General Cho or the military base, then Hong Gil-dong may have suspected something. He may not have, but they wouldn't know that for sure. I think they told the truth and planned to clear up their mess later. As tragic as it is, the crash proves that what Hong Gil-dong said is true. But if we are ever to find the location of the hacking operation, then we need General Cho."

"It's a hell of a gamble, King."

"Well, it's just as well that I'm the one on the ground who's going to find out…"

Chapter Fifty-One

The sea kayak was equipped with a three-horsepower electric motor for silent running at around six knots for a run-time of two hours, but King used the paddle in conjunction with the electric motor both to cover the distance sooner, and to ensure that he had another hour's run-time in reserve if he needed to escape. He had the satphone with him as his two-way radio only had a range of three miles at sea-level. Another factor of elevation and curvature that was called line of sight.

The sea was calm, but there was a gentle, rolling swell, and as he neared the beach, barely visible in the starlight, he could hear pounding surf. King knew that the shelf would be steep, to turn gentle swells into powerful surf in the space of a few hundred feet meant that deep water became shallow in next to no distance. He switched off the electric motor and double-checked the strap of the Sterling sub-machine gun fastened around his neck and shoulder. He could feel the pull of the tide, knew that millions of gallons of water was rushing up beneath him, irresistible force meeting immovable object. The tiny swells started to build, and he paddled tentatively with them rising and falling through the troughs. He could see whitewater now, oxygenated foam from crashing upon the shore, highlighted by sand as black as powdered jet. King felt a swell behind him lift the tiny craft, and he paddled for all he was worth to catch the face. He felt the kayak propel forwards and the wave build behind him. The drop was steep, and he leaned back to balance the craft and put some weight into the rear to avoid nose-ploughing and submerging the entire kayak. He could hear the rush of water, the pounding of the waves in front of him, and was aware of the sky darkening as the wave broke and curved and enclosed him in the barrel. King pushed through the curtain, drenched and suddenly engulfed in the foam, but powered out into the open as the whitewater ran out of energy. The remaining three feet of whitewater washed him up the beach, and as soon as it had arrived and the craft had grounded upon the shore, the water surged backwards, energy spent and receding into the wash. King got off the kayak and pulled it up the beach using the toggle on the prow. He kept pulling until he was past the seaweed and flotsam and jetsam of the tideline. The shoreline was scattered with rocks from cliff falls, and the cliffs were sheer and at least two-hundred feet high. King wedged the kayak between two large boulders and went back to the tideline where he gathered up handfuls of seaweed and covered the olive-coloured craft to avoid detection.

King had chosen the cove because of North Korea's sea defences on the more accessible beaches. Not many landing crafts would have made it over the shore break behind him, and that left a two-hundred-foot sheer cliff to ascend. As he started out across the cliff face, finding finger holds and places to wedge the toes of his trainers, he wondered whether the South Korean military judged other nation's military on their own abilities. What he did now was no different than what young Royal Marines had done in the early hours of D-Day. The Germans hadn't expected that, either.

Defences aside, the North Korean regime did not expect a full-scale invasion anytime soon. After he had rolled over the edge onto the dry grass, King lay on his back, looking up at the stars catching his breath. After a few minutes, he hauled up his equipment on the line and swapped his trainers for military boots, then packed the line and trainers away and checked his equipment. Lying prone, he used the night vision monocular to survey a full sweep from his left to his right, and everything in between. A cluster of huts looked like a likely place for guards, either that, or the world's least luxurious holiday park. There were no fences, but a large field gun facing the ocean and an anti-aircraft battery showed that they were open to the possibilities of an attack, supposing that attack was coming in 1958. There was no sign of surface to air missiles, no radar to operate such a system, merely a large communications antenna. King wondered whether the whole thing was a ruse with a cutting-edge defence system hidden from view, but he doubted it. It wasn't that the West underestimated the DPRK, it was the fact that they had not fought a conflict since the fifties, and tactics, weaponry, technology and battle methodology had changed. NATO prepared for every contingency, and they practised exhaustively. What made the DPRK a threat was the sanity and reality of their leader and the sheer fighting numbers that they could muster. And that could never be underestimated.

King rolled down to a crevice and followed it inland. By the time the crevice flattened out, he was level with the huts and half a mile away. He continued to move steadily, keeping low. Silhouette, smell, sound, shine and shape were the five S's to remember for camouflage and concealment. Pay attention to all five, and you're invisible.

He was using a hand-held Garmin GPS that worked on the triangulation of telecommunication satellites that gave his position and the position of the military base. His mind had flashed back to Iraq and the operation he had been on being compromised by a Magellan GPS unit used predominantly by NATO forces at the time. Of course, there had been an ulterior motive for sending him back in, but he did not want to think about that now. He had been 'the contract man', the man used by MI6 to act when government diplomacy had failed. That now felt like a lifetime ago, and he liked to think that he operated with a far more ethical remit now, but he suspected that he was just kidding himself. The orders never came in now for a simple assassination, but people still died. On both sides. He had not told Rashid about the crash. It had been awkward ignoring it, pretending everything was ok. It felt like a betrayal, but he would jeopardise the operation and Rashid's personal safety if he dumped that onto him now. The man was sweet on Jo Blyth. He had only held off asking her out because of his experience with Marnie, and King knew that the man had vowed never to have a work relationship again, but it wouldn't have made him care any less. Now he had not only lost someone he was attracted to and cared about, but he had lost the potential that could have bloomed between them. King thought it like the *it's better to have loved and lost, than never to have loved at all* line. Rashid had never realised the dream of loving her. The man would take it hard when he found out.

King had twelve miles to cover quickly. He knew that

between the coast and the base there were three villages, but he did not plan on going near them, and had waypoint markers set on the GPS set that would allow him to follow a set route. He checked his laces, tightened his belt and checked the duct tape that he had used to tape over the rattly metal sling clips on the Sterling, then set out at a slow jog. He breathed steadily as his heartrate increased and his muscles warmed, then after around five minutes, he quickened the pace and settled into a good rhythm. King could run a half-marathon in ninety minutes, but given the terrain, his equipment and heavy boots, he aimed for making it in a little over two hours.

Chapter Fifty-Two

The ground was hard and sparse. King was aware of a lack of wildlife, too. Walking through the British countryside at night you were awash with the noises and movement of nature. In the African bush or the jungle, it seemed that there was more nocturnal life than in daylight. But here? Here it was silent and still. As the miles rolled on, he could tell that the land was farmed out. No topsoil left, no fertiliser other than the human excrement that he could smell at an area of intensively farmed land on the banks of a deep, putrid river that he had been forced to wade and swim through. The water was thick with mud, and he shuddered to think what else, and after a few hundred metres trudging on the other side, he was back to barren, stoney ground that was more like the mining waste ground in parts of Cornwall, than agricultural land. The villages were unlit, and he had never experienced skirting a village without the sound of dogs barking. In Iraq, it had been the curse of special forces operations. That and goat herders, if that was to be believed. It had become a standing joke when operations went wrong – blame the goat herder. King thought there couldn't have been enough goats or goat herders in the country for all the botched mission reports to ring true. However, he had certainly cursed his fair share of dogs. Dogs could smell people from a mile away. But here, it was silent. King knew that both North and South Korea had a penchant for eating dog meat, although it was becoming less common in the south. The stillness as he drew close to the areas of habitation was eerie.

He had stopped only to let the water out of his boots and eat some chocolate that he had stowed in a waterproof zip bag. In one of his canteens, he had a mix of water, lemon juice, salt, sugar and soluble aspirin which provided him with precious electrolytes. He had found that his recipe replaced salt lost from perspiration and kept up his energy while hydrating him. It also took the edge off any pain from foot-rub or bruises and grazes he received along the way. His old mentor Peter Stewart had sworn by a generous swig of Scotch and a short bump of cocaine, but each to their own.

A road led to the military camp, but King wouldn't be taking it. He made his way parallel to it, keeping well away. A large section of the road had washed away, and rather than rebuild the foundation and lay new tarmac, a large wooden bridge had been laid over it, linking the two sections of road. Each side of the road boulders the size of small cars made for difficult terrain by foot, and near impossible by vehicle. King edged closer to the road, then when the rocks thinned out, he crossed the open ground to the perimeter fence. He checked his watch. He had an hour until all hell broke loose. He was cutting it fine.

The thermal monocular showed him four sentry towers

All the King's Men

right out of a Second World War stalag. There were two guards to a tower, one for the spotlight and one for the machine gun. The towers faced outwards. The guards had their backs to the camp. They were watching for an attack, not an escape. King wondered if they had heard of LAW rocket launchers or Milan anti-tank launchers, both of which, would blow the turrets to kingdom come in seconds. King could see that two of the guards were asleep in one of the towers, and he chose to make his way closest to that one to start on the fence. Inside the camp, a roaming patrol of four guards paced with lacklustre in a clockwise direction. On the north side where the camp met the road a guard gate was manned by four soldiers, and there were two jeep type vehicles that looked like cheap Chinese SUVs that had been kitted out for a weekend off-roading, with machine guns mounted on the rooves. Sandbags and machine gun posts had been set up covering the road, but other than the guards he had seen so far, the camp was deserted. King could see four rows of Nissen huts and from what Hong Gil-dong and the two North Korean agents had said, knew that these were the barracks for the soldiers. Adjacent to these, three more huts acted as a toilet and shower block, mess hall and recreational room. King had been in better prisons than this place. The stark reality of the DPRK was that it was utilitarian and functional. There were no comforts or luxuries in the country for anyone but the regime leaders. The ruling family had instilled such fear in the population that nobody attempted a coup. They had elevated themselves – generation by generation – to that of a God-like status. Beyond royalty and into the realms of the holy.

King tested the wire mesh fence with a blade of dried grass, leaving it for a few seconds to test for an electric pulse. Nothing. If it had been electrified then he would have felt a mild shock, but no more than static electricity. The fence could well have been fitted with a trembler device, but he would have to take his chances. Above the fence were coils of both barbed and razor wire, so he would have to cut through at ground level rather than climb. He used the wire cutter on his Leatherman, slicing down half a metre to the bottom, then another half a metre across, both top and bottom, before peeling back the section and tucking it back tightly with a few of the loose wire strands. Twenty-five metres to his right, and ten metres above him, the guards had not heard, and for all he knew they were still asleep. It had been risky to cut the wire so close to the tower, but with all four tower turrets facing outwards with up to one-hundred-and-eighty-degrees arc of fire, none of the other three guard towers could see him. Darkness was lifting, and King could see some raised ground to his right. It was a knoll more than a hill, and he imagined that it was man-made from the construction of the base. The topsoil had been scraped back to bedrock to avoid the build-up of mud in heavy rain. King found himself wondering whether they had used excavators or merely forced local labour for the task. He had heard that people would be press-ganged into forced labour, and while not slave labour as they were given minimal pay, they were given no choice as refusal guaranteed them a stay in a concentration camp or 're-education centre'.

King slipped through the fence. The officers did not have to make do with Nissen huts, and the chalet type buildings were worthy of at least a two-star campsite in Devon that advertised 'kids, pets and large groups welcome', but King supposed that this was luxury accommodation for North Korea. Checking all four guard towers in the monocular – using his left eye to retain his night vision in his dominant right eye – needed for aiming the weapon - he walked slowly and confidently across the open ground and into the shadows of the first barracks building. He listened carefully at the side of the asbestos building but could hear nothing. The men or women were sleeping. King checked the dull luminous dials of his vintage Rolex. He had earlier removed the stainless-steel bracelet and replaced it with a NATO webbing strap to cut down the shine element of the five S's. There was an hour left until dawn, and barely twenty-minutes until the extraction. His heart fluttered at the thought, adrenalin surging through him. They were cutting it damn close. He closed his eyes momentarily, recalling the plan of the camp – which had been purely verbal and roughly sketched out on rice paper for him to learn before Big Dave had eaten it – then opened his eyes, the layout fresh once again in his mind. The Sterling sub-machine gun was a simplistic piece of engineering with thirty-four rounds of 9mm and an effective range to two-hundred metres, although King had found all weapons of its type to be more suited to about half of that. His only reservation about the weapon was that it fired off an open bolt, meaning that the chamber was always open with no bullet in the barrel. When fired, the firing pin and bolt dropped, scooped a bullet from the magazine and when it entered the breech, fired instantly. The system meant that the first shot was always fractionally off target because of the working parts driving forward. It also meant that the open chamber was susceptible to debris becoming lodged. King had kept the weapon above water when he waded and side-stroked his way across the river, and checked the breech as best he could, but there was always the nagging doubt that the first shot wouldn't go 'bang'.

King skirted the toilet and shower block, the smell nauseating. The mess hall wasn't much better with overflowing rubbish bins and rats climbing over everything in search of a meal. He watched as some disappeared through hinged lids, realising that some of the bins were indeed traps. *That was probably dinner sorted tomorrow*, he thought. Some of the rats were a foot long, with a tail around the same length, the biggest rats he'd ever seen.

The chalets each had a veranda, and a satellite dish attached, and stainless-steel flues that would be connected to woodburning stoves. North Korea could get cold in the winter and this posting would be a grim prospect. King had only jogged through twelve miles of the country at night, and he could tell that living here would be a gloomy prospect any time of year. He focused on the door, not knowing whether it would be locked or not. For all he knew there was a law against locking doors in North Korea. It seemed like there was a law against everything that protected a person's basic human rights. He had read that if a person committed suicide, then three generations of that person's family could be punished, often with a death sentence. Practising any religion in public was a death sentence, too. As was making an international call. He had wondered how people even got up in the morning, let alone made it through the day.

King stepped out of the shadows and right into a soldier with a towel wrapped around his waist, wearing a pair of flipflops. He held the sub-machine gun squarely at the man's chest, but the man could see King's quandary. He couldn't risk being detected, and the hesitation showed. The man shouted for all he was worth, and King went to punch him, but was met with a block and a counter kick that forced him to stagger backwards. King whipped out his sheath knife and threw it, sinking it squarely in the man's sternum. The man had frozen to the spot, his towel dropping to the floor. King charged forwards, hammered his palm on the hilt and drove it several inches deeper, at the same time, kicking out his opponent's ankles and driving him to the hard ground. There were further shouts and torch beams swept around the compound. King dragged the naked body into the side of the mess hall and withdrew the knife. The man whimpered and without looking at him, keeping his eyes on the area in front of him, King drove the blade down into the man's temple, then withdrew it and sheathed the bloody blade. King watched the torch beams and took his chance. He sprinted across the open ground, took the steps to the veranda two at a time and shoulder-barged the door, splintering the frame with his fourteen stone and a hell of a lot of speed behind it. He grabbed his torch and shone it on the bed, capturing the general's shocked expression, but also that of two women. King had not planned for the man to have company, let alone two people, and he could feel it all unravelling. One of the women reached for a pistol on the bedside table, and King fired a short burst, driving five 9mm bullets into her side. The other woman screamed leapt out of the bed and King had little choice but to fire and she fell to the floor. He cursed out loud, glancing at his watch. Keeping the weapon aimed at General Cho, he fumbled for the two-way radio and switched it on. He pressed down on the switch and said, "It's all gone to shit, you'd better come in noisy..." He paused, then said, "I'm in the target's quarters. Try not to kill me..."

Flymo's voice came over the network. *"Thirty seconds out. Keep your head down..."*

King approached the bed and pulled the naked general

out by one of his ankles. He quickly subdued the man with several hard punches to his ribs and kidneys, then dug the scalding muzzle of the Sterling into the man's neck as he secured his hands behind his back with heavy-duty cable ties, then wrapped duct tape around the man's mouth. He spun General Cho around until he was sitting up and pinched the man's nose. The man instantly struggled, and King kept up the assault for fifteen seconds or more, his weapon trained on the door the entire time. When he finally released his grip, the man sucked in air through his nostrils and had never been more grateful for anything in the life. His nose was working like a bellows when King said, "Now that I have your attention, you will cooperate with me, or I will kill you. As simply as pinching your nose. Now, get on your bloody feet!"

General Cho did so, answering the question of whether he understood English or not without any pretence or deception. King pulled him to the door, the sound of the approaching helicopter seeming like sweet music to his ears. Seconds later, gunfire and explosions thundered across the compound and King pushed the general outside. He needed the man, but he wasn't his bodyguard, and self-preservation was strong with King. He rested the barrel of the Sterling on the man's shoulder and engaged the first two soldiers as he walked the General down the steps, keeping him directly in front of him as a human shield. The soldiers hesitated before a hail of lead peppered them. King changed magazines as he guided the Korean across the open ground towards the fence. He moved the weapon again, engaging two more guards using the sub-machine gun one-handed and controlled his 'shield' so that he was always covered by the man. The men fell, and King pressed on.

The camp was on fire. The petrol bombs had set

anything flammable alight, and Flymo's mass grenade delivery system had brought down a tower, while another was burning fiercely. Huts were ablaze or blown apart and men and women in various stages of undress were running around like frightened chickens. King caught sight of the underbelly of the helicopter, with Big Dave leaning out of the doorway and firing the double BARs across the compound. The Bren guns fired up as Flymo dipped the nose and flew directly over the barracks, peppering the rooves with dozens of .303 bullets. King saw grenades release, falling like cricket balls and exploding seconds apart, ten thumps of concussive blast with little flame, just hot shrapnel raining everywhere. Soldiers fell. Some dressed, many either naked or wearing little loin cloths as they ran into the chaos. Heavy calibre machine guns lit the sky with muzzle flashes, tracking tracer towards the helicopter, but never quite on target as Flymo flew crazy paths across the compound, banking left and right, dipping low and climbing hard. King fired on more soldiers, most not daring to return fire as they realised who he was using as a barricade. He struggled to change over magazines, the general trying to make a break for it, then found himself cornered, two soldiers catching him in a pincer manoeuvre, their weapons aimed at him. He moved the muzzle to the general's neck, staring the nearest soldier in the eyes, leaving no doubt as to what would happen if they shot him. King watched as the soldier's face exploded and he fell onto his knees. The second soldier was caught out by the sight, then he too met a similar fate and fell to the ground. King didn't waste time thinking about it and pushed the general through the fence. The guard tower was still, and as King got clear of the fence, he could see one of the guards slumped over the rail and the other was nowhere to be seen.

He glanced back at the knoll where he saw a muzzle flash. A stream of fifty-calibre tracer sparked across the knoll, then another single muzzle flash, and the fifty-calibre stopped altogether. King caught sight of a figure – that could only have been Rashid - sprinting down the knoll, and he turned away and pushed the general out into the open. More grenades and gunfire engulfed the compound and King heard the pitch of the helicopter change and felt the downdraft of the aircraft above him. It roared overhead and put down just short of the boulder field. King pushed the general ahead of him as he ran towards the helicopter. Big Dave fired past them, the double BARs sounding like pneumatic drills, the bullets 'fizzing' past their heads. King pushed the Korean into the helicopter and turned around, taking the Lee Enfield rifle off Rashid as he clambered inside. Once again, the man had had his back with a sniper rifle. King nodded a silent thanks, and Rashid simply shrugged. He'd lost tally on the times he'd saved King with a rifle. It was almost a running joke now.

King put on a headset as they climbed. Flymo spun the aircraft around and emptied the last of the rounds in the Bren guns towards the camp, then banked and increased speed, flying just a few metres from the ground. "There's a bridge coming up," said King through the intercom. "If you've got any grenades left, then dumping them on it cuts off their only route in and out of the base..."

"That's awfully short sighted of them..." Flymo replied, then hiked up the nose and levelled the aircraft. He pulled the pin on the last of the tubes and ten fragmentation grenades dropped on the wooden structure. Flymo banked hard right and said, "That should do it..."

King craned his neck out of the open doorway to see the grenades detonating just half-a-second apart and the bridge going up in matchwood. Behind them, the compound was ablaze and in chaos, tracer rounds arcing in the sky nowhere near their direction. King looked at the prisoner beside him and said, "Cheer up, pal. We've most likely done a million pounds of improvements to the place…"

Chapter Fifty-Three

Flymo touched down on the deck, the rotors clearing the wheelhouse by less than a foot, the glass of the structure flexing with the billowing wind of the downwash. He powered down, keeping his hands and feet on the controls to prevent the craft's desire to tip. King slid out and pulled the Korean after him. He instinctively placed a hand on top of the man's head ducking him under the rotor, but there was still a couple of feet or so spare. The man started to protest as King pushed him towards the loading bay, and King kicked him up the backside and he stumbled towards the steps.

Behind them, Big Dave was already operating the crane and pulling at two webbing straps that threaded through a winch that Rashid had attached to the skids of the helicopter.

Flymo climbed out of the aircraft and patted his hand on the nose. "Thanks, old girl," he said, then held up his thumb for Big Dave and as he took up the slack and the aircraft shifted, he added, "Rest easy, thank you for your service..."

The helicopter scraped against the hull and groaned as metal flexed, but it seemed like a protest from the aircraft as it slid and splashed into the sea. Water engulfed the cabin through the open doorways and the nose-dived, the tail rotor lifting like a flag as it sunk into the bubbles and wake. It took all of forty seconds for the aircraft to disappear into the depths, and Flymo was already climbing up to the wheelhouse to get them underway.

King secured the Korean to a chair using duct tape, then climbed back to the deck and took out the satphone. It was answered after three rings. "King..." he said.

"And?"

"The package is secured," he replied. The line was secure, but old habits die hard. There was a long pause, during which King could hear Ramsay's sigh of relief.

"Jack is en route to escort General Cho back."

"Are you sure?" King asked. "It didn't work out so well for Jo, last time..." He looked around him to check that Rashid wasn't nearby.

"The Royal Navy are helping with that," he explained. *"The American Air Force are flying them to Perth, and then HMS Dauntless is taking them on the first of three legs meeting other Royal Navy ships that will get them home within twenty-two days."*

"Nice for some," King commented.

"However..."

"Go on..."

"I want the threat shut down sooner. I want the man talking. I want a location, and I don't care how you do it, or how much of General Cho reaches that Royal Navy destroyer." Ramsay paused. *"I don't even mind Jack having a wasted journey and flying back on his own. I just want the location."*

"I get it."

"Do you?"

"I *get* it..."

"Then I'll wait to hear from you..."

Ramsay had broken the connection and King pocketed the satphone and rested his hands on the rail, watching their wake in the pre-dawn light. Rashid wandered over, looking once more like the antithesis of a sailor. What King would tell him next would not make the man feel any better.

"I'm sorry, mate," he said. "I've just spoken with Ramsay, and Jo and the hacker didn't make it..."

"What?"

"Their plane went down in the Arabian Sea. Ramsay is certain that it was the other hackers silencing the Korean..." King watched him, waiting for his reaction. "I've just found out," he lied, feeling about as low as he had felt in years. Then, not knowing what else to say, he gripped his friend's shoulder and added, "It would have been quick..." Again, he had no idea how the end had been, and his words were echoing around his skull, praying that Rashid would say something, anything to distract his thoughts.

Rashid nodded, then turned and walked away to the other side of the boat where he leaned on the portside rail and watched the golden glister of dawn on the horizon. King cursed, shaking his head, irked at the way he had handled it. He paced off to the wheelhouse and climbed into the structure where Big Dave had boiled a kettle and was making tea.

"I'll just borrow this," he said, taking the freshly boiled kettle and a bowl of sugar to the sound of the big Fijian's protests. He climbed back down and made his way down to the loading bay where General Cho looked up at him, fear and loathing in his narrow eyes. He tipped the sugar into the boiling water, where it dissolved instantly into hot, sticky syrup. He tossed the empty bowl onto the floor as an afterthought. "Now, sunshine. You and I are going to have a nice long chat," King said brightly. "But don't you worry; this is going to hurt you a lot more than it's going to hurt me…"

Chapter Fifty-Four

London,
Three days later

Caroline pushed open the door and stepped into Ramsay's office, where she found him staring at the Thames from the window. She knew that the man used the somewhat murky, occasionally glistening waters to arrange his thoughts.

"I should be out there!"

"It's soldiering," Ramsay replied without turning around.

"I *was* a bloody soldier!"

"In Fourteen Intelligence company..."

"I have done everything the men have done for the service," she replied irritably. "Everything and more."

"I know."

"We're finished here." Caroline paused. "I should be helping Alex and the boys. I missed out on North Korea, and now Ukraine?"

"You were needed here."

"And now I'm on the sidelines!"

"What do you want, Caroline?"

"To be involved!" she snapped.

"I mean, out of life..."

She frowned as Ramsay wheeled half a turn and stared at her. "What...?"

"You want to retire, you want to leave, but then you come back. And you keep coming back. You and King, you're not the retiring types. You're both still in your prime, you both have values that are needed to fight crime and terrorism and espionage, and still you procrastinate."

"I..."

Ramsay didn't give her time to counter his attack. "You have a formidable brain, can handle yourself as well as anyone, and still, you yearn for something else. But it's not for you. You can blame King or any number of things for returning to the fore, and don't give me the maternal thing, because you know that you won't be happy living in the Cotswolds with a baby in tow, going to mum and fun coffee mornings, and trust me, if I remember correctly, primary school politics is more ruthless than Westminster..."

"I just want to be normal," she said, still affronted by Ramsay's attack.

"Keep your edge, Caroline. Keep your figure and your healthy bank account. This *is* normal for you and King." He paused. "You both bring different strengths to the team, to what we do in these anonymous offices, and out there in the shadows. I can't lose King because he feels torn by what he does, and was always meant to do, and what he *thinks* he should do." He wheeled himself to his desk, opened a drawer and took out a folder and tossed it down on the desk. "For you," he said, his manner mellowing.

Caroline stared at him, then walked to the desk and picked up the folder. She opened it and read, then sat down heavily in the leather tub chair and continued to read for five minutes. When she'd finished, she looked up and said, "Are you sure?"

"Of course, I am." He paused. "And I'm sure about you, and I'm sure about King. If you need time, then just tell me. If you need a break, then tell me. But please, stay. Let's take on these threats to the country together."

Caroline looked thoughtful for a moment, then said, "I suppose we could see how it goes for a while..."

Ramsay sighed heavily. "Good." He paused. "You and King complement one another. King is a rare breed. He's a killer, but he has a conscience. He's a blunt instrument, but he has a high IQ and knows how to use it. You keep him balanced, because the conscience thing has only really been present since he met you..." He looked up as Mae entered with a tray. She smiled as she placed it down, but something told her that she was interrupting a private matter, and the woman left without a word, closing the door quietly behind her.

"She's good, that one," Caroline observed as she leaned over and poured the tea into the two cups and added a splash of milk, stirring well. She handed Ramsay his cup. "She's an asset to the office."

"Agreed," Ramsay replied. "Speaking of which, I need a personal assistant. Someone to fight my corner, take charge in the field because I can't be there..."

"I'm sorry how it turned out for you," she said awkwardly, her eyes darting to the wheelchair.

Ramsay smiled thinly. "Oh, don't be. I've still got my mind, and I'm getting stronger with physio." He paused. "For me, the challenge has been strangely rewarding. Liberating, even. Of course, my wife and daughters think that I'm quite mad when I tell them that, but I'm not sure they ever truly understood me, anyway."

"Not like Charlotte does," she quipped.

"Meaning?" he asked, quite perplexed.

"Well, seeing how we're giving home truths, I don't mind telling you, she's utterly in love with you. Not just a whim, but on a soulmate level."

"Oh..." He paused. "Well, thanks for dumping that extra emotional weight on me..."

"Life is short. And no shorter than in this game."

"Undoubtedly. And we have lost many good people along the way," Ramsay replied heavily. "As for my personal assistant, I'd very much like that person to be you."

"Me?"

"Will you do it?"

"I'm a field agent; not a carer, Neil..."

"And I don't bloody well need one!" he said sharply.

"No, of course you don't. I'm sorry."

Ramsay sighed heavily. "Caroline, you must be the only person in the world who gets given a file like that..." He pointed at the folder in her hand. "... and worries that she's not being taken seriously." He paused. "Our CIA friend, Newman contacted me. I know what you did in America to take the heat off King. I know what you are capable of, Caroline." He watched her gaze shift to the floor, and he knew from her expression that she was utterly human, despite the things she had been forced to do in her long career. He knew that she lived quietly with the consequences of her actions, and that was why he was having this conversation with her. "Alright, I suppose the position isn't for that of a personal assistant, it's more like deputy. My deputy, for what we do here"

"But..."

"But nothing woman! I want to go into meetings and not have some public school twit try and intimidate me by standing in my personal space and looking down at me when I can't even feel my damned legs, let alone stand and meet the man's bloody gaze! I want someone to look King, Lomu and Rashid in the eyes and tell them not to think with their bloody balls and to look at the bigger picture! I want someone who I trust one hundred percent with my own life to have my back, and that of the team's, and approach problems with reasoning and foresight as much as testosterone! I want that same person with me when I meet the Prime Minister, or Select Committees, or other branches of intelligence or police and law enforcement." He paused. "And I want that person to be you, because believe me, you'd be the best person I know at doing all of these things." He pointed at the folder and added, "And so much more, besides..."

Chapter Fifty-Five

Ukraine

King headed the team, lightly equipped and agile. There were eight SAS troopers with him. All selected because of their experience and the fact that they were all single men with no dependants and all aged under thirty. They had moved swiftly and covertly into Russian lines and had no idea that behind them, Rashid covered them through a Schmidt and Bender scope attached to a .338 Lapua Magnum Accuracy International sniper rifle. Seven miles away, nestled in a copse of trees just before the Russian lines, Flymo sat at the controls of a dull, grey Sikorsky S-70 that had been used for aid work, and stripped of all civil aviation authority tail and identification numbers. The team had infiltrated on foot to avoid detection. They knew that to exfiltrate, they needed to send a coded bubble-burst on the TACBE, or tactical beacon. They did not know who would be providing helicopter extraction, assuming that it would be Ukrainian forces.

King was the tip of the arrow. The other men filed out behind him, their modified and silenced Heckler & Koch UMP .45 carbines scanning the area in front and parallel to them. The weapons were all equipped with bulbous suppressors and drum magazines containing two-hundred rounds of hollow point ammunition. These were shock, awe and dump drums, and the men would switch to single thirty-round magazines when they were empty. Each man carried silenced Heckler & Koch USB .45 pistols in holsters, keeping common ammunition between their weapon systems.

Fifty metres to the right of Rashid, Big Dave manned the Russian 7.62x54mm belt-fed PKM squad support weapon, with a two-hundred-round belt attached and two more boxes of ammunition beside him. A night-vision scope had been attached and zeroed for three-hundred metres. Big Dave manned the weapon, moving it freely on the bipod as he scanned the area. He watched King and the eight SAS troopers reach the perimeter of the encampment, knowing that Rashid would be watching, too. It was imperative that the raiders kept the element of surprise, so both men had been warned adamantly by King that they should only fire upon the enemy as a last resort, or if things went 'noisy', as King had put it.

The muzzle flashes lit the encampment below, shocked faces illuminated milliseconds before death. At this distance, Big Dave could not hear the gunfire, making it a surreal experience. The men did not have the chance to shout or scream, multiple bullets hitting each guard before they fell, and some pounding into them as they lay on their backs dying. Big Dave felt oddly voyeuristic, and had he not

All the King's Men

had King's back, or the other men for that matter, then he could quite happily have looked away until it was over.

From where he was, down and dirty and in the thick of it, King had no time for such thoughts. With his night-vision-goggles illuminating everything in an eerie green, King found his targets – for that was how he thought of the young soldiers – giving each one three rounds, then a further bullet in the head when they were on the ground. Some may have said that was overkill for a .45, but to him, there was no such thing. Vastly outnumbered, and still holding onto the vital element of surprise, he could not afford mistakes or overconfidence. Every Russian soldier that was put out of the picture meant another obstacle had been overcome and the mission was moving ever closer to success.

The whine of the electric turret on the mobile field gun told King that they had just lost their advantage. There was no point firing at the turret with the machine carbine, so King sprinted as fast as his legs would carry him, both away from the direction of rotation of the mounted twin 12.7mm machine guns, and at the same time, wheeling closer to the field gun to disrupt aim. He was soon under the arc of fire, and he darted back anti-clockwise and leapt onto the metal hulk. Often confused as a tank, the mobile gun was exactly that. A vehicle that mobilised and sought cover for its giant field gun to engage targets several miles away. King pulled a fragmentation grenade, opened the turret hatch and tossed the ordnance inside. Slamming the hatch shut, he ducked aside and felt the thud of the explosion through the hull. He opened the steaming hatch again and emptied a magazine into the opening. The .45 bullets bounced around the steel sides, some finding flesh and bone and some simply running out of energy and dropping harmlessly on the floor of the hull. King leapt off the vehicle and caught sight of muzzle flashes on the ridgeline. Big Dave was getting busy with the machine gun and Rashid was picking off soldiers as they leapt out of the vehicles that they had been sleeping in, and the SAS troopers fired upon the neat rows of tents and the helpless souls inside.

The gunshots died down, and then as it does in battle, suddenly stopped altogether with an eerie stillness. The only movement in the encampment was that of the SAS troopers as six of them set up a perimeter against outside attack, and King knew that both Big Dave and Rashid would be changing belts or magazines, finding new positions and keeping a watchful eye on the area. The two men were now like Greek mythological gods. Looking down from on high and prepared to strike down those who would harm King and his team of soldiers without mercy and with extreme prejudice.

The six mobile launchers carrying the 9K-720 Iskander hypersonic cruise missile system were 'at rest' with their destructive payloads inert. However, the two SAS troopers now in the process of arming the first launcher were hard at work with pre-programmed tablets plugged into the guidance system and bringing two long days of classroom-based training to fruition. There was an electrical whine and the ballistic missile, weighing some 3,800 kg and measuring 7.3 m in length rose slowly like one half of a drawbridge. King watched as the two men clambered out of the launcher and climbed up into another, tablet in hand and moving more efficiently now they had completed their first task for real in the field, instead of a classroom. Within twenty minutes, five of the launchers were set to fire. At the two trooper's orders, King and the other four SAS troopers pulled back from the encampment and one of the troopers started a countdown from ten. The missiles rumpled and whined and as the count reached one, the man's voice was drowned out as four of the launchers fired their lethal loads into the sky.

King send the bubble burst on the tactical beacon, then looked skywards and watched the missiles climb, then their second-stage burners caught, and they shot off across the sky towards Belarus. The fifth missile remained in place as the Sikorsky banked in the sky and came down sharply, entering a hover and maintaining perfect stability a hundred metres from them. King caught sight of Rashid and Big Dave running towards the aircraft and when he reached the helicopter, Big Dave had attached the PKM to a mount hanging in the open doorway and was nestled in the gunner's seat. The last two troopers hopped inside and Flymo climbed and banked and powered up. The fifth missile shot up, its booster engaging second stage and tore across the sky, turning sharply on a three-hundred-and-sixty-degree course back to the encampment and the remaining missile and ordnance that would destroy everything inside the perimeter and any trace of them ever being there.

Chapter Fifty-Six

Belarus

Sangita Raj stepped outside with her coffee and stared at the night sky. It was peaceful here. Soon, the world would change. Iron Fist had wanted an E.L.E, an extinction level event. And so, they would have one. But not for the poor souls on the planet who toiled and survived and endured despite capitalism and the West's hold it had on money, technology and the pharmaceutical industry. No, it was time to level things, to give other nations the chance to evolve and grow on their own terms. Not host the sweatshops for greedy capitalists to post record profits, not to mine the lithium for wealthy soccer mums to drive a Tesla, to dig for diamonds for the wealthy to declare their undying love, or to hand pick the cotton for hundred-dollar T-shirts. Sangita had chosen the targets and the means of their demise, and as she watched the sky, she tried to imagine

All the King's Men

what the ICBMs would look like in the sky as they left their silos in South Dakota, Wyoming and Idaho, spreading out to destroy each of America's state capitals. What action the American missiles falling on London, Manchester and Birmingham would provoke from the UK and NATO when they realised that no threat had indeed come from Russia, that they could not respond without counter-attacking a fellow NATO member state. As she sipped her coffee, she wondered how the socio-political and economic landscape would change, how the countries on the periphery would seize the opportunity. How would the view change from space? Cities wiped out; no lights emitted at night. Total darkness where once lights were visible from satellites in low earth orbit between eighty and a thousand miles above the earth.

There was little light pollution here, and the sky seemed darker in Belarus than other places she had known. She wondered what the sky would look like in the depths of the Russia interior, or in the Sahara. Total dark skies, punctuated only by a billion stars, each one a sun to another universe. No, that was wrong. She frowned as she watched the sky. Every sun was a star, but not every star was a sun. She remembered now. A sun needed to be still fusing elements and releasing heat, and it needed to be orbited by at least two planets. Some stars were no more. If it was indeed possible to travel instantly to them, then you would find that they were no longer there, and all humans had seen for centuries, and would see for centuries more was the light emitted at the point of explosion. It was a marvel, and as she sipped her coffee and stared blankly into the night sky, she was only spared travelling down the existential rabbit hole of the quandary of extraterrestrial live versus size and probability. Spared by the four glowing lights in the sky. Travelling in a line, red and yellow flame contrasted by the white dots of the galaxy. She frowned, squinting her eyes to better see, better process the sight, drawing ever closer, arching downwards following a trajectory that would leave even the most lacking in IQ of no doubt to the curvature of the earth, maintaining height by retaining a perfect arc. Were they accelerating? Her keen analytical mind told her that they were not. The objects were merely growing ever closer, perceived speed an illusion to proximity. The colours were brighter now. There was a perceivable movement to the colours, and she realised that they were flames. Meteorites perhaps? She followed the trajectory, realising that the arc that the objects made were not only on a direct course with her, but increasing in speed. She turned and looked at the hangar where Mishkin, his bodyguard and the team of hackers were oblivious to the sight, and when she looked back at the objects, she was only aware of an incredible blur. No longer could she see the flames, and no longer could her brain register the oncoming speed and shape of the objects, merely that an irresistible force was upon her before everything went black.

Chapter Fifty-Seven

Luger paused to watch the blue, cloudless sky. Contrails cutting swathes through the blue, airplanes carrying passengers to places both old and new, for holidays and business, to see family, friends or colleagues. He thought about Jo Blyth and what she would have felt at the end. Terror and fear, certainly. Regret? Things undone, possibly. He wondered whether it was true that your life flashed before your eyes when death was certain. He hoped that her last thoughts had been enough to calm and console her.

Luger's voyage back with General Cho had been short. Once King and the team had neutralised the hacking threat in Belarus, Luger had been dropped off at Diego Garcia military base in the middle of the Indian Ocean, and an RAF Globemaster C-17 cargo plane had taken them the rest of the way. General Cho was soon whisked off to the safehouse in Scotland where he was about to learn just how tough, resilient and utterly relentless the interrogators of Britain's intelligence services could be.

Luger wasn't sure how Ramsay would feel about him

using the department's resources for something so unrelated to the case, but he had quickly shrugged it off. Better to beg forgiveness than ask permission and have it refused. At least some good would come out of it, even if it had nothing to do with national security. Even an emotional ice cube like Ramsay would surely see what he was doing as a good thing. He wasn't so sure, but he was past caring. He climbed the steps and rapped on the door, and as was his habit, glanced both ways down the street. The door opened just a touch, secured by a thick brass chain.

"Hello..."

"Hello, Lillia," Luger smiled.

"I'm not sure if it's such a good idea that..."

"I just need five minutes of your time," Luger said quietly. "I'm not fishing, I'm not asking you out, but I'd like to talk with the door open. If you don't mind?"

Lillia closed the door briefly, the chain rattled, and she opened it wider. She was dressed in pyjamas and her hair was tied back in an untidy ponytail. To Luger she looked every bit as beautiful as when they had dined at The Ivy.

"I've done some digging," he explained. She frowned, but he continued. "Banking records, transaction timelines and a forensic deep dive into the man's finances. There's no court in the world who would not find the evidence compelling. The aircraft investigation officer in charge of the crash, of Brad's crash, was being bribed handsomely..."

"You're serious?" she asked, then shook her head and snatched the envelope in Luger's hand. "Oh, of course you are, I'm just... well..."

Luger smiled. "Not only does the evidence point towards him blaming Brad for the disaster, but it's highly likely that he took a bribe from the aircraft manufacturer in the Malaysian disaster last year, and the tragedy in Egypt a few years before. The transactions correspond with the datelines. Our head analyst reckons that there's enough in that file to nail him and blow the international air crash investigation sector apart. Heads will roll, people will go to jail, but more importantly for you, Brad's name will be cleared."

Lillia stared at him, tears in her eyes and her lower lip quivering slightly. "Why? Why would you do such a thing, go to such trouble?" She paused, then it dawned on her. "For sex?"

"No!" Luger said sharply, then softened his tone as he said, "I like you. I feel for you. And frankly, I was a bit of a dick coming on so strong and confident that you'd fall for me. I wanted to go after you and to hell with the consequences, and to hell with your feelings. Yes, if I slept with you, then I probably wouldn't have taken it further. But your vulnerability showed a human side that I have been ignoring. I would like to think that one day, someone would miss me as much as you miss Brad. That's a special quantum, immeasurable, even." He leaned forward and kissed her cheek, still wet and salty from her tears. "You have my number," he said. "Perhaps one day, after you've cleared Brad's name, and put that investigator in prison, then you could give me a call and we could go and get a coffee. If not, then take care and I hope you can find happiness and joy in whatever you do."

He turned and dropped agilely down the steps. Twenty metres down the quiet street and out of sight of Lillia, he pressed the key fob and the gleaming, blue Bentley Continental GT's lights flashed as the doors unlocked. He opened the door, sat down heavily on the sumptuous leather and closed the door with a resounding and solid 'thud'. The black labrador's wet tongue lapped across his cheek and he pulled a face of disgust, that soon turned to a smile. He had put a blanket across the rear bucket seats, and that blanket was now bunched up in the limited footpace. His seat was warm, too and he imagined the dog had leapt back into the rear of the car when he'd seen him returning.

Luger sighed heavily as he thought about Lillia. He had never left his heart out there like that. Never self-reflected and assessed himself to be the problem. *It must be love,* he said to himself with a smile in the rear-view mirror. Well, he'd have to see about that. For now, he would take a long drive down to the coast and head west to the New Forest, let the dog out into the woods for a run. He'd enjoy his new toy and enjoy his time with the dog. He wasn't even sure if he should keep him but giving him up seemed unlikely now. He had grown quite attached to the company, if not the hairs on his trousers and the scratching at the door of his flat for walks in the rain. His neighbours liked the dog, too. They had been more than happy to take him in for a few days at a time, and the elderly husband had quietly assured him that it was no problem if he had to go away for work at a moment's notice.

Luger smiled as he thought about the joyful expression on Lillia's face as she had been rocked by his kindness. Perhaps one day, in the not-too-distant future, he would get a call from her and they could both start an adventure that was unchartered and unfamiliar, yet wonderful and exhilarating.

Chapter Fifty-Eight

Berkshire, England

Harriet had not ridden in ages and enjoyed the weightlessness of the gallop of the 16.2hh bay mare. The horse had been bred for racing but lacked finishing speed, making her an ideal showjumper. Harriet had won many local events on her, and even qualified for Hickstead alongside professional showjumpers. Harriet did not compete as much now, but she enjoyed hacking out and the hunt meet when it met in the nearby villages surrounding her country home. The advent of scent and drag hunts had fulfilled the chase and riding experience and ending the chase early and finishing the fox with guns or falconry had enabled the hunt to continue unabated.

The house was a large Georgian manor house with some original features dating back to Tudor times. Set in three-hundred acres of prime Berkshire farmland, the managed farm produced mainly hay and silage, enabling Harriet to have miles of gallops marked out either around or through the grass. She had enjoyed a spirited ride, and Elenor, her groom, had put the sweat rug out for her and mixed up the rolled oats, mashed bran and vitamin and mineral sachet, loosening the mix with some molasses syrup. The stall had been freshly mucked out and bedded down with barley straw, and the automatic drinker cleaned and checked for blockages. The two geldings and the yearling had been put to bed, and with just the smallest tasks left in equine terms for Harriet to complete, had left the yard until next morning.

Harriet rode through the concreted yard, the mare's shoes clipping crisply on the hard surface and echoing around the stables and barn. She kicked her feet out of the stirrups, swung her left leg forward and loosened the girth a couple of notches to make untacking easier when her weight no longer pressed down the saddle, then dismounted. She stretched her legs, then lifted the saddle flap and unfastened the girth and removed the saddle, placing it on a wooden saddle stand on wheels before leading the mare to its stall. She put the sweat rug on, a thin rug that resembled a string vest aiding the animal to cool down slowly and prevent it from either over-heating or getting a chill. Once fastened, she removed the bridle and stepped back out of the stall, closing the door and fastening the bolt into place. When she turned around, she physically jolted as she looked directly at Caroline standing to the side of the door.

"Goodness!" she said, startled. She looked at Caroline, faint recognition dawning on her. "What are you doing here?" she asked, then added calmly. "My husband is home..."

"We don't need to bother him." Caroline paused. "And I'm quite sure he won't bother us, either."

She looked worried. "Why are you here?"

"Answers."

"To what?"

"Don't play dim, Harriet. It doesn't suit you."

"How dare you!" she scowled.

"Russian GRU agents, SIS section chiefs getting killed in hit and runs, Security Service officers stabbed on buses and getting gunned down in broad daylight..." Harriet raised her hand to her neck, her thumb and forefinger failing to take comfort from an old habit. "What's wrong, lost your comforter? Not wearing your pearls today."

"They're being cleaned," she replied quickly. "You have to be careful cleaning natural pearls. They're porous and don't take well to some silver cleaners..."

Caroline stared at her. "You're a class act, Harriet. I almost believed you..." She paused watching her take her coat off a tack peg and slip it on against the late summer evening chill. Harriet placed her hands in her pockets and shivered. "I had the displeasure of speaking to Devonshire, just before he died. He made it sound like he was involved with Iron Fist," she commented flatly.

"I think that's right."

"We don't. We think Devonshire found out about you playing with fire and found himself being played by the Russian GRU agent, Igor Reznikov. That or he figured out how to turn him and had it confirmed that you were his contact."

"You should write a novel with an imagination like that. God knows, you're no good in this line of work..."

Caroline shrugged. "I'm not doing too bad. I know a liar when I hear one."

"You know nothing," Harriet said acidly. "That autistic cripple, Neil Ramsay, can't last much longer in his role, if I'm being honest."

"Well, that would be a first," Caroline retorted. "The honesty part, that is."

"Oh, darling, you have so much to learn about this work."

"I think I'm catching up quickly."

Harriet sighed. "Probably not quick enough, though. Iron Fist represent the biggest threat we've had in recent years. So naturally, we need them to survive."

"What?" Caroline asked incredulously.

"Oh, dear girl, the enemy of my enemy is my friend! NATO countries are upping their spend percentage on defence, cyber defence is a rapidly growing industry, our own newly elected government are recruiting for all three branches of our military, and by having an inside track with the enemy, we weaken countries who don't have our interests at heart. France, for instance."

"Our own country has been affected," Caroline said dubiously. "The first flight affected by this was a British Airways flight rammed full of UK citizens."

"Not the first," Harriet replied. "The system was tested on a Malaysian flight that went missing. The technology has evolved since then."

"We stopped hackers from launching American ICBMs onto their own cities, and upon us," Caroline said, eyeing the woman carefully, and for the first time seeing a flicker of doubt in her eyes.

"I don't believe you."

"I think your Russian contact played you..." Caroline sneered. "And all the while, Iron Fist were planning more than holding the world to ransom through hacking, they were planning to annihilate the West. You really were playing with fire, when all you were doing was playing the fool..."

Harriet scoffed. "I'm a realist. With an enemy like Iron Fist, SIS will never be obsolete. Our budget will increase year on year. You lot may get swallowed up if we merge, and from what I hear, that's a distinct possibility. Especially as your bungled surveillance on a Russian GRU agent resulted in the death of an SIS section chief and a Security Service freelancer. That's the angle I'll come at it from."

"There's only one person with their death on their hands..." Caroline glared at her. "I get why you ran down Devonshire..."

"I did not!"

"Bullshit!" Caroline spat at her. "You knew that Devonshire had worked with Igor Reznikov before, passing information to each other for quid-pro-quo. Not traitors, merely for mutual benefit. To keep the peace, even. But Igor Reznikov defected to Iron Fist and when he found out that Devonshire was your boss, he tried his hand at recruitment. But you knew that despite being a colossal idiot as a man, utterly hateful, even, Devonshire was in no way, a traitor." She paused. "You planned the hit, but you needed to get away from your tail and get to the car you had waiting for the hit and run."

"The plot for that novel is getting more complex..."

"Jim Kernow made it," she said. "Oh, he was extremely poorly for a while. Touch and go. But he talked and he said that there was no way that the Russian could have stabbed him in the back. For a while we all assumed that it was a mugging or simply another day on London streets, but it made sense. You killed Carter, then crossed the road and got on the bus. We were trying so hard not to be seen by the

Russian that we didn't notice you. You knew what Jim looked like, because he sat down in SIS headquarters and had a drink on your account. The bus got you closer to the scene of the hit and run as well."

Harriet laughed; her expression seemingly resided to the fact that she'd been found out. "That has-been Carter snatched my bloody pearls as he died..." Her right hand left her pocket, a tiny Beretta pistol in her hand. "I'm sorry, sweetie, but I seem to have got the upper hand again..." She squeezed the trigger, then her eyes flickered as the hammer struck the firing pin on an empty chamber. She racked back the tiny slide but could see that the weapon was empty.

It was only now that Harriet noticed that Caroline wore a pair of gossamer-thin leather gloves. She reached into her pocket retrieved a handful of .22 cartridges and dropped them onto the ground, where they scattered around Harriet's riding boots. "Sorry, but I guess I know more than you give me credit for. If you feel that you need a gun, then you should never leave it unattended." Caroline took the .32 Beretta model 81 out from her inside jacket pocket. The weapon had a suppressor attached, leaving no doubt about the task at hand. "I suppose that peashooter will match the ballistics of the bullet in Carter's heart?"

Harriet didn't answer. Instead, she said, "There's CCTV in here, you'll never get away with it!" She paused. "Look, we're on the same bloody side! Ok, so I was played by Iron Fist. I didn't know they planned hacking missile silos, I thought we could stop them from further hacking, while still being seen as relevant. For God's sake, GCHQ does most of our spying now. I was just looking at the bigger picture. You can't kill me; it would be cold blooded murder!"

Caroline scoffed. "That's rich after you already pulled

the trigger on me." She paused. "Anyway, I disabled the camera system. Easy enough when you know how. We've had control over it for a month. Just like you had over Jack's flat. Poor Jack. He let Ramsay know about your pearls, too. It must have been hard for him, because he was certainly sweet on you."

"Darling boy..." Harriet said warmly, her eyes glistening.

"As for Carter, I don't know whether Carter was a good man, or not," she told her. "But he was *our* man. We look after our own. Jim is a good man, too. And he may never be the same again..."

Harriet did not seem concerned about the death of Carter or that Jim Kernow had been fighting for his life, but she asked, "Does Jack know you're here?"

"No," she replied. "Poor Jack actually rather likes you."

"Me too. I'm very fond of him."

"It's a shame that you hung him out to dry in Russia."

"It's all games, nothing personal, you should know that by now. Will you tell him that I was also very fond of him for me?"

"No."

Harriet remained in the present long enough to register that something was wrong, and that the muffled gunshot had indeed come as a surprise. The blood spread across her forehead and dripped into her eyes before her knees buckled and she fell in a crumpled heap on the ground. Caroline removed the suppressor and tucked it into her pocket. She picked up the ejected shell casing and pocketed it. Harriet rested perfectly still, blood dripping from her forehead onto the spotlessly clean concrete. Caroline bent down and unfolded her, offering her some dignity in death as she laid her carefully on the ground.

Chapter Fifty-Nine

Tuscany, Italy
Six weeks later

"I have something that you will want," the Russian said, staring at the muzzle of King's pistol in the same way that one does with a snake poised to strike, eyes daring not to move but wishing that he could be anywhere else but here. "I mean it, do not shoot. Please, give me time to talk..."

They had hunted Igor Reznikov since the day he had given them the slip. The hunt had started with Charlotte and her technicians in the floor below Ramsay's office. When the digital intelligence had yielded locations, Rashid and Luger had travelled to Finland, and then Sweden in their search for the GRU officer-turned Iron Fist saboteur. Big Dave had taken over when the trail led to Berlin – a city he was familiar with having lived there for a while. Caroline and King had picked up the mantel in Switzerland and

All the King's Men

Italy. All the while, Charlotte had used banks, credit cards, hotels, traffic systems, finance companies, letting agencies, vehicle hire companies and even the databases of mobile phone companies and Uber to find the Russian. Luger had even followed a lead to South Africa, but only now, in the hills of a small Tuscan town, had Igor Reznikov become something more tangible than a spectre.

"Then get talking..." King said coldly, the pistol unwavering in his steady hand. "Like your life depends on it, because it does..."

"I need a guarantee!" the Russian protested vehemently.

"You'll need an undertaker soon..."

The time had passed quickly since King had returned to Britain after Ukraine. Caroline had seemed invigorated with her new role, and King had been secretly pleased that he could concentrate on looking forwards. He hated to admit it, but he loved what he did for a living, and he enjoyed the quiet satisfaction as he passed people on the street and they never knew what he did, or indeed if he had saved them or the people they loved and cared for. Ramsay had seemed like a weight had been lifted from him, and he knew that it was because of Caroline and the support that she gave him, and the fact that he was surrounded by people that he could trust. King knew, too, that Ramsay would have his back, because Caroline was right there with him, and she would never let King down.

A service had been held for Jo Blyth and Carter, and Jim had been able to attend. He was expected to make a full recovery physically, but King knew that there would be mental scars. As King and Caroline had left for Italy, Jim Kernow had returned to work as Ramsay's driver and minder and had been busying himself in the building's underground carpark with some *Autoglym* on the Jaguar, which he proudly treated as his own.

"It's big," said Reznikov. "Nobody outside of the GRU knows. Seven people, tops. Not even the Russian president. Obviously, the design and development team, but that is only fifty men and women, and they are working in a secure facility."

"And you know..." King shrugged. "Sounds like the sort of bullshit a dead man walking makes before he sees the muzzle flash."

"Don't," the man pleaded quietly. "It's an aircraft. A helicopter."

"We have helicopters," said King. "So do the Yanks. The best there are."

Igor Reznikov chuckled, which was both brave and foolish in his position, but King could see that the man genuinely believed it. "An attack helicopter. A prototype. But a working one."

"We've got the Apache," said King. "I think we're good..."

"I mean it!" Reznikov persisted. King had heard men say the craziest things before they died, but there was something believable in the man's desperation. "Five hundred miles per hour, a ceiling climb of twenty-five thousand feet! Loop and victory roll capability, and stealth technology..."

"Helicopters don't break, or even bend the rules of physics," he replied, the pistol weighing heavily in his hand. He checked his watch. Caroline, waiting in the car, would be worried and come up to check on him soon. King didn't want that. He wanted to keep this clean, not leave anything to chance.

"Trust me. Our scientists are the best in the world, with

proper funding. And that's what they have. Funnelled funds from various means. The aircraft has mirrored camera projection technology..." Reznikov said, desperation in the timbre of his voice. The man knew that he was on borrowed time. "Like in that movie, *Predator*..." He paused as King frowned. "Mirror-finished panels that absorb a camera's images and project it. It looks a little weird, but it makes it invisible, kind of. Certainly, invisible to the naked eye at half a kilometre. And smart weapon systems..." He shook his head, almost sensing that his time was up. "All new missiles and cannons more advanced and ballistically capable of that of the A-10 Warthog. If produced, they will change the battlefield. Some have called it the flying tank, while others have said it takes the fight to fighter jets because of the weapon systems and stealth capabilities."

"Remind me how many Russian attack helicopters have been lost in Ukraine?"

"Three hundred and thirty," Igor Reznikov replied. "And now because of this well-documented fact, which was purposely overlooked when planning strategies were made, the project will be revealed to the president and his military chiefs and production is guaranteed."

King stared at the man. His eyes were lie detectors. Intense and cold, he could make any man blink, but liars blinked soonest. King pulled out a pair of handcuffs and tossed them at the man's feet. "I'll check out your story," he said. "I'll present it, and my people will question you. But count on one thing. If this is bullshit, then I'll put a nine-millimetre bullet in your brain and won't lose a moment's sleep about it."

"I believe you," Igor Reznikov said, relief spreading across his face. "And you won't have to kill me."

"We'll see," King told him, the pistol aimed at him, his

hand still steady, his eyes as cold as glacier water. "What's the name of this project?"

"*Operatsiya Orlinyy kogot'*," Igor Reznikov said in his mother tongue, then added, "Operation Eagle's Talon..."

Author's Note

Hi - thanks for making it this far - which means you hopefully enjoyed my story!

I'm lucky enough to write full-time, and it goes without saying that I couldn't do it without your support. As always, I'd appreciate a rating or review and thank you for doing that.

Did you know that you can sign up to my mailing list? You will receive extra content, new release information and promotional offers, and if you don't like it then you can opt out at the bottom of the email.

Alex King will return in The Eagle's Talon which you can find here: The Eagle's Talon

Thank you, and I hope to entertain you again soon.

A P Bateman

Printed in Great Britain
by Amazon